The Mantle of God

God

A Dottie Manderson
mystery

Caron Allan

ISBN-10: 1533453004
ISBN-13: 9781533453006

DEDICATION

For my family, with love and gratitude.

ACKNOWLEDGMENTS

A huge thank you to Alana, without whom this book, would still be a total mess. If it is a bit dodgy here and there, it's not her fault.

I am so grateful to the Victoria and Albert museum in London for the inspiration I gained from their wonderful *Opus Anglicanum* event last winter (2016-17), it was truly magnificent. As was the Flemish Tapestry hall. And the café...

.

THE MANTLE OF GOD:

A DOTTIE MANDERSON MYSTERY

Chapter One

Hertfordshire, November 1605

As soon as the sound of horses reached her ears, Lady Gerard knew her greatest fears had become a reality. She fell against her husband, half-swooning, clutching at his coat with trembling fingers.

Sir Gerard was a man of courage and action. He had planned for this day, though hoping it would never come. It was a vain hope however, and he spared a brief second or two to be thankful that he had not only planned for this event, but had the support of his loyal staff to help him see it through. He shouted for the servants, and even as they came running, he was leading Lady Gerard up the broad staircase, calling for the children to be brought down from the nursery, and giving instructions to each man or maidservant as they appeared.

'Williams, send a man in first with the children. The nurse shall follow behind, then Greene with Lady Gerard and a lantern. Beyond all else, you must get

them away safely as we arranged. You know how I depend upon you both. Maria, help Lady Gerard. Constance, bring candles and her ladyship's cape.'

The servants, white-lipped and terrified, nevertheless hastened to do his bidding without hesitation. He could smile, even at such a time, that he was so fortunate in his companions.

Through the window they could see the first of the horses entering the long carriage drive. They had a bare minute, no more.

'My dear!' Gerard said to his wife, and his voice was sharp only to stir her to action. 'We cannot delay,' and by now they had reached the upper hall. 'There is not a moment to lose.'

'I will not leave you...'

'You must.' Pausing, he took her face in his hands, and kissed her for the last time. Looking into her eyes, he insisted gently, in a half-whisper, 'You must, Katherine, my love. Think of the children, I beg you.'

There was silence. She nodded, a tear spilling over onto her cheek, and she said, 'I know.'

'Mama, what's...?' asked their eldest daughter, but was instantly shushed. The panel in the upper hall was opened, and a manservant stepped through, then another immediately thrust the four children, their nurse and a female servant through the gap after them without pausing to light torch or candle. One child whimpered, fearful of the darkness. My little Roland, thought Gerard with a pang.

But here was no more time for partings, and he pushed his wife through the entrance, handing her the precious wooden box. 'Keep it safe, and may the Holy Mother watch over you all, my love.'

From the downstairs hall came a shout. Gerard quickly closed the panel, the suit of armour was returned to its position, and by the time the soldiers broke down the door and burst into the house, Sir

Gerard was sitting calmly at his desk, reading from his prayer-book. He had dismissed those few servants who remained, fervently hoping they would get away to safety; they had been loyal beyond anything he could have asked or hoped. How he prayed they would not pay for that loyalty with their lives as others had elsewhere. As he himself was certain to do. So many things to hope for, he thought, at the very time when hope seemed the least of his commodities.

The charge was read out by the captain even as the soldiers grabbed Sir Gerard by the arms and hauled him to his feet.

'Where is your family?' the captain demanded.

'They are gone to the south coast for their health, we have all suffered so much from the influenza this past spring.' He got a slap across the face for that, and the men were despatched to search the house.

'Tear it apart if you have to! These papists have so many secret places in their homes. Rip up the floors, tear down the walls, smash out the stones of the fireplaces!'

Sir Gerard felt no fear for his family. The passage would be found eventually, but the men would never be able to open it. By the time the soldiers had taken an axe to the panel, his family would be long gone, and family, treasures and the precious relic would never be found.

'You will end your days in the Tower,' the captain told him with a smirk, 'and in great agony, I've no doubt.'

'If God wills it,' Sir Gerard responded with calm. 'And afterward I shall be received in heaven.'

The captain spat at his feet and turned away. His men searched for the remainder of the day, and even returned the next, but they found neither Lady Gerard, nor her children, nor the famous Gerard relic.

Two weeks later, when the cold blade of the axe was

laid upon his neck, Sir Gerard died secure in the knowledge that all was well, and that neither plans nor friends had failed him.

London, February 1934

'Do sit down, Mr—er—Inspector. How nice to see you again.'

'Thank you, Miss Manderson. It's been a couple of weeks since we last met, I'm very glad to see you looking so well recovered.'

'Would you like some tea? Or perhaps you prefer coffee?'

'Thank you, a cup of tea would be most welcome.'

Dottie crossed the room to ring the bell. She moved slowly, mainly because part of her was astonished at how she, how both of them, managed to keep up this polite banality, when their last meeting—the one he had referred to—had been so... so... She fought to find the right word. Dramatic was not nearly dramatic enough. It had been chaotic, hellish, like something from a nightmare.

Resuming her seat, she turned a polite smile on him. He seemed to have run out of small-talk. His right knee bounced nervously. He was trying not to stare at her.

The door to the morning room opened and Janet the maid came in almost at a run and bobbed to a halt in front of Dottie. Of course, Janet had probably opened the door to him, and taken his coat and hat. No doubt the tea had already been made downstairs, just waiting for her to ring. Dottie smiled at Janet and said, 'Please could we have some tea?'

'Yes'm, right away,' said Janet, flashing a look and a quick smile at her favourite policeman as she went out. Janet had hopes of a match between Dottie and Inspector William Hardy. Although admittedly she harboured hopes of each and every man who might whisk Dottie away to a life of excitement and adventure, not only because she wanted Dottie to be happily married almost as much as Dottie's mother did, but also because Dottie had promised that when she did eventually marry, Janet could go with her to her new home. Janet's main goal in life was to be the housekeeper of a large and beautiful home in what she termed a 'nice' part of London. Briefly Dottie wondered whether Janet would insist on looking over any future marriage proposals to ensure the most suitable establishment was chosen for herself, rather than for Dottie. Certainly it was likely be a toss-up to see if it was her mother or their maid who had the final say in whom Dottie accepted.

The door closed softly behind the maid, and Inspector Hardy again tried to bring himself to the point of asking Dottie whatever it was he had come there to ask.

He complimented her for a second time on her healthy appearance, then cast about him for something else to say. Dottie, often the despair of her mother in social situations, simply leaned forward, fixed him with her large, hazel eyes and said, 'What's up?' in the modern style her mother often criticised.

'Ah, well, I—er...'

'It's no good pretending, I know you wouldn't have called on me unless you simply had to. So, as I said before, what's up?'

He gave her a grin, cheeky and almost boyish, and just for a few seconds, the grave policeman persona was gone. 'I might call on you, especially if I thought your mother might be out.'

'She's not,' Dottie said, 'she's upstairs bullying my father who is in bed with a cold.'

He looked uncomfortable again. 'Ah, oh dear, then I'd better...'

'Be quick? Yes, you better had.'

'I was going to say, I'd better ask you to give both your parents my best wishes.'

The door opened.

'Tea,' said Janet and she set down a tray. She seemed to take an age to pour out a cup of tea for the inspector only, then she performed an odd hybridised bow-curtsey and, cheeks flaming, left the room once more, leaving Dottie to pour her own drink.

'I'm sorry there's no cake,' Dottie said, 'Mother's put Father on a diet, which means none of us gets any treats at the moment. Cook's under strict instructions.'

'Never mind,' he said. He clutched his cup and saucer. Perhaps having something to do with his hands gave him courage, for then he said, 'Do you remember when Archie Dunne died?'

Dottie raised an eyebrow. 'I'd hardly forget,' she said, 'seeing that it was I who found him bleeding to death on the ground. And it was only a couple of months ago.'

'Ah, oh yes, indeed. Dreadful business.' He allowed the clock above the fireplace time to loudly tick four times before adding, 'I have been wondering if he said anything to you that night. Anything that might have slipped your mind?'

'No,' Dottie said, and watched him closely. What on earth did he mean?

'Oh? And you're quite, quite sure about that?'

'*Quite* sure, thank you. If he'd said anything other than just singing those few words from that song, I would have told you.'

'Well, if you're sure...' he repeated doubtfully.

'I think I would have remembered,' she replied somewhat waspishly. Then, curiosity getting the better of her, she added, 'Surely this is all old news? I thought that case was all finished with? Why do you ask?'

He poured himself another cup of tea, stirred in milk and one teaspoon of sugar. Her mother wouldn't like that, Dottie thought. As far as Mother was concerned, the milk absolutely *had* to go into the cup before the tea. There was a pause. The clock ticked loudly. She began to think he wasn't going to reply. He gulped down at least half his tea before finally saying, 'If I was to say to you 'the mantle of God', what would that mean to you?'

She shook her head. 'I've never heard that before. What *does* it mean?'

'It doesn't mean anything to you? You've never heard anyone say those words?'

She shook her head again. 'I told you, no.' She blushed a little as in her mind's eye she saw a kind of gigantic shelf over a huge fireplace in Heaven, and a clock and a few photos in silver frames sitting on the shelf. She pushed the image aside and told him firmly, 'This is the first time I've ever heard those words, and I can't imagine what they might mean.'

He said nothing, but drank the rest of his tea. Two can play at this game, Dottie thought, irritated, and forced herself to hold back any more questions that might be begging to be asked. She sat back in her chair, her arms folded, and regarded him in silence. Silence filled the room. Silence and the ticking of that dratted clock on the mantelpiece, she thought. She looked at his face. She saw now how pale he was, and that great hollows lay beneath his eyes. He looked as if he hadn't slept for a week. She wanted to reach out to him, comfort him, help him in some way. She poured him another cup of tea, adding milk and sugar as he had done, and passed him the cup and saucer.

'Tell me about it, if you like,' she said gently.

He drank his third cup of tea in two huge gulps and set down his cup on the table. He ran a hand over his eyes and forehead as if trying to wake himself up. Dottie wondered what he would do if she were to go over to him and sit on his knee and stroke his tired face. But no doubt, she reminded herself sternly, if I did such a ridiculous thing, that is precisely the moment Mother would walk into the room, and she'd have forty fits and pack me off to a convent. Dottie therefore remained where she was, her hands neatly folded in her lap.

He cleared his throat. He offered her a crooked smile.

'Sorry,' he said, 'we've got so many cases on at the moment, yet all can I think about is this—this conundrum.' He sighed, and she waited. In his own time he would tell her, she realised.

'I don't know if I'm cut out to be a policeman,' he said suddenly, and very quietly. She looked at him in astonishment. That was the last thing she had expected to hear. Before she could comment, he continued, 'I can't remember the last time I slept for a whole night. We've had a suicide, two armed robberies, an attack on a pr—er—on a good-time girl, a domestic battery, a kidnapping, and three break-and-enters in the last two weeks. You'd think that would be enough to keep me busy. But no, all I can think about is this wretched thing.'

He took a small brown envelope from his inside pocket and handed it to her. 'It's quite all right, you can open it. Have a look at what's inside.'

She pulled up the flap, peered inside and saw a tiny scrap of fabric, badly faded, no more than the length of her little finger and only twice or three times the width. There was a line of stitching across one corner. There was also a small piece of paper which had once been folded over and over to create a parcel around the scrap. She smoothed out the paper on her knee. There were words printed in scrawly black ink: 'The mantle of God.'

She stared at the items, then looked up at him questioningly.

'The scrap of material was wrapped inside that piece of paper to make a little package as you can see. And this little package was found by the police doctor when he examined the body of Archie Dunne. It was tucked in the inside pocket of his evening coat. Officially it's been set down by the chief superintendent as 'of no significant value' in the investigation. But yet...' He rubbed his face again, this time with both hands.

'The mantle of God,' Dottie repeated, pondering the meaning. 'Mantle as in a cloak or something? An ancient word for a coat or something similar.'

He nodded. 'I assume so, but...'

'Shall I ring for some more tea? Or what about a sandwich? Are you hungry? You look completely...'

'I'm sorry, I really must be going. Thank you for your time.'

She held out the scrap of fabric and the paper but he shook his head and gestured for her to keep it.

'Will you do me a huge favour? Will you see if you can find out anything about it? As a mannequin, you must come into contact with dressmakers, costumers, people who might know a bit about dress materials. I really can't afford to spend the time on something my superiors have already dismissed as of no importance. And at the moment I don't have any free time or I'd try to do some research myself. It's just that—it *feels* significant in some way I can't understand, or at least, relevant, but I haven't the proof to justify the manpower or the time...'

'Of course.'

He was on his feet, heading for the door, when he recollected his manners and came back. He shook her hand, and then seemingly on impulse, bent to kiss her cheek.

'Bless you,' he said, and squeezed her shoulder before leaving.

Dottie sat and gazed into space. She felt on the verge

of tears, suddenly, and wanted so much to call him back. The front door banged. She heard the sound of his feet hurrying along the street. The room seemed full and highly charged, yet at the same time, strangely empty.

*

Chapter Two

She looked at the fabric again. Going to the window, she couldn't resist looking down the street in case she could still see him, but he had gone. With an effort she ignored the unsettled state of her emotions, turning her attention to the scrap of fabric, holding it up to the natural light and examining it. The material was badly faded and worn, but a few traces remained of some variation in the surface texture.

The scrap felt warm and butter-soft in her hand, and had no great weight or stiffness to it. It was a sort of faded greyish green colour, but here and there in the less-worn places, there was a trace of a deeper emerald shade, with more—she couldn't quite think how to describe the texture—it was— denser, plusher.

The stitches were a pale warmish colour like that of oatmeal or old stalks of wheat. They were worked close together, with no discernible fabric showing through. At one end of the piece of fabric, where the line of stitching reached the edge, a short length of thread hung loose, perhaps an inch and a half in length.

She sighed. She still knew nothing. It was the kind of scrap that one would normally throw away, or a very thrifty housewife might save to add to the stuffing of a new cushion or a child's toy. Insignificant. Worthless. Yet it meant something to William, as she privately called him, and so if it was important to him, she would find out everything she could about it.

The hall clock chimed the hour, and Dottie, suddenly panicking, swept up the packet he'd given her with the mysterious writing, and ran upstairs to get ready. She had to be at Carmichael's for a late afternoon show, followed by a cocktail party for the firm's best clients.

She was almost late. A road accident held up the bus she was in, and she sat there, hands gripped tightly in her lap, as the precious minutes ticked by. Inside the bus it was stuffy and musty-smelling, whilst outside, a chilly rain fell upon the now-dark streets. How she wished it were Spring. It was only mid-February, and winter had seemed to last forever. She longed for lighter evenings and sunshine.

The bus showed no sign of moving, stuck as it was in a crowd of traffic at a junction. Up ahead, there was shouting and a glare of lights. Dottie brought her thoughts back to the scrap of fabric and the enigmatic words on the paper it had been so carefully wrapped in.

What could it mean, she wondered. The mantle

of God. She smiled as she recalled her first mental image of a crowded overmantel. Wrong mantle, she thought. This clearly referred to a garment, not a piece of furniture. But how could God wear an item of clothing? Then again, she thought with a smile, what would God want with a mantelpiece?

The bus lurched forward suddenly as the road ahead finally cleared, and it was all she could do not to shout, 'Hurrah!' She mused on the words 'mantle of God' again.

What kind of garment would God wear? She thought of the statues in churches, of the paintings she had seen in galleries and museums.

Usually the Christ-figures in those were shown on the cross, clad only in a modest cloth, or if depicted in other scenes from the Bible, speaking to crowds for example, wearing long robes covered by a cloak...

...A cloak. That had to be it! The cloak. Was this anything to do with the Daughters of Esther and their gold cloaks? Dottie's thoughts leapt from the memory of the gold cloaks to Leonora and her bloody knife, to Susan Dunne, sitting dead in her armchair, her eyes wide and staring, her throat ripped apart and gushing blood.

Nausea passed over Dottie and she shivered with it. The plump matron beside her patted her knee and said, 'Never mind, Dearie, we'll be there in a minute, and you can get yourself warmed up with a nice cup of tea.'

The show went well. Dottie moved and turned mechanically, her mind busy on the puzzle of the fabric, her body well-versed in the movements required to show the gowns and costumes to the small eager group of Mrs Carmichael's exclusive clients.

Everything went without a hitch, and when the show was over, the food and drink was carried in and set out upon tables in the long room. The mannequins went backstage to change into their ordinary clothes, and the few of them favoured by Mrs Carmichael were invited to join the great lady and her clients for the cocktail party.

Dottie, a glass of sherry in her hand, stood in the middle of the room and wondered where to go. Mrs Carmichael didn't like her girls to huddle in a corner and chatter: they were still at work, so she expected them to be out in the room, circling, smiling and talking to the clients. Now that the show was over, some of the ladies had been joined by gentlemen, and more than one man looked hopefully in Dottie's direction, far too openly admiring her tall slender figure, dark hair and eyes, and her smooth fair skin.

Avoiding those she already knew to be insufferable, she wandered aimlessly about the room, a smile fixed on her face, occasionally nodding to someone or calling out a non-committal, 'Good evening, lovely to see you again.'

Mrs Carmichael was in full flow with a group of people, three ladies and a gentleman gathered about her like chicks around a plump hen. One of the ladies was clearly hanging devotedly on Mrs Carmichael's every word, the others appeared merely polite, not really attending to everything the great woman was saying, just content to bask in her rough-diamond glory.

Dottie smiled to herself as she heard Mrs Carmichael's robust East End tones outlining all the advantages of natural fibres over the new man-made artificial fabrics. Certainly Mrs Carmichael knew her stuff when it came to fabric and style, which was to be expected, as she had often told Dottie she started in the business ten years before the Great Victoria had passed away.

A thought now came to Dottie. She made her way over to join the group. Standing at Mrs Carmichael's elbow, she seemed to see her employer anew, now recognising for the first time the knowledge and expertise contained behind the vast bosom and the unflattering spectacles that reposed thereupon on a beaded ribbon, ever ready to decipher the ridiculously tiny writing everyone seemed to employ these days.

When there was a lull, and Mrs Carmichael's admirers had turned away to greet friends, Dottie said, 'Mrs Carmichael, please could I have a few moments of your time after the party?'

Mrs Carmichael cast a practised eye over Dottie.

'Well, you've not got yourself into trouble, I know, so you must be going to leave me to get married.'

'Not at all,' Dottie responded, blushing furiously, 'I just want to ask your advice about something.'

Noticeably relieved, Mrs Carmichael told her to come along to the office once everyone had gone. Pleased about that, and confident she was going to make some progress, Dottie felt lighter and happier, and applied herself vigorously to socialising with the clients and enhancing Mrs Carmichael's considerable reputation for quality garments and exclusive designs for the discerning lady.

Mrs Carmichael, ushering Dottie into the little windowless room she called her office, began to divest herself of the less comfortable parts of her attire: first, the tight, high-heeled shoes, then the heavy necklace and earrings, then the tiny hat was yanked off and flung on the desk, followed by the silvery stole, the heavy gold bracelet and the spectacles on their beaded ribbon. Mrs Carmichael, much lighter and more at ease, sat, and invited Dottie to do the same.

'Takes it out of you, all this socialising. At least it does when you get to my age,' she told Dottie. She stretched out her stockinged feet with an expression of blissful relief, wiggled her toes and rotated her ankles several times in each direction. 'Coo, that's better. My poor feet. The things we do to sell a few frocks.'

Mrs Carmichael waddled over to a drinks cabinet and poured herself a neat gin, then quirked an eyebrow at Dottie who hastily declined.

'I've been meaning to have a chat with you, Dot,' Mrs Carmichael said as she returned to her chair and sank into it once more with a groan. 'I can't tell you how worried I was when you said you wanted to talk to me. I made sure you was going to say you was getting married or had got yourself in the family way.' She glanced at Dottie's hot and embarrassed face again. 'But there, you're a good girl, and a sensible one. Now I've been approached by a friend of mine who works for a big studio. They need some girls to help out. There's a picture being made, it's about a mannequin who falls in love with a duke or something, and all set in the fashion world. I was thinking of you. Oh, it's all perfectly decent,' she added, seeing Dottie's expression, 'Nothing nasty. It's a proper film, with some well-known people in it.' She reeled off a few names, and Dottie recognised two of them. 'The money will be very good, I should think. They need a couple of girls, as I said, for background scenes, catwalks, a few tasteful dressing room scenes, no nudity, nothing *riskay*. Just girls in outfits patting their hair or putting on lipstick, that sort of thing. What do you say? Shall I put you forward, or do you need to check with Dear Mama?'

Mrs Carmichael was a clever woman. A clever, self-made woman. There was no Mr Carmichael. There never had been. Like many women of her time, she found it expedient to adopt the title *Mrs*, it lent an air of respectability and wisdom to her business. She had worked her way up from scullery-maid for a designer at age 12—she'd lied about her age—to where she was today: owner of her own fashion house, owner of her own home in London, possessor of cars, jewels, furs, servants, and a holiday villa in the south of France. All the girls who worked for her, including Dottie, would have been surprised to know she was a self-made millionaire, and that was entirely due to her own good sense and understanding of others. And nothing could have been better calculated to push Dottie to make the required decision than her last comment, *'Or do you need to check with Dear Mama.'*

Dottie, blushing, immediately said, 'No, of

course I don't. I'll do it, Mrs Carmichael. Please put my name forward.' She paused then added, leaning forward, and speaking softly, 'And you're quite sure it is perfectly—*respectable*? I couldn't do anything...'

'Nor would I ask you to, Dottie, dear. No, take it from me, it will be perfectly respectable. Leave it with me and I'll get in touch with them. No doubt but what they'll be in touch with you in a week or so. Now I just need to think of one or two more to send them.'

'Gracie?' Dottie suggested.

'Bless you, dear. You haven't heard, then? Got herself into trouble. That boy from the docks. He's a bad 'un too, I told her when she first started seeing him. Men are all the same, only interested in one thing.'

Her face crimson again, Dottie tried to nod sagely, feeling quite proud of herself for discussing such a topic so matter-of-factly. 'Oh dear, poor Gracie. I wonder what will happen?'

'Well that mother of hers is a poor stick, so it's hardly surprising. And I don't s'pose as how the mother'll make him marry her.'

'Things have been very difficult for Gracie and her family since her father died, it must be two years ago now.'

'Must be. As you say, poor Gracie. These girls will fall for a smooth-talker who takes 'em out and splashes the money.' Mrs Carmichael finished her gin and set the glass aside, along with poor Gracie and her predicament. She looked at Dottie and said, 'No young man in your life?'

'Oh no,' Dottie replied hastily.

'Good thing too, don't want to throw yourself away too young. Not that you'll need to. I expect they're queuing round the corner to take you out dancing. Did I hear your sister's had some good news?'

'Yes, um—Flora is expecting a baby. She's delighted, of course. In fact, we all are.'

'Very nice too. Is she keeping well?'

Dottie affirmed that Flora was well apart from a little nausea now and again. She sensed the time had come. 'Mrs Carmichael,' she began, 'I would like to ask you something. Do you know much about fabric? I mean, not about patterns or fashions, but the material itself?'

'Well, a bit more than most, I daresay,' Mrs Carmichael admitted, and her interest was definitely piqued.

Dottie carefully extracted the tiny scrap of fabric from the paper wrapping. She held it out to Mrs Carmichael, who took it, and after a glance, she laid it on her desk, turned on the desk lamp, and opened a drawer to fish out a magnifying glass. She turned the cloth this way and that under the lamp as she examined it carefully for several minutes.

When at last she handed it back to Dottie, she seemed a little put-out, or—well, Dottie wasn't sure what Mrs Carmichael was—she could only sense that there was a change in the room and the change came from Mrs Carmichael herself, and it wasn't a happy change, nor an interested change. It was a tense, angry, odd change and the room felt unfriendly.

But Mrs Carmichael simply shrugged her ample

shoulders and turning away to put off the lamp and put back the glass, she said, 'Well it's not much to go on, is it, just an old bit of something, I suppose. What did you want to know about it?'

Dottie was watching her closely, feeling rather puzzled. 'What sort of fabric is it?'

'Don't know. Could be cotton, I suppose. Looks like it's been in the wars a bit.'

'Yes, it is rather tattered,' Dottie agreed. She put the fabric away again inside its much-folded paper. There was a flash of the writing, but Dottie hoped Mrs Carmichael hadn't seen it. In spite of William Hardy's request for help, she wasn't sure how much to say.

'So, where did you get it?' Mrs Carmichael asked. 'What's it from?'

Dottie smiled. 'Oh, it's just something I found. I just wondered what sort of fabric it was. Thank you so much for your time, I mustn't keep you any longer. I think the party went well, didn't it?'

Mrs Carmichael seemed to have to pull her attention back to Dottie from a long way off. As Dottie stood, and made her way to the door, Mrs Carmichael was still nodding her head and putting out her hands to heave herself onto her aching feet once more.

'Well if there's anything else,' she said, but Dottie simply made herself shake her head and said no thank you, then with a bright smile, she added, 'Well, goodbye!' She turned and hurried away, banging the street door a moment later as she set off for the bus stop.

Behind her, alone in her big warehouse, now all in darkness save for the single electric lightbulb burning in the little back office, Muriel Carmichael sat deep in thought for a few moments. She came to herself after a while, gave herself a little impatient shake, then picked up the phone and got through to the operator. She asked for a number. At the other end of the line, down the miles and miles of cable strung along the streets, twisting and turning across the vast busyness of London, she could hear a bell ringing, once, twice, four times, six, before the receiver was picked up and a refined voice said, 'Mrs Gerard's residence, this is Aitchison speaking.'

'It's Muriel Carmichael. I must speak with Mrs Gerard immediately. If not sooner.' Muriel Carmichael bellowed, being of the generation for whom the telephone was less of an instrument of communication and more of one of torture.

The butler ahemmed politely and said, 'I'm afraid Mrs Gerard has not yet returned from her trip. I expect her back in a few days. I shall inform her that you rang.'

The butler then hung up the receiver and left Mrs Carmichael swearing furiously and in a most unladylike fashion at her own now useless apparatus.

*

Chapter Three

It was Flora's idea to take the scrap of fabric to the London Metropolitan Museum. Dottie had her doubts, and tried to insist they would be wasting everyone's time.

'They've all sorts of costumes and things,' Flora had said, 'they're bound to have some kind of crusty old fossil who is the world's expert on tatty old bits of cloth.'

The crusty old fossil was gazing at Dottie now. There was a quality in the gaze that reminded her of the cook's dog when it spied a string of sausages. Dottie wondered what her own expression revealed, because certainly, the London Metropolitan Museum's tapestry, textile and costume consultant was worth looking at.

He couldn't be more than thirty-two or thirty-four, she thought, and he was easily six inches taller than her own five feet seven. He was more thin than slender, had eyes of a piercing blue over which his fair hair repeatedly flopped, requiring him to push it back continually. His fingers were like paintbrushes, long, thin and pointed-looking, yet as he took the scrap of fabric from her hands and turned it over to study it, his touch was that of a mother with her newborn child.

Dottie exchanged a look with her sister. Flora's eyes were wide and amused, making Dottie blush, and turning her back on her sister, Dottie began to apologise to Dr Melville.

'I'm afraid it's probably nothing of interest. I'm afraid we're simply taking up your valuable time, I'm sure you're exceedingly busy...'

'Nonsense,' he murmured but didn't take his eyes off the greyish piece of stuff.

'Perhaps we ought to just...' Flora offered, but he ignored her completely. Silence seemed to envelop them. Dummies stared from behind glass screens. All of life seemed to pause, waiting on his pronouncement. Flora fidgeted, bending forward to relieve her aching back. Her tummy was a little larger now she was well into her fourth month of pregnancy, and her back sometimes complained.

At length, the museum's expert on tapestries, textiles and costume indicated he was ready to deliver his verdict. Flora and Dottie regarded him with bated breath.

'Perhaps you'd like to come this way? I need to look at this properly,' he told them, and now Dottie was able to register his soft Scottish accent, which added to his many other alluring attributes. Without waiting for them to respond he strode away, bearing Dottie's fabric scrap in his right hand.

They quickly lost him. Turning this way and that between the displays, they came face to face with a door marked 'Private' which was just closing.

'Well, go on, you ninny,' Flora said. Dottie hesitated.

'It might not have been him who just...'

'He said, 'come this way',' Flora pointed out. 'He's not here, so we need to find him. There's a jolly good chance he went through there. If he didn't, we'll just apologise like sensible human beings and come out again.' She turned the handle and bundled a still-hesitating Dottie ahead of her through the door.

Beyond the door, the corridor was long and dark, lit only from the opposite end where a single door stood ajar, allowing a combination of electric light and daylight to spill out into the darkness and chase away the deepest shadows. All the other doors were closed. They made towards the light. But before they got that far, a face peered out at them and an impatient Scottish voice said, 'Oh there you are. Do come along.' And suddenly Dottie didn't think him so very attractive after all.

An irritated, 'Well, shut the door, then,' welcomed them into his inner sanctum. They entered the room that seemed so bright after the dim hallway, but found he had already turned his back and was bending over a microscope, the scrap of material on the specimen glass between two thin slides. Dottie felt an urge to snatch the fabric back, but held herself in check, waiting, her foot tapping on the tiled floor, for his verdict.

It was a long time coming. Flora seated herself

on a convenient chair, exchanging eye-rolling with her sister.

'Hmm,' he said. They waited for more, but nothing came. The two sisters exchanged another look of annoyance mingled with amusement.

Dottie looked about her. It was an office not unlike that of experts and academics up and down the country; books were piled on shelves that vied for living space with stands, cabinets and table-tops. An attempt—no doubt when the present incumbent had first moved in—had been made at some kind of order, as the book case nearest the door contained books arranged in neat rows, clearly in a particular sequence but further along, these neat rows gave way to tottering stacks, and other items had been introduced: the handles of scissors, knives and other tools poked out here and there; small items of historical clothing were displayed on wire figures or preserved beneath dusty glass domes. Drawing closer she saw that there was a little group of clerical vestments in miniature—tiny wire priests stood ready to offer sacraments and prayers. Another shelf held the more prosaic examples of everyday dress of bygone centuries, again all perfectly replicated in a tiny scale, as if designed for the doll of the most indulged of royal offspring. A far cry, Dottie thought, from the rag doll her nurse had made for her some fifteen years earlier. Anna-Maria still sat on a chair in Dottie's room, in her patchwork shawl, apron and cotton frock, and the uneven petticoats sewn by Dottie's own childish fingers.

Beneath the book shelves, on both the right and the left-hand walls of the room, were many, many shallow drawers, some half-open and stuffed with envelopes and packets from which spilled threads, ribbons, small samples and great swathes of fabric, all labelled in the same small, neat hand. Dottie was about to pick one up to get a better look, when Melville's voice suddenly bellowed:

'Don't touch that, it's priceless!'

Jumping half out of her skin and biting back the retort that perhaps, in that case, it ought to be more carefully stored, she instead offered an apologetic smile and folded her hands in front of her.

He turned back to the microscope and said, 'Hmm,' once more. Then queried, 'Where did you say you found this, again?'

Flora stifled a yawn. Caught off-guard, Dottie wracked her brains to think of something plausible. 'Er, well I didn't say. I—er—that is to say, we—um...' She directed a look of sheer panic at Flora, shaking her head as if to say, I don't know what to tell him.

'We came across it in our granny's attic. She recently passed away and we've been clearing out the house so it can be sold,' Flora said, and she managed to inject a note of boredom into her tone that was not entirely fictitious. Not for the first time, Dottie wondered whether she should be concerned over her sister's ability to lie so convincingly and without the least qualm.

'I see. Just this tiny scrap? On its own?' He sounded politely disbelieving.

'It was part of a larger piece of fabric,' Flora said.

'How large exactly?' He turned to stare at Flora with those beautiful blue eyes. Dottie had the feeling he was still peering through the microscope at a specimen, trying to discover its secrets.

'It's hard to say,' Flora hedged, 'it's so dark in granny's attic. And it was amongst lots of bits and bobs in a trunk.'

'Hmm,' he said and turned away.

There was another long silence. Dottie's attention was beginning to wander again. She looked at the desk beside the table which bore the microscope. It was a very neat desk. No typewriter, no papers, no photographs of a loving wife or doting parents. There was a neatly folded length of black silk, and a pair of dressmaker's shears. It was the only tidy space in the whole room.

He straightened and turned away from the microscope. 'I'd like to keep this, if I may, and run some tests.'

'What kind of tests?' Dottie asked.

'Oh, well it's rather complicated to explain to the layperson,' he told her with a patronising smile, 'but to put it simply, I shall combine microscopic samples of the cloth with various solutions, and these will help me to learn more about the nature of the fabric.'

'But surely...' Flora began, and at the same time, Dottie said, 'But surely that will destroy this piece of fabric?'

There was an odd still moment that seemed to stretch between them like a taut wire. No one spoke, or even seemed to breathe. Then he looked from one to the other of them and he flashed Dottie another smile, this time more charming, 'Well yes, but at least then we'll know what it is. You still have the rest of the fabric in granny's attic, after all.' His tone was gentle, persuasive, almost teasing. Dottie felt like an unreasonable child.

'But I don't want...'

'Look, you asked me to help you,' he said with a touch of asperity, 'that's all I'm trying to do.' He raked a hand through his floppy fringe.

'I realise that,' Dottie said in a small voice, 'and I'm sorry to have wasted your time, but I don't want you to cut this up into tiny pieces. I thought you'd just take one look at it and say, 'oh yes, that's 18th century Indian cotton', or something like that. I don't want it destroyed.'

'You've got the rest of the fabric,' he pointed out again, and his tone was sharp with annoyance. Dottie felt herself blushing. She felt embarrassed for having taken up his valuable time with her childish errand then refusing his help when he offered it.

'I'm terribly sorry,' she repeated, 'please let me have it back. I'm afraid we have to go now.'

He stared at her for a few seconds, jaw clenched and lips pressed together. Dottie felt he was going to be very angry, but finally he simply took a little inward breath, then smiled and said, 'Certainly,' and he removed the scrap from the microscope slide and put it into her hand.

She felt an unaccountable relief to put the scrap back into its paper and safely away in her handbag.

Without quite noticing how, she realised they were walking along the dark hallway again, back to the public gallery of the museum and as he held the door open for them, he smiled once again, and in a warm, friendly voice, said, 'Do forgive me, I'm afraid we academics are rather prone to getting wrapped up in our work and have a tendency to forget about social pleasantries. I'm afraid I got a little carried away. Sorry for trying to cut up your fabric—I forgot myself there for a moment.'

There in the brightly lit colourful gallery, it was easy to relax and feel that she had imagined that odd moment in his office. Dottie smiled back at him and told him he was forgiven. Flora was looking at some royal robes in a nearby glass case, and when she ventured a comment about them, he hurried to her side to explain. Dottie drifted after him.

He really was so very—intense. Physically attractive, yes, but on top of that he had a kind of magnetism that sparked her interest. He turned, caught her staring at him, and she blushed and turned away. For another ten minutes they followed him around as he pointed out some of his favourite exhibits. As they were about to leave, he held out his hand to Flora who shook it, and then to Dottie, who did the same, but he trapped her hand between both of his and said, 'I'm really so sorry about my madness earlier. Please let me make it up to you. Will you allow me to take you to dinner?'

Surprised, flushed, Dottie answered a shy 'yes', and gave him her address and telephone number which he scribbled down in a tiny notebook with an even tinier pencil stub, then he promised to call for her the following Wednesday at seven o'clock.

'Well!' said Flora, when they reached the chilly street.

'Oh dear!' Dottie groaned, 'do you think I should

have declined?'

'Don't be silly, he's gorgeous!' Flora told her with a laugh, 'even if he is a bit—how did he put it? Academic?'

'Hmm,' Dottie said, wrinkling her nose. 'I can't picture him making polite conversation with Mother, can you?'

'It's only dinner,' Flora reminded her. 'You don't have to marry him. You realise we still know nothing about that dratted bit of fabric?'

'It's odd,' Dottie said coming back to her main concern, 'As I said in there just now I really thought that, being an expert, he would take one look at it and immediately know exactly what it was. I really thought he would just shrug and say 'oh yes that's cotton from somewhere-or-other' and that would be it. But no, he had to try and turn it into a chemistry experiment.'

'Your face! I thought you were going to slap him, or burst into tears, or wrestle him to the ground for it. I hate to think how possessive you'll be over something really important, like a baby or a wedding ring!'

Dottie halted in the street, and had to apologise to two people who cannoned into her. She bit her lip. 'I wish I hadn't said I'd have dinner with him.'

'Don't be silly, he's very charming when he puts his mind to it. I'm sure you'll have a lovely time, and if you don't, well, you don't need to see him again.'

'But...'

'Dottie! Come along, and stop worrying. It's only one dinner. Dinner with an extremely handsome—and, no doubt, interesting—man.'

'I know,' Dottie said, and they continued on their way. It was only dinner, that was all. Not a life-sentence. She would have to keep reminding herself.

William Hardy was on his way out the front door of the police station when a call came through to the front desk and the duty sergeant called him back.

Hardy leaned against the tall counter with a sigh and waited for the sergeant to write down the particulars and end the call.

'Another robbery?' Hardy said as soon as the sergeant had hung up the receiver.

'Yes sir. Kensington. Here's the address. The home of Mr Ian Smedley-Judd. Stockbroker. Was having a dinner party; said they'd barely had time to take their seats when masked men burst in, holding them at gunpoint and demanding all their valuables. Said the men left within ten minutes of their arrival. All very polished and well-rehearsed.'

'They would be, it's not the first of these we've had. Right, call Maple and get him to meet me there. And as many uniformed constables as you can find.'

'And the fingerprint chappie?'

'Yes, though I doubt he'll find anything. It seems all criminals these days know to wear gloves. It's such a shame there are so many novels to teach crooks how to run the show!' Hardy began to turn away and then turned back to offer a wry grin to the desk sergeant. 'And please telephone to my mother and let her know I won't be home for dinner.'

The sergeant sketched him a salute. 'Very good sir. I'm afraid this latest bunch don't much care if people get their dinner.'

'No, indeed. And I don't know which is worse, the robbery they've committed or them keeping me from my evening meal. Goodnight Sergeant.'

Mr Smedley-Judd resided in a rather lovely part of Kensington: quiet, leafy, close to the park, far from the unsightly slums and the docks. The residence was an imposing one, built over six floors, including a basement of kitchens and storerooms, and an attic full of servants' quarters. Even in the gloom of a late winter's evening, the house shone startling white, the doors and windows the easily picked-out rectangles of a child's drawing.

A butler opened the front door as soon as the inspector knocked, and made none of the usual difficulty of suggesting the police officer should avail himself of the tradesmen's entrance. Clearly the evening's events had shattered the butler's customary placid confidence.

'Come in, come in, Inspector, you're a sight for sore eyes, I can tell you.' He was already halfway along the hall, leaving the front door wide open. He collected himself, and pushing past Hardy, hurried back to close it. 'Forget my head if it wasn't screwed on,' he said with a worried smile. 'What a thing. Come this way, come this way, sir.'

'My men will be arriving any time now,' Hardy said, 'along with our fingerprint expert. I hope I can count on everyone being amenable.'

'Oh definitely. You'll have no trouble anyone, sir, I guarantee it. Come this way, Mr

Smedley-Judd said he would see you immediately.'

The carpet was thick and quite new, and in a deep shade of peacock-blue that was a little over-bright for Hardy's more conservative sense of style. All the walls appeared to be in good decorative order. A few paintings hung on the walls, spaced out neatly where only forty years earlier, a Victorian taste would have crowded in many, many more. Altogether the home gave the impression of comfort and wealth without ostentation.

The sound of voices came from a large room on his immediate right, but the butler, who told Hardy his name was Morris, led him further along the hall and in through a doorway on the left, behind the main staircase.

It was a modest but attractive study. Here again the décor was immaculate, and of superior quality. Well-polished wood gleamed, the glass of cabinet doors and lamps were shining and streak-free, and the leather of the chairs looked waxed and supple. One man was seated behind the wide expanse of a desk, and another man stood nearby. They were talking, and drinking brandy from lovely crystal glasses.

'Inspector Hardy, sir,' the butler announced and withdrew.

'Ah Inspector. I'm so glad to see you.' The man behind the desk got to his feet. 'I'm Ian Smedley-Judd. And this is my brother Gareth.'

'How do you do, sir. And you, sir,' Hardy said. Reassured by Hardy's 'one of us' accent, Smedley-Judd shook Hardy's hand then resumed his seat and invited Hardy to take a seat too. Gareth

Smedley-Judd pulled over another chair for himself, and sat. Hardy noticed the strong family resemblance between the brothers in spite of an age difference of probably ten years or more. Hardy said, 'So tell me what happened.'

'Well Inspector, I had invited a few friends and business acquaintances to the house for dinner this evening, and just after seven-thirty, we took our seats in the dining room, and before the soup was even served, five men rushed in and held us all at gunpoint. They demanded our valuables. Everything happened so quickly. They made us hand over cigar cases, rings, pocketbooks; the ladies had to give up their necklaces and other jewellery. Then, with two of the men holding guns on us, and one guarding the doorway, the other two swine went around the house, helping themselves to other things. My wife's jewellery box, my daughter's, a few small paintings, some silver and gold items.'

Hardy glanced around the room, and noted two places where empty nails indicated a small missing picture. The crucifix was still in place above the bookcase on the back wall of the study. Ian Smedley-Judd had broken off to take a sip of his brandy. Now he added, 'The footman tried to call the police but one of the robbers caught him and coshed him. There's a doctor with him now.'

'No one else was hurt?'

'No. And I'm jolly grateful for it. Thank God they only coshed the footman, I half-expected them to shoot the poor fellow.'

'And then they left?'

'Yes, out the back, through the service yard.

Gone before any of us reached the gate.'

'Well thank you, sir. I'm afraid there will be quite a lot of rather tedious questions for you and your guests to answer, but I promise you, we will do everything in our power to catch the men who did this and hopefully to restore your property to you.'

'That's the second time within a month it's happened,' Smedley-Judd said. 'Oh, not here. There was a robbery at my brother's house three weeks ago, same circumstances. Exactly the same situation. Shouldn't be at all surprised if it wasn't the same villains too.'

'Really?' Hardy said. 'I haven't heard of it.'

Gareth Smedley-Judd lit a cigarette. 'You wouldn't have, old chap,' he said, 'Different police force. We come under Hertfordshire Police. I live just outside Hitchin.'

'I'll contact them, sir,' Hardy promised. 'We may be able to assist one another in this. And now sir, I'd like to speak with your guests.'

It was almost six hours later that Hardy finally reached his home. In the kitchen, the fire had long been banked up for the night, and his food was covered by a cloth and left on top of the range. The food looked rather the worse for wear. Then with a powerful sense of gratitude he saw that either his sister or his mother had put ready a tray of sandwiches with a huge slice of cake and a thermos flask of hot tea.

When he finally went up the stairs to his bed, it was half past two. As he came out of the bathroom, his mother was there on the landing, tying her dressing gown about her, her face an expression of concern. She kissed his cheek.

'Is everything all right, dear?'

'Yes, Mother. Just a robbery. Nothing for you to worry about. Thank you for the sandwiches, I was very pleased to see those. But you shouldn't have troubled to get up, I'm going to bed myself now, I'm all in. Good night.'

His bed springs creaked as he sat on the side of the bed and pulled off shoes and socks, then his tie, and unbuttoned his shirt. He thought of looking out of the window to see the moon which was full, but it was too much of an effort, and without undressing further, he lay down, and immediately his thoughts plunged down into darkness and sleep.

*

Chapter Four

As it was growing light, Hardy stirred in his sleep. A foreboding enveloped him, and he knew a new day had dawned, a new working day that yawned ahead, tedious, unending, exhausting. And worse still, he knew with a sinking feeling that when he opened his eyes, the face that, in his dream, had smiled at him from the pillow beside his own, would be gone. He would be alone. He kept his eyes closed for a few moments longer. The alarm had not yet gone off so he knew he could afford a few more minutes to lie there and attempt to recall the vivid colours and emotions that were his only when he slept. The coming of day chased away romance, passion and the sense of someone warm and near, someone who loved him.

Before the money had run out and his father had died, William Hardy had gone to Oxford to study law. His future, as he had imagined it back then in those arrogant, rose-tinted days, had consisted of comfort, wealth, status, late breakfasts, long lunches, and rounds of golf with friends, with perhaps the odd appearance in a sensational court case which would bring him the respect and admiration of his peers. It had not entailed getting up shortly after dawn, of working twelve, fifteen or sometimes even eighteen hours a day, often seven days a week, nor the worry of trying to make ends meet. Of ensuring bills were paid on time, or of the guilt he felt at the hardships his mother and sister suffered daily, hardships they had never faced in life until recent years.

And he was lonely. At home, his mother and his sister were there, but he did not want to share his life with them in that sense. A man was supposed to leave his father and mother, and cleave to his wife. He had once been engaged but the loss of prospects had led immediately to the loss of love—if love it had ever been—and now the demands of his profession, whilst he was deeply grateful to be employed, meant that he had neither leisure nor funds to socialise with his old friends, nor to consider romance or courtship.

Yet his dreams were continually haunted by the tall slender girl with the large hazel eyes, the wide beaming smile and the alluring figure. He could never hope to deserve her, and certainly even if he himself, or she, could overlook the gulf between their stations in life, then he knew without a doubt that Dottie's parents would never commit such an aberration.

He opened his eyes. He turned his head and looked at the flat, undented pillow at the top of the empty space beside him and felt a fresh stab of misery. His alarm clock blared out, startling him out of his daydream, and he rose for the new day.

Maple was already there in Hardy's office when he arrived. Now a detective sergeant, and enjoying the status that came with the promotion from uniformed beat copper, Maple was repaying Hardy's belief in him with good solid work and unfailing good cheer.

'Morning, Bill,' he said, informal as ever when they were alone. 'You look a bit rough, mate. Did you get any sleep?'

'A bit. Not enough. Where are we with all this?'

Maple took him through everything they had. It wasn't as much as Hardy had hoped. He raked his fingers through his hair as he looked about the room. But there was no point fretting, they just had to keep plodding through everything.

'Chase up the fingerprint chappie, will you Frank? And phone Hertfordshire and see what time they can see us. I'll go and see about a car. Not sure what time we'll get there, better see if we can see them around mid-afternoon. From what little information we already have, there could well be a connection between our cases and theirs. In fact, I'm almost certain of it.'

The car wouldn't be available until after lunch due to having the brakes repaired, so Hardy settled at his desk with the neverending paperwork. The day ground slowly on, reports and statements were read, yet more reports were typed. Information was gathered, and as expected, every fact seemed to contradict another fact, every clue seemed to be meaningless, all the witness statements told them either not enough or too much of all the wrong things. The witnesses failed to corroborate one another, seeming almost deliberately to say the exact opposite of the person interviewed before them. Hardy felt he was getting nowhere. His head ached and his mood was grim.

They left at half past one, arriving in Hitchin in time for an early tea and a long leisurely chat with the very pleasant inspector in charge of the case. He was happy to allow them to read through his case notes and witness statements. By eight o'clock, Hardy was mentally exhausted and even Sergeant Maple was looking completely fed up.

'Frank, can you go and get a table at the pub? Order us some food. I'll phone the chief super and tell him we need to stay overnight. That way we should finish at a reasonable hour and get some sleep before driving back in the morning,' Hardy said at last, stretching and yawning. His head was pounding. All the information he had read was beginning to blur together in his mind.

The chief didn't seem too surprised that they wouldn't be back that night, and when Hardy had confirmed his opinion that the two forces' cases were linked, somewhat to his surprise, the chief seemed content with paying the bill for their night's room and board at the pub. Next Hardy phoned his mother to let her know he would be away overnight. She warned him to be careful on the roads, and to wrap up warm against the evening chill. Smiling to himself, he assured her he would be fine, she had no need to worry.

'Are you all right?' he asked then, 'you don't sound too good yourself. Coming down with something?'

'I'm just a little tired, William dear, that's all. We'll see you tomorrow evening, then. Take care, dear. Goodnight.'

After a very welcome and filling hot meal at the pub, the two men returned to the police station and continued to go through reports, making notes and discussing anything that seemed significant.

'It says here,' Maple said at one point, waving a sheaf of paper aloft, 'that the two men who went upstairs to ransack the house while the others kept everyone in the dining room, came down with nothing in their hands. That's one of the maids that said this, and she goes on to say that their coat pockets were flat so they didn't have much in them. She says they could of got all sorts of small valuables upstairs, yet it seems like they didn't take anything. So why not? They weren't threatened or in danger of getting caught, all the guests and staff were contained, so they had time to grab a few useful bits and pieces. Apparently there was jewellery, small pictures, silver ornaments, one of those Russian decorated eggs. All sorts of stuff in the hall and the bedrooms.'

'Fabergé,' Hardy said, but he was preoccupied with the report he was himself reading. 'Well listen to this then. One of the gentlemen says, 'the robber who came over to me was an inch or two taller than myself, and I am five feet eleven inches tall...'

'Well if he's right, then we know one of the robbers was about six-foot, six-foot one or so tall. Useful, I suppose but hardly unusual. If he'd said he was six-foot four and the robber was taller than him, that might have been a bit more useful.'

'He goes on to say, 'And as he reached across me

to take my wife's necklace, his sleeve rode up and I noticed he had a tattoo on the inside of his forearm. It was small, in blue ink, and it appeared to spell the word Duck.' He then says as soon as the robber realised he'd seen it, he turned away from them, pulling down his sleeve very quickly, and the gentleman says that was why his wife didn't lose her earrings as well as her necklace.'

'Interesting. But Duck? What does that mean?'

'I don't know, but it could be useful. And it was clearly a mistake, the robber wasn't happy that this chap saw it. That means it can be used to identify him.'

By half past ten they were back in the pub having a last pint before going to their beds. They sat at a quiet corner table. They spoke little, each man too tired and focussed on his own thoughts for idle conversation. It was a relief for Hardy to tumble onto the rather lumpy mattress. He had not expected to sleep, but he closed his eyes and knew nothing more until he was called for his breakfast at seven o'clock the next morning.

Comfortably full of bacon and eggs, they went back to the police station to take their leave of the local inspector and to check one or two more things. By ten o'clock they were on the road again. It was a bright, if chilly day and the journey was somewhat like a half-day's holiday for the two of them. They even stopped for a cup of tea at one point and sat in a warm and comfortable tearoom talking about the case. Hardy felt more relaxed than he had felt for a long time. Perhaps being a police officer wasn't so bad, after all? He just couldn't decide how he felt about his work. But after such a long delay, and with no money, he had no possibility of resuming his studies, so what other choice did he really have?

Returning to the car, they swapped places, and as Maple drove, Hardy again read over and over the notes they had made. He felt he knew the handwriting and the contents of each statement by heart. But he was gaining nothing from them in terms of a breakthrough with either of the cases which were now, in his mind, inextricably linked.

When they pulled into the little parking area behind their own police station just after lunch, he said to Maple, 'Can you check with other local forces, see if there have been similar robberies in their areas. Try Surrey, Essex and Kent for starters, then perhaps we'll contact some of the big cities, Glasgow, Edinburgh, Manchester. I'm convinced our thieves will have spread their net a bit wider than just London and Hitchin.'

Dottie was nervous about her upcoming dinner with Dr James Melville. All that day, she had been torn between the desire to ring up the museum and ask to speak to the doctor in order to cancel their arrangement, and a stoic acceptance which necessitated frequently repeating her sister's comment as a silent reminder: It's only dinner, I don't have to marry him.

By the time she was ready, at a few minutes before seven o'clock, she was a bundle of excited agitation. Her mother had repeatedly questioned her about the young man, inquiring minutely into his antecedents, of whom Dottie was completely ignorant, his financial position, again not an area Dottie was acquainted with, and his prospects, also another grey area in the great field of her knowledge of the man with whom she was about to leave the house on a dark winter's evening. Dottie's mother's opinion was that he sounded decidedly Bohemian. Coming from her mother that was almost the gravest aspersion she could cast, practically the same as suggesting he lived in a pig sty or even a Victorian opium den. None of this helped to calm Dottie's nerves.

Dr Melville arrived at a quarter past seven, instead of the agreed seven o'clock, which irritated Dottie immensely, especially as he made no apology for his late arrival. He spoke briefly but politely enough with her parents, assured them—to Dottie's great disappointment—that he would bring her home on the stroke of ten o'clock, not a second later, and even went so far as to name the restaurant where they were to dine.

It was with great relief that she preceded him out of the house. She was starting to feel horribly hemmed in and constricted. The fresh air of the evening was bracing and cooled her frayed temper, even though Dr Melville failed to compliment her on her dress. She was wearing the moss green silk-satin, it was sleeveless to show off her shoulders, but she had her dark grey moleskin cape over it, and the skirt of the dress flared out beautifully from the knees.

At least they didn't have to walk. He hailed a taxi to take them to the restaurant, and sitting in the back with him—did he have to sprawl quite so much and take up so much room, he really was a very untidy man, she thought to herself—they rode in near-silence. She had enquired after his health in the usual manner, and received a monosyllabic response. And *still* no apology or excuse for his lateness. He had failed to respond with his own equally conventional yet socially essential enquiry about her health. After another minute of silence, Dottie had broken in on his sullen musings with a banal comment about the weather: still so cold, although it was almost March, and of course one always hoped for an early Spring. He gave her a brief if puzzled smile as a reply then lapsed once more into his former preoccupation.

She sat back against the leather of the seat; clearly the situation was hopeless, he had changed his mind about his impulsive desire to see her again but had been too polite to cancel their arrangement. Her own doubts about the evening were all too entirely justified. She exhaled heavily, sending her hair fluttering in the breeze, and she turned to stare unseeing out of the window.

At long last, Dr Melville seemed to realise he was expected to act as if he wanted to be in her company. He rallied, stole a look at the face of the openly bored Dottie, then said pleasantly, 'So, have you and your sister found any more intriguing pieces of old fabric from Granny's attic?'

Caught off-guard both by his sudden remark and the reference to her fictitious grandmother, Dottie stared at him, then floundered into speech.

'Oh, er, haha, nothing else so far.'

'Ah,' said the doctor. After another pause he added, 'Sorry once again about trying to cut up your fabric sample. I got a bit carried away, I'm afraid.'

'It doesn't matter in the least,' Dottie told him. 'I know you were just trying to help.'

'You don't happen to have it with you, I suppose? I wouldn't mind another look.'

She smiled and shook her head. She certainly wasn't going to let him see it again. She really didn't believe he would give it back. It could stay right where it was, thank you very much. He would never know she had it with her. 'I'm sorry, I'm afraid I didn't bring it with me,' she lied, without a moment's guilt.

For a moment, she thought he was angry. He seemed to hold his breath for a second or two and he blinked a couple of times rather rapidly, but in the end, said simply, 'Ah well.'

Any further nuggets were lost as the taxi drew up outside the restaurant. Fortunately, Dr Melville had finally remembered his manners, and he hastened to open her door and assist her to step down to the pavement. Normally such attentions didn't matter too much to her, but she felt it was the least he could do under the circumstances. Ten o'clock began to seem a very long way off.

It seemed almost inevitable to Hardy that as soon as he was ready to go home, his attention would be needed urgently on some police matter. After the long journey to and from Hitchin, he had been looking forward to getting away at the right time for once. He did actually make it out of the building and was halfway along the street when a young constable in uniform came panting after him, calling him back. He was wanted about a burglary, and no one else was available.

Hardy seriously considered saying that he also was not available, but then the youngster told him the name and address, and all thoughts of going home went out of his head.

The evening wore slowly on. The food served at the *Le Pierrot* was more fashionable than delicious, and the staff emitted a sense of injury at being required to wait at table. Dr Melville—'Do, please, call me James,'—had made an endless evening even longer by telling anecdote upon anecdote about his adventures on the golf courses of the British Isles. He seemed to take excessive delight in his membership of two or three prestigious clubs. She didn't understand why he seemed to feel he had accomplished something of a coup in joining the ranks of their members. Dottie abhorred golf, but as she reminded herself for the hundredth time, he was at least talking to her. Or *at* her, to be more accurate.

A waiter approached with a new bottle of wine and proceeded to open it, then refill her glass. Dottie realised all too late she could have done without the wine. The tedium of the evening had made her drink more than usual, and far more quickly, and she was afraid of making a spectacle of herself. Though it would serve him right if I did, she thought. Flora was right, and thank the Lord I *don't* have to marry Melville, if this is how bad it is to spend just one evening with him. What a complete and utter bore.

She rose from the table with an apologetic smile, and Melville, halfway through resetting the table to indicate the position of his ball (pepper pot) and those of his opponents (teaspoons and butter knife), relative to the hole (salt pot), rose in hasty good manners, upsetting his glass of wine as he did so. Dottie smiled a polite apology and hurried for the staircase and the door to the ladies' cloakroom.

In the cloakroom it was much cooler and she had the place to herself, so she sat for a little while at the vanity unit. Her bad temper gave way to humour as she dabbed her dampened handkerchief at her temples and the back of her neck. What a dull man! And given his good looks, it was such a shame that his character was so flawed. Boring, inconsiderate and completely socially inept. I bet he can't dance either, she thought, and he's not even *old*. What on earth would he be like in middle age? She shuddered at the thought. How different he was in reality to her favourable initial impression.

The clock in the cloakroom indicated twenty minutes past nine. With a sigh of relief and a sense of a heavy burden gradually lightening, she told herself, only another half an hour, then I can remind him it's time to take me home. Then I need never see him again.

She rejoined him at the table, and this time as he rose out of politeness, he managed not to knock anything over. The cruet and cutlery had been replaced during her absence, but whether by him, due to abandoning his story, or by the fastidiousness of the waiter, she didn't know, though the latter seemed almost as unlikely as the former.

The wine had also been cleared away, she noted. Coffee cups and a sugar bowl and creamer now graced the new, snowy cloth.

'Miss Manderson, I do hope we have time for a coffee, I've already taken the liberty of ordering,' he said. She nodded and forced herself to smile at him.

'That would be lovely, Dr—er—James, thank you.' Half an hour, she reminded herself, just another thirty minutes and she would be free. It could even be only twenty minutes by now.

Soon the waiter arrived with the coffee pot and left them to pour for themselves. Melville slid his chair back. 'I'll just go and settle the bill,' he said, and again, Dottie simply nodded and smiled.

He was gone a full ten minutes. She was beginning to think he had left without paying, but eventually she saw him coming back, putting a piece of paper into his pocket. He was frowning. She congratulated herself on having only another fifteen minutes at the most left in his dreary, irritable company. She sipped her coffee, grimaced at the bitterness, and heaped more sugar into the cup to mask the taste, stirring vigorously.

'Well,' Melville said as he sat back down, 'I must say it's been a very pleasant evening. We really must do this again. I can't remember when I've enjoyed myself so much.' He stretched a long bony wrist across her and for a fleeting second she thought he was going to take her hand, but then she saw that the sugar basin was his object. He spooned in four little heaps of sugar and stirred his cup noisily before letting the spoon clatter into the saucer. He slurped appreciatively.

Dottie, unable to tell another outright lie to his face, settled for a perfectly true, 'I can't remember ever having an evening quite like this,' which he luckily took as a compliment, and looked really pleased with himself, whereas she was wondering about the mark she had just observed on his wrist.

'Alas we must leave if we are to have you home at the time I promised your parents.'

Dottie glanced up in surprise as he came around the table to pull out her chair for her. She couldn't help commenting, 'Well the coffee is here now, and you've paid for it, so we may as well drink it, it's not quite time to leave.'

He turned to say, 'Of course.' Then leaning past her to reach his cup, he downed the beverage in one long swallow. He stepped back and signalled to the waiter for their coats. He helped her on with hers, draping his own over his arm, and hurried off towards the exit, leaving her staring in surprise at his retreating form. In less than five minutes she was closing the front door of her parents' house, and he was already driving off in his taxi. He hadn't attempted to kiss her, had barely even troubled himself to see her up the steps to the door, before calling out heartily, 'Well, goodnight!' In fact the taxi was already driving away as she stood on the step looking for her latch-key.

'Well really!' Dottie said to herself as she took off her cape and hung it up. Then she smiled. It didn't matter, nothing mattered. The evening, the ill-fated dinner with Dr Melville she had so been dreading, was finally over. It hadn't been a success, but at least it was over. She could tell Flora in the morning that she was never going to see Melville again.

Dottie went into the drawing room and halted just inside the door. Her eyes took in the scene: her father was standing beside her mother's easy chair, his face stern, his hand on her mother's shoulder. Her mother was dabbing at her eyes, clearly distressed. Cook and Janet hovered uncertainly in the background, grim-faced and worried. And seated opposite her mother was Inspector Hardy, pale, tired-looking, a notebook balanced on his knee, a pen poised to write.

'Hello Mother, I'm home. What's going on? Good evening, Inspector Hardy.' What a contrast in her feelings between her first glimpse of Dr Melville earlier that evening and how she felt on catching sight of the handsome young inspector now. Her heart fluttered. She blushed. She couldn't look away from his mouth.

Hardy, ever polite, rose to his feet and came forward slightly. He almost bowed but settled instead for a grave smile. 'Good evening, Miss Manderson. I'm afraid your family has suffered a break-in during your absence. I'm afraid we haven't quite finished checking upstairs yet.'

Nothing had been taken. Her parents had been at dinner when the intruder or intruders had gained entry to the house via the back door. Neither of the staff—of whom only two were on the premises at the time, the daily help having gone home for the day—had seen or heard a thing until the back door had slammed shut, shattering the glass. It appeared the door had not been locked. In fact, Dottie was surprised to discover, the back door was rarely locked before eleven o'clock.

Anyone could have walked in off the street and along the side alley to the back of the house.

Her father was shouting angrily and her mother, uncharacteristically womanly and clinging, continued to grip his arm and dab her eyes with her handkerchief.

'As soon as our specialist has checked for fingerprints, you can all move about the house again as normal,' Hardy told them. 'I've asked him to start upstairs, so that the ladies can retire to bed as soon as possible. I'm afraid it is rather a long process.' He was preparing to leave, Dottie could tell, and neatly side-stepping Janet and Cook, she walked with him into the hall, wracking her brain for something, anything, to say to keep him there a little longer. A thought occurred to her.

'Did the thief or thieves actually go upstairs, then?' she asked. He halted and turned to face her.

'Yes, your mother found that things had been disarranged in her room and I believe there was a possibility that someone had also entered your room. There's no one there now, obviously. I'll ask that your room is checked as soon as your parents' room has been done. It shouldn't be too much longer.' He paused on seeing her expression, and held up a hand to calm her fears. 'Your mother is certain nothing has been taken. She says all your jewellery is still in its case. You can go in the room, just try not to touch anything.'

Dottie felt genuinely nervous of going upstairs alone. She flashed a glance at him, hesitating. Lacking her mother's overly particular attitude to social convention, Dottie would never normally feel the least concern or embarrassment about asking any other male friend to come upstairs and check inside the wardrobes or under the bed, and she would be perfectly comfortable leaning on any other male friend for emotional support or reassurance. Yet still she hesitated.

Hardy noted her pale face, the long slender fingers of her restless hands entwining, her large dark eyes gazing up into the shadows at the top of the stairs. As a friend, he wanted to put an arm around her shoulders and hug her, to tell her he would check under her bed for monsters. But were they friends? That was a point of deep uncertainty. Sometimes he felt they were, yet at others, he couldn't quite define their relationship. At this point he firmly, if reluctantly shoved aside those thoughts as they tried to intrude.

As a policeman he had the authority to ignore social niceties and to say with great officiousness, as he did right now, 'On second thoughts, Miss Manderson, I just need to check something upstairs, I shan't detain you long.'

Her relief was immense, and undisguised. She made a play of stepping back and indicating with a gesture of her hand that he should precede her up the stairs. 'Certainly, Inspector. Please feel at liberty to go wherever you wish. We're only too glad to help the police.'

He mounted the stairs, aware of her following behind him. He made a few unnecessary examinations of the handrail with a small magnifying glass he took from his pocket, after spending a full minute polishing it with his handkerchief. She pointed to the door to her room, her cheeks charmingly aflame. His heart melted a little more. With difficulty, he kept his mind on his role as detective. Further along the hall, a figure was bent over a door handle with powder and brush. 'Good evening Sergeant Carson.'

The figure turned, and the brush was waved in salutation, a small amount of powder drifting down onto the carpet.

Hardy examined the door handle carefully before reaching out and gripping it with his handkerchief to open the door. Glancing back at her, he looked directly into her now-laughing eyes. She was not fooled for a second. He cleared his throat. She snapped on the light before he could stop her, even though he already knew the room was empty, any intruder long gone, yet the switch had not been fingerprinted. Not, he reminded himself, that the intruder was likely to have touched the light-switch. The room was bathed in the brilliance of electric light.

He looked about him. An instinct prickled the back of his mind, niggling away at his good-natured charade and filling him with disquiet. He held a hand out to her, to tell her to stay back out of the room, but she misunderstood and stepping to his side, she took his hand in hers, wrapping her other arm around the arm he held out to her, her body shaking against him.

'What is it?' she whispered, and the laughter was gone from her eyes.

'I don't...' he murmured, and looked about the room. It was the typical room of any single young woman of a well-to-do family, very like his sister's own room, in fact, in spite of his own reduced circumstances. A bed, a chest of drawers, a screen behind which was a tallboy with a jug and basin set on the top, and a mirror. A much-loved rag-doll sat on a small chair in a corner. A pair of wardrobes. A dressing table. A few items of clothing were strewn across the bed including, even now he couldn't help noticing with masculine interest, some very filmy, lacy night-attire in the soft petal pink often seen on babies. The room was a lot neater than his sister's, actually, though Dottie's room held far more storage for her possessions than his sister at present had, and of course Dottie was a crucial two or three years older than Eleanor. And she had a maid.

On the dressing table, the open jewellery box was fairly full. He pointed to it, and turned to ask her, 'Is everything here?'

She peeked round him, glanced at the dressing table then nodded. Her eyes were still as huge as saucers. Lovely eyes, he thought irrelevantly, and not for the first time. He patted her chilly fingers.

'It's all right. There's no one here. You're safe.'

The eyes fixed on his face, then after a few seconds his words sank in, she nodded again, and some of the tension left her. She blushed as she looked down to see that she was hugging his arm, and released him, stepping back. His arm still felt warm from the contact. She looked again at the jewellery box.

'Yes, that's everything, it's all here.'

He took a closer look. If anything, he was a bit surprised at how little proper jewellery she had. Most of it was the cheap modern costume jewellery his sister liked. There were, in addition, a few items that were undoubtedly valuable. He touched a ring and a pair of earrings.

'My grandmother's,' she said, 'other than those, and the pearls I'm wearing, I don't have anything of real value. Nothing to tempt a thief. I'm so glad they didn't take Grandmama's jewellery, that would have broken my heart.'

A silence settled over the room. They stood side by side in the pool of light, their shadows stretched and bent by the light, seeming to lean in and touch one another. Hardy couldn't seem to make his brain function. All his instincts screamed at him to kiss her. Yet good sense told him it would be an unpardonable liberty that would blight their friendship. If indeed, he reminded himself, they *were* friends.

He forced himself to step back and turn away from her. Behind him, he heard her exhale slowly and realised she too had been holding her breath.

'What about this?' He reached a hand out to point to the scrap of paper that was on the bed, barely visible beneath the folds of her nightgown, not that the flimsy item really was substantial enough to warrant such a name, he added to himself yet again. He refused to dwell on the sudden mental picture of Dottie dressed in the garment. Why did these thoughts plague him so? She stared at him, a little surprised by the odd sudden shake of his head that seemed not to match his actions.

She reached out to take the piece of paper from him. She flattened it out on the palm of her hand with trembling fingers. It was the paper the tiny scrap of fabric had been wrapped in. He could see the ink, the spidery words scratched on the surface, 'The Mantle of God'.

'That wasn't there when I went out,' she said immediately. 'That's not where I keep it. I keep it in the back of the top drawer of the tallboy, under the towels.'

He wasn't surprised to hear she had hidden it; he had known he could trust her to take care of it. But where was the scrap of fabric? It wasn't by the paper on the bed. 'I think we have to admit at last that something has been taken after all,' he said, and felt as though his heart had sunk to his heavy, ill-fitting boots.

She smiled, and reaching for the hem of her skirt, she turned it back to reveal the tiny piece of fabric pinned there.

His eyes glowed with admiration. Blue eyes, Dottie decided, were definitely what she was looking for in a man. Blue eyes like William Hardy's, deep, expressive, now pensive, now laughing, and full of life. That was what she wanted in the man she would marry.

'Thank God,' he said fervently.

'Is everything all right up there?' her father's voice called from the hall below. Dottie, startled, bit her tongue, but nevertheless managed to call back in a perfectly normal voice, 'Yes, Father, everything's perfectly fine. The inspector is just making some notes.

'Hmm,' her father replied, 'Don't care what he does so long as he catches the blighter.'

The sense of intimacy dispersed, the atmosphere lightened. To her amusement, Hardy insisted on checking inside her wardrobes for intruders, then he made certain the windows were secure. Lastly, with a teasing grin, he flung back the fringe of the deeply-draping counterpane, and bending over, peered beneath the bed, then turned back to assure her gravely that no robbers lurked in her room and that she could sleep in perfect safety.

She laughed softly and made a playful slap at his arm, turning to plant a quick soft peck on his cheek. He moved at the crucial moment and she found her lips on his.

He froze. She leapt back, horrified but laughing, her hand going to cover her mouth, her cheeks infused with pink. He cleared his throat to hide his confusion and turning for the door, began to stammer his goodnights and hastily took his leave.

She reached the top of the stairs in time to see he was already turning away from her father and heading towards the big front door that Janet was holding open for him. And then he was gone.

Dottie went to sit in her parents' room whilst the fingerprint man carried out his examination of hers. All she wanted was to go to bed. She just wanted to shut out the world and think about what had just happened. At long last Sergeant Carson called out to her that he had finished. Everywhere seemed to be covered in grey patches of dusty powder, but that would have to wait until morning.

She said goodnight to her parents, unwilling to risk any conversation with them regarding her all-but-forgotten dinner with Dr Melville. Under the covers a minute later, she thought about that accidental kiss. She saw—or thought she saw—in her mind's eyes, his surprise at her action. She felt his unmoving mouth against hers.

Sudden realisation struck her. He had been

chivalrous and charming, a gentleman, allaying her fears about the break-in, and she had acted like a thoroughly brazen and fast modern girl of the worst kind, flinging herself at him, in her *bedroom*, of all places, and how disgusted he surely had been by her behaviour. He hadn't lost a second in leaving the house. She felt this small disaster assume greater and greater proportions, and her evening with Melville now completely forgotten, she sobbed into her pillow at the thought of losing William Hardy's regard.

*

]

Chapter Five

After leaving the Mandersons, Hardy went directly to the police station where he wrote up his report. That done, he spent another half an hour looking over the evidence that had been accumulated for the dinner-party robberies. Maple had used a table on one side of Hardy's office as a central point for all the documents and files relating to their investigation. A large metal box labelled 'Property of Hertfordshire Police' took up a lot of space. They had borrowed it for all their notes and copies of the Herts' case documents. He was too tired now, he decided to wait until the morning when he was fresh to start going through its contents again.

He stretched and yawned. Time to go home. His watch showed him a few minutes short of one o'clock in the morning.

On leaving the station, the desk sergeant gave him a solemn nod, one that conveyed sympathy and fellow-feeling. At least someone knows I'm putting in all these extra hours, Hardy thought.

Outside, the breeze was far too damp and cold to be called bracing, and as he made his way home, walking as quickly as possible, turning up the collar of his coat, he hunched his shoulders against the chill. The streets were silent, almost pitch black in the long gaps between the lamps. He remembered how Dottie Manderson had found a man dying in the street just before Christmas, in just such a dark patch between two streetlights. He thought about her as he walked along, his steps echoing through the air. Her lips had been soft and warm. He had so longed to give in to his desire to really kiss her.

Turning into his road, he could see that his house was all lit up. At first he felt a little curious about that, then puzzled, then finally his emotions turned to fear and he quickened his walk to a run.

One o'clock, and every light in the house was lit, and the front door standing open... Alarm bells shrieked in his head. He raced in at the gate, up the three steps, in at the front door, colliding with a dark-suited gentleman who carried a black bag.

'Wh-what?' Hardy said but didn't wait for a response. He went straight into the little sitting room and recoiled at the scene.

His sister sat on the floor, weeping quietly. She held their mother's hand. Their mother, still wearing her now-customary white apron over her day dress, was seated in the chair beside the fire. Her eyes were closed, her head tilted back against the cushions. No longer her normal pinkish colour, her face was a mask of strange, dull grey.

Hardy stared. He became aware of voices. A

woman whom he recognised from the house next door was speaking to him. Eleanor turned her face up to look at him, her eyes reddened with weeping. She broke out afresh as she saw her brother. The dark-suited gentleman had followed Hardy back into the house, and he was speaking. They were all speaking. But he could only look and look at the body of his mother, neatly seated in her chair, neatly arrayed in her dress and apron, her hair smooth, her hands neatly folded in her lap, a gleam from the light bouncing off the plain gold wedding band on her finger.

He fell into the chair opposite her, unable to wrench his eyes from the sight of her face. Eleanor ran to fling herself into his arms. He rocked slightly with the force of her slender body, automatically catching and holding her, but still, still he couldn't fix on what she was saying.

He turned his head. The man in the dark suit gave him a small glass of something. Hardy knocked it back, still not sure why he had even taken it from the man or why it was thought he needed it. The brandy seemed to set fire to his throat, burning inside him and making him choke.

And all sound suddenly fell upon his ears. They were all speaking at once. Eleanor, sobbing as she explained, clearly feeling it was all her fault. 'We had just sat down with a cup of cocoa before bed. She said she felt tired. I went upstairs for a book, and when I came back... Oh William! When I came back...' She was sobbing again, clutching at his jacket.

'I'm so sorry, Mr Hardy. I'm happy to stay and help as long as you want me. All mine are tucked up in bed, so they won't need me. I'm free to sit up with Miss Hardy all night if needs be...' the neighbour woman was saying.

'Nothing to do, I'm afraid. Very sudden. Acute and fatal cardiac arrest. She wouldn't have suffered, not that that will be much comfort to you at the moment, I fear, but...' The man in the dark suit was watching William with concern. He was the doctor, it came to William now.

He felt an urge to cover his ears, cover his eyes, run back out into the chilly night air, back to the time when his only concerns were his work and imagining Dottie Manderson in that ridiculously flimsy nightgown. He just wanted to go back to all that.

But he couldn't.

Dottie knew nothing of Hardy's personal tragedy. On the morning following the robbery, she received a phone call from Mrs Carmichael. It began without preamble and ended equally abruptly.

'That you, Dot? Look here, I've spoken to my friend what I told you about, told him you're willing. He wants to see you this afternoon at two o'clock. It's a Mr Cecil Greenwood. Take down this address.'

Dottie hastened to take down the address then found Mrs Carmichael had hung up at the other end, and the line was dead. Golly, Dottie thought, it's actually happening. She wondered what sort of outfit one wore to meet a film producer.

She stepped out of the taxi, paid the driver and turned to look about her. She was unsure exactly what she had been expecting, but she had definitely pictured something more glamorous than the rather dull, suburban landscape that now confronted her. On one side there was a long row of respectable, identical housing, with pots of daffodils and primroses, the odd starched matron or plump cat walking along, then on the other side was a tall fence that seemed to stretch for miles. The fence was easily eight feet high and topped with coils of barbed wire. This was not the ultra-modern, elegant movie studio of her imaginings.

In the fence, a narrow door was cut, with a peep-hole at eye-level. A sign proclaimed 'entrance' but the presence of the peep-hole made Dottie doubt whether anyone was ever actually admitted. She knocked. Her heart was pounding in her chest. What if they wouldn't let her in? She didn't want to let Mrs Carmichael down.

Two bloodshot eyes peered out at her. 'Name?' said a harsh male voice.

She stammered, 'Oh, er, Dorothy Manderson.' She felt flustered. The eyes disappeared.

A moment later a muffled voice said, 'Would that be Miss Dot Manderson of Carmichael's?

'Oh yes!' Relief flooded through her as he opened the door, stepping aside to admit her.

'Sign here,' he instructed and held out a clipboard and rather chewed pencil. A grimy fingernail tapped the page against her name. Dottie signed and gave back his pencil.

'That way.' He pointed, then turned and went back inside a kind of sentry box and vanished from her view behind a large newspaper.

She faced the way he had indicated. Spread out

before her was a veritable estate of avenues, buildings, carts, horses and scurrying, bustling people who all too clearly knew just where they were going and were already five minutes late getting there.

Dottie regarded the scene. There was nothing to say where she should go. She dithered for a few moments before summoning the courage to speak to the doorman again.

'Where exactly am I supposed to go?' she demanded of the newspaper, a little louder and more crossly than she'd intended. He dropped the newspaper, glanced at her, and clearly decided that she was not to be trifled with, though she was unsure why.

He carefully folded his newspaper—the Times—and with a heavy sigh laid it to one side. Then from the doorway of his sentry box he gave a long piercing whistle followed immediately by the cry of, 'Oi Anthony!'

Almost at once a round-faced boy with freckles and blond hair appeared.

'Take this lady to Mr Greenwood's office,' the doorman told him.

Anthony nodded, and turning to give Dottie his arm in a very adult fashion, said, 'Allow me, Ma'am.' He winked at her, which made her laugh.

Thus they set off along the broad avenue ahead, and Dottie had reason to be glad of her escort as he turned left and almost immediately right, turned again, opened a door to lead her through a warehouse that turned out to be a set containing a full-sized baronial hall, where a sword fight was about to take place upon the long banqueting table, then they exited upon an alleyway, turning twice more before running up some metal stairs and in at another door.

'Nearly there,' Anthony informed her with a cheeky grin.

'I'll never find my way back again,' Dottie said, panting a little as he hurried her along an upstairs corridor.

'I'll wait for you, Ma'am, and excort you back.' She smiled at his mispronunciation.

'Oh, thank you, Anthony.'

He halted abruptly outside a door. A small brass plate proclaimed *Cecil Greenwood: Producer* rather in the manner of those outside a doctor's or lawyer's office. Anthony rapped smartly then stepped aside and sank down onto the dusty floor, pulling a crumpled comic from the pocket of his elderly tweed jacket.

'I'll be right here, Ma'am. If it was up to me, I'd give you the part. But don't let him take advantage.'

Dottie fervently hoped that would not be part of the role. The door opened. A platinum blonde in a tight jumper and skirt inspected Dottie critically, then told her, 'Step this way, Miss.'

Inside was a desk. In front of the desk were half a dozen hard wooden chairs. 'Wait here. I'll just let him know.'

With a clacking of heels, the blonde disappeared through a door, and Dottie made out the muffled sound of voices. The clacking heels returned.

'Mr Greenwood will be with you shortly.' And the blonde, having lost interest in Dottie, took a seat behind the desk. Presently there was the sound of hesitant typing of the two-fingered variety, and whispered cursing as she halted almost at once to make a correction to her work. Dottie sighed and sat back, eyes closed. She waited. She was wishing fervently she had not agreed to come.

The door was flung open with a crash about fifteen minutes later. A large gentleman bounded through the aperture, his form filling the space.

'Miss Manderson, my dear! Do forgive the delay. Most unfortunate. Most unforgiveable. Come this way, come, do, and let's have a chat. This way to my boudoir, dear lady.'

Dottie exchanged a look with the blonde who, suddenly human, rolled her eyes and smiled at Dottie. Dottie's nerves evaporated.

She followed the gentleman through to his 'boudoir', which she quickly discovered was a rather ordinary-looking office. So ordinary, it might have belonged to any businessman in any institution or corporation in the city of London.

'Sit, my dear, sit yourself down and let's have a look at you. Oh Margaret, do come and take the lady's coat and hat, my dear!' The blonde appeared and took away Dottie's outdoor things, then retreated with them to the outer office, shutting the door behind her.

Mr Greenwood sat, and through the blue haze of his cigar smoke, regarded her with shrewd, steady eyes rather as a farmer might size up a possible purchase at a cattle market. It was a look she had seen many times before, though not usually focussed on herself. It was the same assessing look worn by the women who came to Carmichael's warehouse to view the gowns and costumes Dottie modelled.

'Hmm,' he said after a moment. 'Slim. Pleasing figure. Tall. Pretty hair, good skin. Shame the eyes aren't blue but I suppose one can't have everything. Yes, my dear Miss Manderson, you'll do. You realise of course you'll have no lines?' Dottie hastened to reassure him that she was aware of that.

'Hmm. Well, there you are then. Be here at six o'clock tomorrow.' He was looking at a ledger on his desk, taking up a pen to make a mark on the page. Dottie divined she was dismissed.

She rose to her feet, dropping the hand she'd held out to shake his absent one. She didn't know whether to just leave, but her mother's early instructions could never be set aside.

'Well, thank you very much for your time,' she said, 'and I look forward to working with you.'

'Good God, girl,' he said in an abrupt change of manner, 'You shan't be working with *me*. But—er— very nice meeting you too, Miss, er... Margaret, show Miss—er...'

Margaret the blonde hurried in to chivvy Dottie out of the great man's presence. He'd already turned back to his ledger.

In the outer room, Dottie said, as she put on her coat and hat, 'He said be here at six o'clock tomorrow. Would that be in the evening?'

Margaret stared at her then laughed. 'Gawd, love, you are a bit green, aren't you? No, six in the morning that would be. And not a minute late, mind, they're dead strict.'

'Do I need to bring my lunch? Or will I be

finished by then?'

'Gawd knows, but there's a cart with food for everyone, you don't need to bring it with you.'

It was evening. The Daughters of Esther had said their opening prayer and listened to a few mundane announcements. Then their leader rose to her feet to address the circle of women all clad in their identical black cloaks with the hoods pulled up to cover their heads and thrown their faces into deep shadow.

'Sisters, it gives me great pleasure to welcome into our midst our newest member. I hope you will all greet her at the end of our meeting.' Holding out a hand, she invited the recruit to stand and say a few words.

The new lady was confident enough to accept the task without embarrassment or awkwardness. She spoke in a clear voice, a voice known to many, and therefore immediately recognisable. She said simply, 'I am so happy to accept the invitation to join the Daughters of Esther. I hope I shall be a useful member, and I look forward to working with you all in the Daughters' programmes to support the needy of our city.'

There was a polite ripple of applause, and she resumed her seat. Then the leader closed the official part of the meeting with the customary prayer: 'Good Queen Esther, bride of the King, help us to walk with modesty and self-sacrifice in this world of men, ever ready to perform any office, without reproach, criticism or demand. Help us to remember to serve our Kings selflessly, as you served yours, and by so doing, to preserve our nation in the day of reckoning. Amen.'

Mrs Manderson said 'Amen' with all the others. She felt a bit impatient with all the secrecy and the cloaks, and so on. It was all rather childish in her view, and dangerous. It was this very pretence at secrecy that had made previous members of the Daughters of Esther feel they were above the law, and that was, in Lavinia Manderson's mind, both a dangerous and an immoral position.

And it wasn't as if any of them were truly anonymous. There were a dozen ways to identify someone, even if you hadn't heard their voice in your own drawing room, or just seen them putting up their hoods over their heads before coming into the hall. Membership was by personal invitation. Names were sometimes accidentally used. So the whole notion of anonymity was a farce. Yes, it was definitely childish.

She wasn't sure about the prayer, either. She loved her husband, that much had never been in doubt, but her love for him was rather like old Queen Victoria's ankles—everyone knew they were there but no one ever saw them in public. Certainly she couldn't see Herbert as a kind of kingly Lord Protector, or look up to him with the deep reverence the daughters of Esther seemed to think necessary. She began to feel she might not last very long with the Daughters of Esther, in spite of her enthusiastic acceptance speech.

The next morning, Anthony met Dottie at the gate at a quarter to six as arranged. Dottie felt as though she hadn't slept. The scene with her mother the night before had left her drained and emotional. She was dreading a repeat of the same recriminations when she got home, which would hopefully be by mid-morning, she told herself.

Anthony delivered her to the door of a large echoey warehouse. Outside, the streets of the 'studio' were deserted, but as she stepped through the doorway, she found the place was noisy and bustling with people. There were screens and chairs, piles of stuff on tables everywhere. There were cameras on wheels, cameras held in the hand, dazzling lights making the place hot, and everywhere, worried people with clipboards hurried back and forth. She hovered inside the door, unsure what to do or where to go.

'Quiet please!' a voice yelled, and all sound abruptly ceased. Dottie could hear the sound of her own breathing.

A man stepped forward and began to read names from a list, adding instructions as he did so. People nodded and ran hither and thither according to his bidding.

When he had finished, and still not called her name, or perhaps she had missed it, she thought anxiously, Dottie went over to him and introduced herself, then quickly explained why she was there.

His face, haggard from the early start, was impassive. As he turned away from her, he said, 'We'll get to you later, sweetheart. Or perhaps tomorrow. Go to Wardrobe.' Dottie was left staring at his back.

Desperately wishing even more fervently she had said a firm 'No!' to Mrs Carmichael's request, Dottie asked first one person then another, and finally a third who gave her some rather sketchy directions, and at almost seven o'clock she found herself in yet another warehouse and what was undeniably 'Wardrobe'. The vast room was crammed with rack upon rack and rail upon rail of dresses, suits, gowns, hats, bags, shoes, gloves, fans, jewellery and even swords and other items of weaponry and armour. In fact every single item a human being could conceivably put on or hold in front of the camera was stored here waiting for its own special moment.

A busy little woman draped in tape measures bustled over, shouting over her shoulder, 'No, Esme, I quite clearly said the *silver* tulle!' With scarcely a breath she turned to Dottie, giving her the once over, and demanding, 'Well, where is it?'

Dottie stammered. The little woman glared at her, tapping an impatient foot on the wooden boards. 'The French navy for the third act? You *are* the girl from Martinsons'?'

'Ah, no, sorry,' Dottie said, and seeing the woman's quick frown, hurriedly introduced herself, adding apologetically, 'I was told to come here, I'm afraid I'm not quite sure why.'

'Oh Gawd, they'll be wanting me to measure you up, I s'pose. What's your part?'

'I'm not quite...'

'Well, what scene is it?'

'I'm afraid...'

Exasperated, the little woman clicked her tongue and already turning away, indicated that Dottie should follow her into the dim recesses of the back-room, demanding, 'Well, for the dear Lord's sake, at least tell me what I'm supposed to give you to wear?'

Here again Dottie was unable to offer any insight. A young woman stood at a table, ironing in a drooping, listless manner what appeared to be an acre of spider-web fine, silvery-grey fabric. The tulle, Dottie surmised, and therefore this must be Esme.

'They only has it on two minutes, I don't know how they gets it so crunched up and filthy. And that lot over there has just come from Martinsons', only on the other side of town, but it looks like it's come by yak from outer Mongolia. But that's Martinsons' for you. Do you know them?'

Dottie said she did, which surprised the little woman, and when Dottie went on to remark upon the ill effects of the firm's transportation of forty yards of chartreuse rough silk suiting for Mrs Carmichael, a friendly light began to shine in the other woman's eyes.

'Come this way, dear, I'll check my list, see what it says. There could be something in there, you never know.'

Dottie trotted obediently at her heels, exchanging a sympathetic smile with Esme who then practically disappeared behind a cloud of steam. I hope that's not the tulle she's steaming like that, Dottie thought. They went past miles of fabric rolls and stacks of shoes and boots, and past the rather scary-looking dressmaker's models, all standing about with vacant stares peering into the unknown.

At the furthest corner of the back-room was a little crowded desk with a dim lamp burning low over the table-top. The woman sat down on a creaking wooden chair and indicated Dottie should do the same.

'Judith Parsons, by the way, Miss. I'm the wardrobe mistress, and that useless drip out there is my niece Esme Barker, and a terrible trial on my nerves, let me tell you, but I promised her mother... Now this here's my list. I'm not saying you're on it, but you just might be. If you're not, we're no further forward.'

She scanned page after page. At length, she peered at Dottie. 'Carmichael's, did you say?'

'That's right.'

'Hmm. Says here, four girls from Carmichael's, various mannequins, for set-dressing in back-room scene. No nudity.'

'Thank goodness for that!' Dottie said.

'Should be four of you though,' Miss Parsons pointed out.

'Mrs Carmichael said she would speak to the other girls. I'm afraid I don't know what the outcome of that was. Perhaps the other girls might be still at the other...?'

'We'll see soon enough, I imagine. So, you'll be in the scene where the star, that's Marguerite Hutchings, playing the part of Ginger Richardson, the would-be actress, what comes into the dressing room to get ready for her big stage debut which is so affecting, her millionaire sweetheart proposes to her there and then, and whisks her off to his palace and she never acts again. We should all be so lucky.'

On hearing this synopsis, Dottie couldn't help wrinkling her nose. Miss Parsons nodded.

'Exactly. Between you and me and the gate-post, I wouldn't give it six months, but this is the Silver

Screen, and all our scenes are rose-coloured.'

They got to business. Dottie's measurements were taken and a list drawn up of likely costumes. Less than an hour later, Judith Parsons set down her tape measure, notebook and pencil.

'Well that's it. It's almost eight o'clock, I'd say that's your day's work finished.'

'Oh, but won't they need me later?'

'Trust me, dear, they won't get to your scene for at least a day or two. They've got to do the wedding scene, don't ask me why they're doing the final scene first, they just are. They always do it in a funny order. And then the next few days is taken up with the suicide bid and her stay in the convalescent home where she meets her future intended as he sits with his dying mother. Like all the actors, I'll be here all the weekend, I expect, it usually ends up like that. So many things crop up at the last minute, it takes me half the weekend to get straight after the week, then I need to get a start on the coming week before that all goes to pot too. There's no possible way they'll need you before Tuesday or Wednesday. If you give me your number, I'll get young Esme to ring up if anything changes, sometimes there's something crops up and they have to rejig the shooting.'

Dottie thanked her but still didn't feel able to just go home. 'Is there anything I can help you with?' She'd noticed that Esme was still at her ironing table and making slow progress. Several times in the last hour, people had run in to drop off a bundle of garments or to collect a bundle, mostly errand boys or girls, mostly young and exhausted-looking.

Miss Parsons appraised Dottie for a few seconds then nodded. 'Well thank you, I can't deny I need all the help I can get. That Esme's a useless lump.'

Esme, on hearing this, glanced up, sniffed, and turned back to the neverending length of tulle. Clearly she was used to such insults.

'How it takes her so long to do the least little thing is beyond me, so yes, I'd be glad of your help. You look like you've got some sense in that head of yours.'

High praise indeed, Dottie thought. For the rest of the day, Dottie worked hard to help Miss Parsons check her catalogue of costumes, ensuring they had all the right garments on the right rails for the scenes in order of shooting. The sizes were checked and double-checked against the lists of measurements of those who would be wearing the clothes, and after all that, they had to ensure all costumes were perfect and not in need of repair or laundering. On a couple of occasions an actress came running in to try on a garment, notes were taken regarding alterations and the young person would disappear again into the outside world.

By the time Dottie went home, she was almost too exhausted to put one foot in front of the other. She had barely sat down the whole day and her head was pounding. She declined any dinner, taking a cup of tea straight up to her room, where she fell asleep, leaving the tea to grow cold. Needless to say, she still didn't know when her screen debut would take place.

*

Chapter Six

For the next two days, Dottie helped Miss Parsons and Esme in the wardrobe department. It was exhausting work, and when she reached home she ate almost nothing, but fell immediately into bed to sleep dreamlessly until her alarm woke her at five o'clock. It was a rare thing for her to be up before the maid Janet in the mornings, and not at all a welcome experience. But she enjoyed the work enormously, even though it meant working over the weekend, the cause of a further rift with her mother. Mr Manderson remained behind his *Times* newspaper for the entirety of Saturday and Sunday. It was safe there, and he couldn't see the furious looks and pursed lips of his wife.

How quickly life can change, Hardy thought. On the previous Tuesday, his life had seemed to be going along on a normal, if unrewarding, path. Looking back, he wondered that the Hardy of a week earlier did not have some inkling of the change that Fate, or whatever controlled the world, had in store for him and his family. A week ago, his mother had still been alive.

'I'm just a little tired, William dear, that's all,' she had said to him on the telephone. Almost the last words she had spoken to him. Why hadn't he realised?

And now, not only was she gone from him, his siblings and their wider family, but she was already buried in the ground too. In just a week. Hardy had an arm about his younger brother's shoulders. Although in his mid-teens, the sudden loss of their mother had pierced Edward's fragile maturity and left him vulnerable and grief-stricken. In spite of this Hardy was glad of his brother's company. Hardy missed the time they used to spend together. There were almost fourteen years between them but in spite of the age-difference, they got on well. He led Edward away to the waiting black-draped carriages pulled by black-plumed horses.

After a lunch at a nearby hotel paid for, to Hardy's great shame, by his mother's brother, he said an emotional farewell to his sister and brother who were travelling back to Derbyshire to stay with their uncle and his wife. He thanked his uncle for all his assistance and promised to telephone in a day or two.

'Leave the police force, come back with us,' Uncle Joe urged, and not for the first time. 'There's a place in my business for a bright young man like yourself, and I've no son coming after me to take it on when I hang up my hat. At least promise me you'll think it over. There's nothing left for you here, Bill.'

Oh, but there is, Hardy thought, and he thanked his uncle again for all his help and kindness. Once they had left, he had others to thank and speak to, then it was time to go back to the house. It was the part of the day he had dreaded even more than the sight of his mother's coffin being lowered into the ground.

He walked from the hotel back to the house. The air was crisp and held a promise of spring warmth. Birds sang. He noticed here and there a daffodil holding a golden head to the sky. He waved hello to the kindly neighbour woman who had sat up all that first night with Eleanor, but he was in no mood for conversation. He had already spoken to her at the funeral, and thanked her for her kindness. Everyone, it seemed, had been kind, so kind. He had had enough of it. All he wanted was to get inside the house and shut the door on the world.

It was the chair that caught his eye as he entered the sitting room. A sudden rage swept through him at the very sight of it, at the memory of that evening only five days earlier when he had come into the room and seen her sitting there. The rage swept away all his sorrow and his lethargy, and he gripped the arms of the chair, wrestled it through the sitting room door, out into the hall and flinging the front door wide, with a howl of fury he threw the chair down the steps and watched it as it splintered, scattered, and came to a rest at the gate. He slammed the front door shut and marched into the kitchen.

There his rage left him and he felt exhausted and unable to think. The fire hadn't been lit for two days. The kettle hadn't boiled. No meals had been prepared. He sank onto a hard, upright chair beside the table. Tears filled his eyes and he put his head down in his hands on the table-top and sobbed for the first time.

Ten minutes went by before he realised the room was cold and dark. Only three o'clock in the afternoon but the kitchen was located in the back basement, and was never truly bright.

He didn't know what to do. There *was* nothing to do. Relatives had sorted his mother's belongings the previous day, taking away everything but the one or two items Eleanor had wanted to keep. It was as if she had never been there at all.

His cases had been divided up between colleagues, but he would be returning to duty in the morning. What a relief, he thought, with irony, it would be to really lose himself in work once more. The endless routine he had grown to hate would be most welcome. He wondered what had been happening in his cases, especially the robberies.

He pushed away worries about the future, and getting up to pour himself a glass of whisky, carried both glass and bottle up the stairs to his bedroom. He sat in the chair by the window, sipping from his glass from time to time and thinking.

He hoped the case wasn't yet closed. He had vaguely noticed a newspaper stand from the hearse as they drove to the cemetery. The headline *Dinner Party Thieves Strike Again* had curiously heartened him. He had no idea how things were proceeding in the case but clearly there was still work to do. He just hoped he would be the one to do it.

By the end of Tuesday, Dottie had still not had her moment of glory in front of the camera, as predicted by Miss Parsons, and she was well and truly fed up with hanging about the film studio trying to fill the time. She half-considered just not going in, but concern that this might be the day she was called, coupled with the fact that she had given her word, made her dismiss that idea almost immediately. She spent most of her waking hours in the company of the rather terrifying Miss Parsons and her much-criticised, rather spineless niece Esme.

So it was an immense relief to meet her sister for a late afternoon tea not too far from the studios. Dottie sat stirring milk into her tea, half in a daydream, half asleep. Every part of her seemed to ache and she struggled to stay awake. Flora was chattering on and on. Her voice formed a kind of backdrop to Dottie's fatigued and confused senses, and she only began to surface when, somewhat belatedly, she distinguished the words, 'Poor William and Eleanor! It came completely out of the blue, apparently, there'd been no previous indication. So very sad.'

Dottie stared at her sister, aware of a growing sense of dread. 'What? What is so sad?'

'Have you listened to a word I've said? I told you, it was in the newspapers, under the obituaries, 'Mrs Isabel Hardy, suddenly at home, beloved mother and wife of the late Major Garfield Hardy, interment at St Frideswide's, all friends and acquaintances welcome', with today's date. They must be absolutely devastated, not to mention the younger brother at Repton, and of course their older sister, the one with the young baby. What a terrible time they must all be going through.'

Dottie stared at her sister even harder. Her eyes glistened with the start of tears. 'Isabel Hardy? William Hardy's mother? Dead? *Our* William Hardy, or...?'

Flora gave a wry smile. She reached into her bag for a handkerchief and pressed it into Dottie's hand. 'Well, technically I'd be rather inclined to say *your* William Hardy, but yes the very same. Heart attack, very suddenly, last week. So sad. They must be completely...'

'Oh my God! How terrible!' Dottie gasped. 'How bloody terrible!' People at a nearby table glared at her and shook their heads over her bad language. Flora patted Dottie's hand.

'Yes, dear,' she said, 'that's what I've been saying for the last ten minutes. The funeral was this morning. I sent a wreath from George and myself, and Mother sent one from the rest of you. And of course, I shall send a note of condolence. Poor William.'

Dottie noticed the broken remains of a chair scattered on the little path. She stepped over the cushioned seat of it as she made her way up the steps to the front door, rapped smartly and waited for someone to answer. Looking about her, she saw a fairly pleasant little townhouse in a respectable, if not particularly affluent, neighbourhood. Certainly a much nicer home than their last, from what she'd heard of that. She turned back to the door. No one was coming, and so she knocked again, a little louder this time.

Perhaps no one was home, she thought, but nevertheless, after waiting for another long, long minute, she tried the handle and the door opened.

She stepped into the dim hallway, ignoring a slight queasiness in the pit of her stomach and pushing away memories of walking into another, similarly dim hallway just a few weeks earlier, and of the dreadful sight that had awaited her in the drawing room of that other house.

A glance at the coat stand showed only William's great coat and his suit jacket. His sister must be out then, and there were no other visitors. Of course, William himself might be out, the day was less chilly so he may have left his great coat at home. But where would he go on the day he'd buried his mother? Surely not to work, or out socialising. In any case, she had always had the impression he had few friends since the loss of his family's wealth and position. So where was he?

There were no lights on, the house felt abandoned. But if the door was open, someone had to be at home, or else, they had just forgotten to lock the door... She made her way through the hall and into the back of the house. She quickly scanned the tiny, old-fashioned kitchen, the even smaller and terribly gloomy dining room, and the much nicer sitting room, but they were all equally empty and chilly. No one was there.

Feeling uncomfortably aware of how intensely her mother would disapprove, Dottie mounted the stairs, telling herself he might be ill, or the house might still be empty and therefore vulnerable to burglars.

She went into the first bedroom. Clearly it had been his mother's. The curtains were closed, but she could make out that the bed had been stripped, and everything looked bare and abandoned. Tears prickled Dottie's eyes as she remembered chatting with sad, tired Isabel Hardy only a few weeks earlier. What a thoroughly nice woman she had been.

The second bedroom was evidently Eleanor's. There was a pretty feminine counterpane on the bed, and a few knick-knacks and personal items about the room: a picture, a scarf, a pair of gloves. Some jewellery in a small, battered-looking leather case. One or two other things on the dressing-table.

The bathroom door stood open, the room cold and empty, lit only by the light from the street coming in at the tiny window. A tap dripped.

The last door on the upper landing was closed. He was in his room then, she surmised, and here again she hesitated. Her mother would have been scandalised and had a great deal to say about the propriety of a single young woman entering the bedroom of a single young man. At any time of day, let alone after dark, and with no one else there as chaperone. It was yet another thing she must ensure her mother never, ever, heard about.

She tapped on the door, and listened. Hearing nothing, and rather surprised at her own boldness, she gripped the handle and turned it. The door opened on a room in darkness, and her senses were assaulted by the overwhelming stench of alcohol. She could make out his form, sprawled and oblivious, in the chair, a bottle on the floor by his feet.

She felt suddenly angry, and completely forgetting about any of the things her mother might think or say on the matter, Dottie marched right into the room, and before she even knew what she planned to do, she had slapped him hard across the face.

It had its immediate effect. He sprang to his feet, confused and swaying, but furious, and swearing loudly and comprehensively, before he realised who he was speaking to. His words stuttered and failed. He stared at her. With an attempt at gaining back his advantage, he demanded with some aggression, 'What the hell do you want?'

His temper, his shock, restored her balance and she was able to tell him quite calmly and coldly, 'I came to see if you were all right, and to offer my condolences. I've only just heard about your poor mother.'

They glared at each other. His chest was heaving as he attempted to pull himself together, and at the same time, get a grip on his temper, borne as it was out of shock. He said nothing.

'You smell terrible,' she told him, and was aware that this was not the polite conversation of guest to host. 'Go and have a bath and change your clothes. I'll make you something to eat. You've got twenty minutes.'

'I don't...'

'Do as you're told, William!' she snapped, and turning on her heel she marched back along the hall to the stairs, praying that her dignity would hold until she reached the kitchen.

She had no idea if he would take any notice of her. She had seen her sister employ such tactics with her husband George after he'd come in from a night of carousing with his chums, although Dottie herself had never had the opportunity to tell a man what to do before. But as she entered the kitchen, she heard the sound of a door closing upstairs, and almost immediately a bolt was slid home. Next, as she stood looking about her and wondering what to do, she heard the sound of water running into the bath-tub. She smiled to herself. It had worked!

Eggs, she told herself. Simple to do, and hopefully wouldn't make too big a hole in the policeman's budget. *If* there were any eggs.

By the time William Hardy entered the kitchen, smelling a good deal better than half an hour before, and looking utterly ashamed of his bad language, there was a pot of tea on the table, and beside it, a plate of thick, buttery toast with scrambled eggs.

She was seated on the other side of the table, cradling a cup of tea in both hands, and had she but known it, in his mother's place. If he was surprised that a posh girl from a home with servants knew how to make scrambled eggs, or indeed even simple toast and tea, he said nothing, merely taking his seat, and with a nervous glance, saying first of all, 'I'm so sorry for the...'

'My mother would have been horrified,' she told him bluntly, adding in a softer tone, 'and so would yours.'

He nodded, blinking, and bent his head to pour the tea and add a splash of milk. The clock on the mantelpiece ticked loudly. Damn all clocks, Dottie thought. No matter where one went, there they were, ticking away, and making a fearful racket.

'I'm sorry,' he said again.

'It's all right. You've had a rotten time, I know. I'm so sorry I wasn't there this morning, I just hadn't heard what had happened somehow. And I'm so sorry about your mother, she was such a nice lady. I would have liked to come to the funeral.'

He nodded, but looked a little teary again, so to change the subject, she asked simply, 'Where's Eleanor?'

That he could answer safely. 'Gone to stay with my uncle in Matlock for a time. My younger brother has gone too. It'll do them good to get away for a while.'

'And when do you go back to work?'

'Tomorrow.'

'So soon? Golly! But perhaps it'll be a help to get back to work and keep busy?'

'No doubt.' He had finished the food and was pouring himself another cup of tea. He offered her more, but she shook her head. They observed one another in an uncomfortable silence then she rose from the table.

'Well, I'm glad to see you looking a bit better,' she said, unsure quite how to actually take her leave. 'And once again, I'm awfully sorry to hear of your sad loss.' How trite that sounds, she thought. I sound just like my mother. She dithered in the doorway. Then finally simply held out her hand to him. 'Well, goodnight.'

He took her hand, pulled her and brought her up against his chair. His arms came around her waist and for a few minutes he leaned his head against her, then recollecting himself, cleared his throat, releasing her, and got to his feet. He led the way to the door, holding it open for her.

'Thank you for coming,' he said, as if it was an ordinary social occasion, as if he hadn't been slapped by her, sworn at her, eaten the food she prepared and held her in his arms. And before he could say anything more, halfway down the steps, she stood on tiptoes to kiss his cheek, then practically ran out into the night, hailing a cab almost immediately.

He leaned against the door for a moment, then with a shake of the head, William Hardy closed the door and returned to the kitchen, which seemed warm and welcoming now, even though Dottie was no longer there.

*

Chapter Seven

The next day, the Wednesday after she had started work at the studio, and ready to drop from the exhaustion of hanging about waiting, Dottie was finally called to do her part.

If she'd thought this indicated a sudden flurry of activity or excitement, she was wrong. There followed two long hours of standing beside a mirror with a hairbrush in her hand, clad only in a pale pink silk negligee over her underwear.

'This is most definitely not the glamorous life I expected,' she told the mirror crossly.

'I know what you mean, love,' confided another voice. It belonged to a young girl positioned on the other side of the mirrored partition. She began to tell Dottie all about her hopes for getting a proper start in the acting profession, ending with, 'It's taken me a year to get this blooming part. If it takes another year to get my next job, I'll be out on the street, I won't be able to pay my rent. And there's no way I can go home to my mother.'

Dottie cast a rueful look down at her attire. 'No indeed. Mine will be furious if she hears about this. She'll probably pack me off to a convent.'

'Mine will think I'm possessed or something. She'll have the priest round straight away to exorcise me. I'm not exaggerating.'

'Hmm,' Dottie said, and at that moment the director's assistant called for quiet on set. Dottie held her breath, waiting to see if the star could finally remember how she had to move and stand. Dottie was supposed to be conveying the impression of someone who had just that moment snatched up a hairbrush to do her hair between dress models, and not at all like a young woman who was cold, bored, and absolutely certain she'd need to stay with her sister for a few days to escape the maternal wrath that awaited her at home.

Everyone's patience was finally rewarded. The star, Marguerite Hutchings, renowned for her ravishing figure and long blonde hair, though not for her intelligence or wit, successfully entered the scene without knocking over the set wall. She then closed the door slowly and carefully behind her without pulling off the doorknob, moved across the short space to position herself in front of the mirror beside Dottie, managing to achieve this object without tripping over the rug on the floor, or her own feet, or losing the feather boa from about her shoulders.

At the mirror, she successfully picked up the other brush, started to brush her hair with it then flung it down, this time without smashing the mirror, and threw herself into a sobbing fit on

Dottie's chilly, waiting shoulder.

Dottie's sole action, to pat the star on the back consolingly, was accomplished without a hitch and the director's assistant shouted 'Cut!' in ringing triumphant tones.

'Well done, that was remarkable,' Dottie told the star perfectly sincerely. Dottie was genuinely surprised the actress had finally done everything required of her. The mood in the place had lightened considerably.

The star was taken off to lie down and recover from her exertions, and the director's assistant told Dottie she could go, adding that she could draw her wages from the clerk, and he gave her a chit of paper to enable her to do just that.

Dottie went to say goodbye to Judith Parsons and Esme. She needed to return the negligee in any case, and she wanted to ask Miss Parsons something.

She found the wardrobe mistress engaged in yet another heated dispute with Esme over yet another piece of tulle, this time in a violent shade of purple.

Dottie was relieved of the negligée by a tearful Esme, still muttering, 'Evil old bag,' under her breath. With a sympathetic smile, Dottie followed Miss Parsons to her desk in the corner, where tea was made. Dottie was really glad to receive a cup, warming her hands on the china. She unburdened herself regarding the morning's work.

'There's a reason some girls choose the stage,' said Miss Parsons, 'and it's not because of their looks. Here even the plain ones can pick up a wealthy husband, and all they need to do is look just slightly decorative. They'd never make a living for themselves. Let's face it, most of 'em don't have the brains the good Lord gave a rabbit, so they've got to marry well or find themselves a sugar daddy. And that Hutchings girl is walking out with a cabinet minister, by all accounts. He's bought her a flat and everything. Though of course, his wife don't know that.'

They talked of this and that. Dottie had a second cup of tea. Over the last few days she'd developed a respect for the formidable wardrobe mistress and her wealth of knowledge, both general and more specifically costume-related. Having debated with herself over and over again since her arrival at the studio, Dottie had come to a decision.

Feeling rather like a magician pulling a rabbit out of a hat, Dottie pulled up her hem and unpinned the tiny scrap of fabric William Hardy had given her. She lay it on the desk in front of Miss Parsons.

'What do you make of that?' Dottie asked. She found she was holding her breath, her heart was pounding as she watched Judith Parsons set down her teacup and with a puzzled look, take up the tiny piece and turn it this way and that in the dim lamplight, as Mrs Carmichael had done, as Dottie herself had done, and even the loathsome James Melville.

Even before Miss Parsons spoke, Dottie knew she was finally going to hear something significant. Here at last was the answer she'd been looking for. Goosebumps stood out on her arms, and she hugged herself to prevent a shiver.

Miss Parsons gave the scrap back to Dottie and

turned off the little green-shaded desk lamp. She took her glasses off her rather long thin nose and set them down on the desk. She fixed a straight look on Dottie.

'Well, I don't know where you got that. And I'm not going to ask. But, seeing as you've asked me about it, I'll tell you what I think.'

Dottie's heart pounded, if possible, even harder and faster. If Miss Parsons next words were, 'And don't tell anyone you heard this from me,' she could not have felt more excited.

William Hardy presented himself to Chief Superintendant Smithers promptly at nine o'clock on the morning after the funeral. He reflected that the fact he was capable of doing so, and looking fairly neat and tidy, able to talk sense and stand upright, was entirely due to the intervention of Miss Manderson and her splendid right hook. And of course, her scrambled eggs and toast. When he thought about how close he had come to just throwing it all away... it was amazing how different things could look in the light of a new day.

'Well, well, Hardy, come in, sit down, my dear fellow. Dashed hard lines, losing one's mother. Condolences. Must say you're looking better than I expected under the circumstances. All credit to you. Ready to pick up the reins, I expect. As you know we've had in an officer from the Metropolitan Police headquarters at Scotland Yard. An arrest was made, some crooked antiques dealer who had some of the items from the first burglary. But you'll no doubt have seen yesterday's paper, so you'll know that there was another robbery on Sunday evening. I had hoped to be able to tell you that you could cross the dinner party robberies off your list but it now seems otherwise. Must be the same people, I'm sure. Everything about this latest case looks the same.'

'Have we released the suspect, sir?'

'Um no, it seems likely he's just one of the gang, operating out of the docks, or so we thought, supposed to have contacts in Holland, none too particular about the provenance of the stuff. We haven't got anything useful out of him as yet. I say 'we', I know nothing about it really, it was the new chappie, very efficient, I'm sure, if a bit too public school for my...er...' the chief super seemed to suddenly think better of what he was about to say, possibly because Hardy was wearing his old school tie. After a pause, Smithers continued, 'What we need, Hardy, is information. We need hard facts. We need to put this whole sorry mess to bed, and be damned quick about it.'

'Indeed, sir. I'll certainly get straight to it, sir, you can be sure of that.'

'Good, good. I've decided to take all your other cases off your plate, so to speak, let you focus on these robberies. Sergeant Maple's already passed on all the paperwork for the other cases, so you'll have no distractions. The higher-ups are getting pressure from the public and even Parliament itself about this, so I want you to get on with it. We need a quick resolution to these robberies. Well I'll let Hayward fill you in on what he's been up to in your absence. You'll have to look lively, he's on his way back to Scotland Yard. Right, well. Glad to have you back, of course. Hard lines, of course, but that is life, I suppose. Dashed hard lines. Let me know if you need anything else. Door's always open. Good day to you.'

And he was out again in the corridor, nodding to the chief super's assistant and the secretary, and making his way back down the draughty stairs to his own office.

A man of about forty-five was there, carefully slotting papers and notebooks into a cardboard box. He had a toothbrush moustache and slicked back, mirror-smooth hair. Hardy detested him on sight. However, he made an effort to remain polite, and entered the room, a smile on his face and his hand outstretched.

'Inspector Hayward? Glad I didn't miss you. I'm William Hardy. I hear you've been holding the fort while I've been off.'

Hayward set down the notebook he was holding, and advanced round the desk to shake Hardy's hand, his own hot and sticky, and as small as a woman's.

'My dear fellow. Very nice to meet you, and of course, sympathies on your loss. Very, very sad indeed. A boy needs his mother. Very sad. No doubt you'll be glad to get back to work to take your mind off things.'

It was what Dottie had said, but delivered without her compassion and sincerity. Also that comment about a boy needing his mother rubbed his pride up the wrong way. Hardy saw no reason as yet to change his initial opinion of Hayward. Who, it appeared, still had things to say. 'But take it from me, it does get a little easier with time. I've been through most of life's crises at one time or another, and I'm usually right about these things.'

Clearly, Hayward was quite the sage, thought Hardy irritably. He tried to maintain his friendly demeanour in spite of feeling patronised. After all, the fellow would be gone soon, and things could get back to normal.

'Yes indeed, nothing like routine, is there?' Hardy responded. 'Well, once again...'

'You'll no doubt have heard that I've cracked your case for you. I expect that's been playing on your mind too. Quite the little teaser, wasn't it? But there, all done bar a little rounding up of the rest of the gang. There's nothing worse than feeling as though one is bumping one's head against a brick wall. I've found that often all it takes is a pair of fresh eyes going over what you've no doubt gone over a hundred times already. Can't see the wood for the trees, what?

'But don't blame yourself, young fellow, I've got a good few years' more experience than you. It'll be the work of a moment to pull the rest of the gang in and get the confessions we need. I've got rid of all your other cases for you, pulled a few strings, called in some favours, all done and dusted. So there's nothing too onerous for you left to do, but it'll ease you back into things, give your confidence a much-needed boost. Well, I'll be off. Got to get back to the Yard, you know. All the paperwork's been done, and as I said, no doubt the chappie we've got in the clink has had time to think and is ready to tell you the rest of the names. I think that's everything.' He patted his suit pockets, found his pipe and tobacco pouch, and began to fill the pipe. 'Could I trouble you for a light, old chap?'

Hardy felt a small victory in being able to say perfectly honestly, 'I'm sorry, I don't smoke. Perhaps my sergeant...?'

Taken aback, but not deflated, Hayward clamped his pipe between his teeth, picked up his cardboard box and held out his free hand to Hardy. 'Short and sweet, wasn't it? Nice to meet you, laddie. Good luck. Take my advice and don't worry so much, it'll come with time, it'll come. Who knows, we might even see you at the Yard one day.'

Hayward then side-stepped Hardy and left the office. Hardy was aware of a simmering rage. He sat at his almost empty desk—was it really that bright shade of ochre, he didn't recall ever seeing the surface of the desk before—and waited for a full five minutes. By the end of that time he felt slightly calmer, and he went in search of his favourite sidekick, Sergeant Frank Maple.

'I'm back, Frank, thought I'd better let you know.'

Maple got to his feet and gave Hardy a hearty hand-shake that in the pub would have turned into a back-slapping, saying in a lowered voice, 'Bill! I've never been so glad to see anyone in my life. Has that idiot Hayward gone?'

'Yes. Though before he left he very kindly treated me to a lecture on how good he is at his job and how bad I am at mine. I feel so greatly edified by his wisdom.'

'He's a total w...' but whatever Maple had been about to say was drowned out as the telephone bell jangled, making both men jump.

A few minutes later they were setting off on a

drive to an address well outside of their London jurisdiction, in Hemel Hempstead, Hertfordshire, a short distance further north than Hitchin where they'd been before, but at least they knew most of the roads now. The local police had rung in response to Maple's widespread enquiries about armed robberies, and thought they had found another, related robbery that bore similar traits to that of the one in Hitchin, and could therefore be of interest to the Met. It seemed that an armed robbery had taken place at the home of a Mrs Emmeline Foster just a few days earlier.

'The lady had been having a dinner party when gunmen broke in. Sounds like another one for our list,' Maple added.

'It's old. Very old. I'm sure it's velvet, though the pile has rubbed away over time. It's as thin as tissue paper in places. Velvet used to be made and imported from abroad, Spain, the Middle East, places like that, then embroidered, by hand obviously, in this country by skilled craftsmen or more often, women. There was a time, and I'm going back five or six, even seven hundred years, now, there was a time when the finest embroidery was found in this country, and royalty, nobles and all manner of influential people all around the world sought out the expertise of English artisans.'

'But not *this*,' Dottie stammered, shocked. 'This can't be...you're not saying, surely you're not, that *this* is hundreds of years old? The best part of *five or six hundred* years old? It can't possibly...half a millennium...'

'Or more. Yes, I am, my dear.'

'But...' Dottie opened her hand, damp with the heat in the crowded warehouse. The scrap curled and stuck to her skin. She flattened it out, pressing it gently, reverently, until it was straight. In a whisper she continued, half to herself, 'Not *this*. This can't be...' Her voice failed her. Everything was falling into place in her mind. Her thoughts adjusted themselves and began to make sense. She looked at the innocent scrap again, and felt the prickle of tears.

Miss Parsons patted her hand, gently folding Dottie's fingers down over it. 'Yes, my dear, it's the best part of easily five or six hundred years old. I'm not an expert, but I've seen something like this before. But if you go to a museum or to Westminster Abbey or any cathedral or an important country house, you might see one, though probably not as old as this. It's a piece from a chasuble or a cope or something of that sort, I'd stake my reputation on that. It's a pity there isn't more of it.' She fixed Dottie with a sudden sharp look. 'Unless of course you have the rest of it?'

To Dottie's hasty shake of the head, she added, 'Oh well, it'd probably only bring you worry, anyway.'

'A chasuble?'

'Or some kind of clerical vestment. The chasuble is the colourful, sleeveless, open-fronted thing they wear over the alb, which is the white, long-sleeved loose smock-type garment. Or it could be from a cope worn about the shoulders, a kind of cape. They still wear these in churches everywhere. Anglican as well as Catholic. The churches used to commission these garments for the priests. Or they might be ordered for a special service, such as the marriage of royalty or nobles, coronations, investitures, special visitations, anything like that. Or they could even be donated by wealthy patrons. In any case, they were fabulously crafted, complex works of art really, not just a simple covering for a priest to wear when conducting mass.'

'So, it's velvet. And it's from a much bigger piece. And rather old, which explains why it's so faded and patchy,' Dottie summarised. The act of doing so calmed her nerves.

'Yes dear. The thread was usually flax or silk. There were two main stitches, I'll show you on this bit of cotton.' Judith picked up a small remnant of fabric, left over from the shortening of a petticoat, and from the pincushion she took a needle with about eight inches of purple thread hanging from it. She leaned towards Dottie, and made a couple of stitches.

'Now you see, that's your basic split-stitch. And this one,' she made a few more stitches, this time bringing the needle back up from underneath to 'pin' long, single stitches in place. 'This one is the underside couching. And these were the two main stitches used for creating the outlines of shapes and patterns, and for filling them in. All the decoration would be worked in thread across the ground of the fabric, like painting on a canvas, but with thread. For the very wealthy patrons, or for special pieces, the thread could be covered in pure gold or silver. There would be figures, scenes from the Bible or lives of the saints or kings. When the garments were brand new, they would have been marvellously bright and colourful, and incredibly skilful, intricate creations. The mainly uneducated congregation could learn about the Church and God from looking at these images, just by watching the priest as he celebrated Mass.'

'Would it be worth a lot of money today?' Dottie asked. 'A whole one, I mean?'

'Well it could be,' Miss Parsons said, though she sounded doubtful. 'I suppose a really avid collector might pay whatever it takes to get hold of one. Otherwise, it probably depends what the decoration was made of.'

Dottie didn't understand. 'I thought you said it would be flax or silk, possibly covered with gold or silver? That doesn't sound terribly valuable.'

Miss Parsons nodded, saying, 'But they would often use real gems, pearls, rubies, emeralds, to create shapes. A pearl might be the eye of a saint, for example, or a teardrop, or just part of a pattern. Or dozens of tiny ones, possibly even hundreds, could be used to create hair or a garment or a flower. These would all be held in place by the stitches I showed you. I suppose there might have been a market for the gold and silver thread too. The individual components of the decoration could be very valuable. Churches in those days were ransacked for silverware, candlesticks, statues, paintings, carvings, and even for these little bits and pieces. Vestments were often cut to shreds in the ransacking. And little gems were easy to carry, easy to hide, easy to sell. Even today, that could still be true... That's all I can think of.'

Dottie said goodbye in something of a daze, promising to keep in touch, and if she found out more about the scrap or its major piece, to let Miss Parsons know.

At the gate, she was directed to the wages clerk and drew her pay, a rather astonishingly large sum of money which she hoped would go some way towards mitigating her mother's annoyance. She tucked the large banknotes into her bag, and made her way out to the gate. She gave Anthony the messenger-boy a shilling, which thrilled him, and a kiss on the cheek which thrilled him even more and made him blush bright pink.

Stepping out into the bustling street and back into the real world, still with a strange sense of moving in a dream, Dottie began to make her way home, mulling over what Miss Parsons had told her.

*

Chapter Eight

Dottie arrived home with a profound sense of an unpleasant task behind her. Next time, she said to herself for the dozenth time, Mrs Carmichael asks me to do her a favour, I shall politely but firmly decline.

Janet, opening the door at once, had clearly been on the lookout for her. She took Dottie's scarf and coat, and the signed photograph of Miss Hutchings Dottie had obtained. The photograph she put into her uniform pocket immediately; she would have to wait until she got back to the kitchen to gloat over that with Cook and Margie. The scarf she hung up, and the coat she gave a good shake then hung that up too on the hall stand.

'Tea will be in about another half an hour, Miss. Would you like a cup of tea or anything before then?'

'No thank you, I won't. I must just go and say

hello to my parents. Come up to my room later, you can tell me everything.'

'I was rather hoping *you'd* tell *me* all about the film studio and whatnot,' Janet said.

Dottie smiled. 'I promise you it's far less exciting than you'd think.'

'I bet that Miss Hutchings is quite something,' Janet added, and didn't understand Dottie's sudden giggle.

'She certainly is. Any messages for me?'

'Yes, several...'

But Dottie cut her off before she could embark on a recitation. 'Any *urgent* messages?'

'Well, not to say urgent, Miss...'

'Good, they can all wait. I'll say a quick hello to Mother and then go and have a bath, I'm absolutely frozen. I suppose the old dragon is in its lair?'

Janet pretended not to know what she meant. 'Mr and Mrs Manderson are in the drawing room, Miss.' She spoiled the dignified moment with a giggle as she ran down the hall to the kitchen, already pulling out the photo.

In the drawing room, her father leapt up to hug her, more from relief at the arrival of reinforcements than from the pleasure of seeing his younger daughter. Her mother afforded her a cool nod from behind her book. Dottie noted the book was entitled 'Moral Perils of the Modern Age'. She felt an inward groan, but nevertheless managed a bright smile as she seated herself next to her mother and remarked, 'Well, thank goodness that's over with.'

The book was closed and placed on the lap.

'Really?' her mother queried, her neatly pencilled cupid's bows rising almost to her hairline.

'Oh yes, they shan't need me anymore. I've done my bit and I shall go to the bank tomorrow to deposit my wages.' She fished in her bag for the money, waving the notes aloft with a certain air of triumph. Her mother tried to conceal her surprise.

'So that's that?'

'Yes, Mother, I thought you'd be pleased to know it's all over and done with.'

'I don't have any particular feelings about it either way,' her mother replied.

'What did you have to do?' her father asked. Dottie shot him a furious look which he failed to notice. Seeing the promise of awakening wrath in her mother's eyes, Dottie decided to skirt the truth somewhat.

'Oh you know. Just spent about four hours standing by a mirror pretending to brush my hair, whilst Marguerite Hutchings attempted to enter the scene and sob on my shoulder without knocking everything to kingdom come. She's a horribly clumsy woman.'

'Got the looks, though,' her father pointed out.

'Really Herbert!' Unable to snap at Dottie's blameless account, Lavinia Manderson turned her temper on her husband.

'Sorry, m'dear,' Herbert retreated once more behind his newspaper, but spared a second to direct a wry grin at his daughter.

'I spent such a lot of time with the wardrobe mistress, a Miss Parsons. She was a tremendous fount of knowledge on fabrics and costumes. She'd get on famously with Mrs Carmichael, I'm quite certain.' The whole time she was speaking, Dottie was wishing the tea would be brought in. In the end she found she just couldn't keep sitting there. She jumped up. 'Just got time for a quick bath before tea, I feel horribly dusty from the warehouse. Won't be a tick.'

She hurried out. Her mother, looking after her, said, 'Horrid vulgar expression.' And returned to her book. Peace descended once more on the drawing room at the Mandersons'.

There were two large bowls of hot-house flowers in Dottie's room. Both sported cards, handwritten in small neat print, and signed with a flourish 'James'. The first card said simply, 'Do let me have the pleasure of your company for dinner tomorrow evening.' The second, imbued in Dottie's imagination with a certain petulance, said, 'I was so sorry to find you out last evening when I called to take you to dinner. Your mother informed me that you were otherwise engaged. Perhaps next time you would let me know if you are not available.'

'He's called about a dozen times, too, Miss,' Janet told her, and fished a sheaf of notes from her apron pocket. 'He's being a bit of a bother, to be honest with you. And not the most polite of gentlemen.'

'No indeed,' said Dottie with feeling. 'Please could you get rid of the flowers, Janet, their heavy scent is giving me a headache. Just put them outside in the rubbish bin.'

'Not very nice, are they, all show and a smell you'd sooner forget. Reminds me of a funeral home. When we went to see my Auntie Mamie in her coffin last September, the place stank like this.' She hefted a flower-bowl in each arm, and somehow managed to give the sheaf of messages to Dottie on her way out of the room. She called over her shoulder, 'I'll just get rid of this lot then I'll air your room out for you, Miss, whiles you're down having your tea. It's because of the smell Mrs Manderson didn't want the flowers downstairs.'

While Dottie waited for her bath to fill, she reflected that only a few years earlier, when she was a little girl, two maids used to run up and down the back stairs with buckets of hot water to fill the tub. Now the water was piped in, and saved Janet a lot of hard work. Not to mention saving heaps of time, too.

Dottie undressed, and sat on her bed in her dressing gown until the bath was ready. She began to leaf through the messages. Janet had been right, there were in fact thirteen messages from Doctor James Melville, ranging from the first, 'Thank you for your delightful company last night, I do hope I may see you again,' to the final one, dated just the evening before, and saying, 'Since I have not been able to speak with you and have not heard from you, I can only assume I have somehow caused offence. Do allow me the opportunity of begging your forgiveness, and please join me for afternoon tea at the new tea room opposite the Museum, tomorrow at half past four.'

Well she'd missed that, it was already almost five o'clock. No doubt a very annoyed young man would telephone shortly and demand an explanation. He really was being surprisingly persistent for someone who appeared to take no pleasure whatsoever in her company.

There was also a short message from Inspector Hardy, saying simply, 'Thank you for your kind wishes.' Clearly, 'wishes' here was a euphemism for a good hard slap across the face. She couldn't help but smile, though she cringed with embarrassment at the thought of her behaviour. She hoped he was all right.

The final message came from Mrs Carmichael, just a short note to say Dottie was needed at the warehouse for a fitting, and could she be there either at nine o'clock or ten o'clock the following morning. 'Tell her either's fine' was scrawled across the bottom of the sheet, almost disappearing into obscurity in the corner, and perfectly encapsulated both Mrs Carmichael's manner of delivering a message and Janet's method of taking them.

Dottie had her bath in record time and joined her parents once again, to find both mother and father in good moods.

One of the first things Hardy did upon his return to work was to re-interview the man held in the cells for the robberies.

Maple accompanied him, and they sat in the gloomy little room side by side and faced the miserable specimen who was supposedly their intrepid armed robber. The man, five feet two inches tall, hollow of cheek and chest, with a rasping cough as a memento of the first world war, could not have looked less like the popular image of an armed and ruthless gunman.

'Meet Wilfred Walter Wotherspoon, outwardly an antiques dealer, but really just a receiver and fence of this parish,' Maple said to Hardy. Hardy, folding his arms and sitting back in his seat, surveyed Mr Wotherspoon in a lazy manner. After a few seconds he remarked,

'That sounds like one of those rhymes children say in the playground. You know, Frank, where you have to say it as fast as you can without making a mistake.'

Frank Maple laughed, his immense shoulders shaking as he did so, and Hardy could feel his own chair shaking as a result. 'What, wilfredwalterwotherspoon-wilfredwalterwotherspoon-wilfredwalterwotherspoon-wilfred...'

'All right!' said the man sitting opposite them. 'I'll not stay here and be insulted about me name. You've got nowt on me, and yer'll have to let me go. I bin here three days already. I've got me business to attend to. I wasn't there, I didn't do it, I didn't see nowt. You ain't got nowt.'

'I love the English language,' Hardy said to Maple. 'We all have our own little ways of communicating, don't we? Every corner of our great nation has its own special sayings and idioms.'

'I like 'nowt', meself,' Maple said, 'Londoners don't say nowt as often as they should. I wish it would catch on more. It's much nicer than that old-fashioned 'nuffink'.'

'The trouble is,' Hardy continued, 'when don't hear your own special brand of English spoken for a while, you start to lose your native tongue and adopt the new one.'

'Like you, sir, if you don't mind me saying,' Maple said with a sideways glance at Hardy. He folded his arms too, and leaned back, both of them now staring at Wilfred Walter Wotherspoon as if he were one of the duller forms of pondlife. 'I mean, there you were just sent down from the actual Oxford University—brawling wasn't it, sir, if you don't mind me mentioning it, what got you sent down—and talking the King's own English, and now, just a few years later, why, you could pass for an ordinary bloke in any part of London.'

'That's why they wanted me for that undercover job last year,' Hardy said, 'they knew I wouldn't mind killing a chap if I had to, and anyway the higher-ups would always sweep something like that under the carpet. It's worth it just to close a big case. I had an in with all the gangs out East. I could get a man's arms broken or, heaven forbid, legs too, in less than five minutes. I must admit, I miss that job. Sometimes sitting behind a desk is a trifle unexciting.'

'Do you still have that stiletto they gave you?' Maple asked. 'Never actually seen one. I'd quite like a quick look, if you do.'

Wilfred Walter Wotherspoon looked distinctly unwell. He fidgeted in his seat. Maple thought, though couldn't be sure, that he heard the little man whimper.

'Oh, it's not a stiletto, sergeant, it's an old-fashioned open razor. You know, the cut-throat sort. Nasty thing, you could have quite an accident with that.' Slowly Hardy began to unbutton his jacket.

'All right, all right!' Mr Wotherspoon shouted, 'I'll tell you anything you want to know, just don't—don't cut me, please.'

Hardy leaned forward. 'Talk,' he said.

Flora's pregnancy was proceeding well. After her appointment with her doctor, she met her sister at their usual table at the Lyons' corner house. Once they were settled and surrounded by sandwiches, buns and pots of tea, Dottie told Flora what she had learned about the fabric scrap from Judith Parsons.

'Forgive me for saying so, Dottie, but if this Miss Parsons, a mere wardrobe mistress, knows what it is, then I find it hard to believe your favourite curator of all things costume would not also have known.' She took a huge bite of her roast chicken sandwich. 'I'm starving!' she said, somewhat muffled by the food in her mouth. She patted her quite plump stomach. 'It's true what they say about eating for two, I'm ravenous *all* the time!'

'You must be having quintuplets, you're definitely eating for a lot more than two. But yes, I've been thinking about that. Melville had to have known. I suspected as much before but now I'm quite certain. But the question is, why did he lie?'

'Perhaps he was just being super cautious in an academic sort of way. You know these intellectuals always hem and haw and don't like to commit themselves. It makes them seem more important than they really are.'

'Do you really believe that was it?'

'Well, no, not if I'm being honest. He knew. It wasn't a case of he thought he knew but just needed to check a few facts, or anything like that. He was certain.'

'Exactly. He knew. He lied to me. Deliberately. I just know he lied. But *why*? That's what I can't understand.'

They ate in silence for a minute or two, then Dottie continued, 'Remember how he asked me if we had more of it? Do you think he was wondering if we'd found and hacked a tiny piece off an actual vestment?'

'Do you mean, did he want to get his hands on the whole thing? Is it possible it is valuable, like your Miss Parsons said it could be?'

Memory succeeded memory and a horrible thought came to Dottie. She looked at Flora with wide, distressed eyes.

'When he took me out for dinner, we went to the restaurant in a cab. It was uphill work trying to get any conversation at all out of him, I can tell you. But one of the few things he did ask was whether I had the scrap with me, as he said he'd like another look at it. He apologised very charmingly and plausibly once again for trying to cut it into pieces. Oh, it was all done so cleverly, but now I have this overriding impression that it was, so to speak, the main business of the evening. He didn't really want to be out with me at all.'

She held her cup to her lips but didn't drink, instead staring into space as she ran over everything he had said and done that blighted evening.

'Flora, I think he just wants to get his hands on the big piece of fabric we said the scrap was taken from. He must know its true value.'

'Or perhaps he thinks it will help him make a name for himself if he 'discovers' it? Have you told our favourite policeman what we've found out about the scrap?'

Dottie shook her head and concentrated on her tea, but grimacing at the overly sweet taste, she set the cup aside, and opted instead for a sticky currant bun with swirls of icing on the top.

'Perhaps you could at least mention your suspicions to William,' Flora suggested. 'It would set your mind at rest, and then if he thought there was anything to it, at least you'd have done your civic duty. What? Now what's wrong?' There was a new expression on her sister's face. She was a picture of utter misery.

'Oh, I haven't told you. It's quite a big thing, actually. Remember when we saw each other the other day and you said it had been Mrs Hardy's funeral that morning?'

'Yes, and you'd not even heard she'd passed away. I do hope he's all right. What? What is it?'

Dottie continued to rip her sticky bun into tiny pieces on her plate, her head bowed. Flora couldn't see Dottie's face, but could tell from the trembling fingers and the growing heap of bun fragments that she was really distressed. She put a hand out to still her sister's fretful movements.

'Dottie, what on earth is it?'

'In the evening, I thought I'd pop round and see if there was anything I could do. I wanted to say how sorry I was. And I was, I suppose, thinking Eleanor might need a bit of support.'

'That was such a kind thought!'

Dottie looked at Flora and seemed to wilt. There

were tears in her eyes as she leaned forward and in a low voice, said, 'Well, at first I couldn't make anyone hear me, then I tried the door. It opened very spookily, just like when I found poor Susan Dunne a month or so ago. It gave me chills. I had to really stop myself from running away right then and there. So I went inside. I went all round the house but couldn't find anyone at home. I felt awfully guilty about being in the house uninvited but I just had to make sure, in case someone was ill or they'd forgotten to lock up and might get burgled, or, well, I don't know, just anything.'

Satisfied now that her sister hadn't actually come to any harm, and with a smile playing about her lips as her imagination leapt ahead to what appeared to be a foregone conclusion, Flora sat back to enjoy watching her sister wrestle with the memory of that evening.

'Or, or...' Dottie floundered to a halt.

Flora wasn't going to let her sister back out now. 'Exactly what I would have done myself, dear,' she assured her, adding, 'Do go on.'

'Oh good. I felt rather...Anyway, finally I found William in his bedroom, dead drunk and passed out in a chair.'

Flora hid her smile of anticipation behind her tea cup. 'Yes?' she enquired mildly.

'Well I'm afraid I lost my temper. Seeing him drunk like that, and his mother only just laid to rest! Before I even knew what I was going to do, I was across the room and I gave him the most almighty slap! The poor man couldn't have known what hit him.'

'Literally,' said Flora, enjoying herself

immensely. She couldn't wait to get home and tell George everything. Both he and she harboured hopes of a romantic intrigue between Dottie and the handsome inspector. And, in Flora's view, a good hard slap delivered spontaneously by an angry young woman was a reassuring sign of emotional attachment to the victim of the slap.

On the verge of tears of shame, Dottie narrated the rest of the story and ground to a halt, too miserable to enjoy any more of her food. She pushed her plate away and added as a codicil to the main story, 'And so I doubt if he will ever talk to me again. Which is a terrible shame because on the night of the robbery, after my dinner with James Melville, William was absolutely wonderful to me. Even though I accidentally kissed him, which I think he was very annoyed about, because he left *immediately.* And to think he went home that night to find his mother had passed away. And this is how I repay his kindness!'

Her eyes brimmed over, she fumbled for a hanky which was supplied by her sister, who added in a bracing voice, 'I wonder if he's back at work?'

'He went back the day before yesterday. It's not very long, is it, a few days to mourn his dear mother and sort through everything. No wonder it was easier just to drink himself oblivious.'

'Hmm. I just hope he doesn't make a habit of it.'

Dottie had nothing to say to that.

Flora leaned forward. 'So tell me more about this 'accidental' kiss that occurred when he came about the robbery.'

She waved Flora off in a cab—George was using

their car—and she gathered the folds of her coat about her, glad of their protection against the chill of the wind that swept the length of the street, its icy fingers snatching at her hat and sending the ends of her long woollen scarf into the air like a kite in front of her. Locks of her hair were driven out from under her little cap—a nonsense of a thing in this weather—and she could hardly see where she was going as she attempted to control all these rogue elements, with her eyes now streaming too because of the cold. Ducking her head to try to minimise the impact of the weather, she turned to hurry away towards home and the warmth of the fire. It was almost pitch black, the low heavy rainclouds bringing an early end to a miserable day. Would the winter never end?

She felt a slight tug on the strap of her bag, and as she began to look down to see what had happened, half-turning her head, she heard a noise, was aware of a flashing pain searing her brain, and somehow she was on the ground, bumping both her shoulder and temple as she connected with the wet pavement. Someone ran off down the street, disappearing from sight. She managed to open one eye in time to see a man's legs and feet, but that was all.

She couldn't get up immediately. Pain seemed to fill her being, and she couldn't catch her breath. It hurt too much to open her eyes. The dim distant streetlamps were like bright needles piercing the back of her skull. There didn't seem to be a soul about, no one heard her whispered pleas for help. The street seemed to be empty yet her mind echoed with the sound of those running feet, though whether that was a real memory or the creation of her imagination, she couldn't understand. It felt very dark and lonely here. She had to move.

After a few moments her confusion lessened, and the pain in her shoulder and the side of her head dulled to a continual throb. Common sense was able to assert itself once more. Lying on the pavement was not a good idea. Gingerly she raised herself into a sitting position, and felt about her for her bag. It wasn't there.

Her head was pounding. She felt she needed to hold it. That seemed to help. With one hand, she pulled herself onto her feet, aided by a sturdy fence-post. Once upright, she waited for waves of nausea to subside, clinging desperately to the fence-post until she was able to marshal her thoughts and decide on a course of action.

She had been mugged, she realised finally. That was a crime, and she needed to tell the police about it. The police station was—she was almost sure—just along the street, around the corner and down a little bit further.

Rather like a drowning man clutching at driftwood, she fixed her thoughts on the help she would get once in sight of the blessed blue lamp of the police station. Infinitely slowly she began to make her way along the street.

It seemed to take her hours to reach the front desk. People had passed her on the street and she'd been vaguely aware of them tutting and shaking their heads over her dishevelled appearance, no doubt thinking she was drunk or destitute or worse. She mused on this as she concentrated on negotiating the steps up to the front door, unable to think what might be worse than being drunk or homeless. The steps were almost too much for her but at last here she was, gripping the counter-top and trying to make herself heard above the pounding of her head.

'Inspector Hardy,' she said, her voice barely above a whisper. The desk sergeant frowned at her, and she could tell he thought she was some disreputable character fit only for a night in the cells. She fixed him with a pleading look.

'Help me. I was attacked. My bag... Please, please, I need to speak to William Hardy. I'm a friend. At least, I think I am... tell him it's Dottie. Please.'

Not entirely believing her but nervous of the alternative if it turned out she was telling the truth, the sergeant nodded and emerged from behind his counter to march off down the long corridor.

Dottie stood there, swaying unsteadily and gripping the counter, knowing if she let go she would fall. Her head swam, she felt nausea from the pain threatening to overpower her, but in her imagination she followed after the sergeant, down the length of the station's main corridor, through some doors, down some steps, along the twists and turns of the hallway, until she arrived at the door to William's office. How lovely it would be to be swept up into his arms and just carried away to a place of safety and quiet, away from this noisy place where all she could hear was the clattering of running feet and the sound of exclaiming voices. And this strange floating feeling she was now experiencing.

'I am *not* drunk,' she announced, suddenly concerned that people might think she was. There was a warm hard pillow at her cheek, and even though it wasn't soft, it comforted her.

'Where's her bag?' she heard a voice demand. I know that voice, she thought, and a smile spread across her face.

'Oh William!' she murmured happily against the hard pillow of his shoulder, and closed her eyes.

'She said something about it, sir, but I couldn't make it out.' That was the nice sergeant. She liked him because he'd brought William to her.

'Get the duty doctor here immediately. I'm taking her to my office. And bring hot sweet tea and a glass of water.'

'Yes sir.'

'Dottie, bloody hell, what happened?' he asked a moment later as he set her down on the only chair in the office that was halfway comfortable.

'Language, darling!' she reproved gently from what seemed like a great way off.

The sergeant arrived with the doctor in tow, as well as a tray with tea and water.

'Been mugged, clearly,' Dr Garrett said. 'Slight concussion, nothing too serious. Get her to bed, a good night's sleep, and a couple of days' rest, and she'll be fine. Isn't this the same lovely young lady I attended outside the house where that murder-suicide took place a few weeks ago?'

'Yes, it is.' Hardy's tone was grim. He didn't want to think about that night.

'Feature in all your investigations, does she? Rather a lovely young lady. Is she walking out with anyone, do you know?'

'I'll kill him if she does,' Hardy's voice was, if possible, even grimmer. The doctor laughed.

'So that's how it is! Then I wish you luck. Let me know when to order the gravy-boat.'

At last they had all left, and he was alone with her. He felt an unreasoning rage at the sight of the bump on the side of her head, the bruise on her cheek, the chalk-white complexion. He pulled a seat over and sat beside her, putting his arm around her shoulder and shaking her gently. 'Dottie.'

She stirred, leaning in to snuggle against his shoulder once more. Her hair tickled his nose and her scent filled his senses. He gave himself a mental shake. They couldn't stay here like this.

'Dottie,' he said again, more insistently. 'Are you ready to go home? The doctor's seen you and he says I can take you home now. I'll go and get a car and drive you.'

'Hmm,' she said. Then a moment later, like a child belatedly remembering her manners, she added, 'Thank you, William darling.'

He sighed. When she remembered this later, she'd be furious with herself. And probably with him too, though he couldn't really see how any of it was his fault. *If* she remembered this.

Her mother was beside herself with anger and anxiety in equal measure when he finally helped Dottie into the house half an hour later. Whilst Mrs Manderson and Janet helped to get Dottie upstairs and into bed, Hardy explained to Dottie's father what little he knew of what had happened.

Mr Manderson, who liked the young man

immensely, poured them both a Scotch, inviting Hardy to take a seat. Soon they were in a deep discussion about their hopes for the coming cricket season. Their peace was broken ten minutes later by the return of Mrs Manderson, with an odd appraising look in her eye as she said,

'My daughter asks me to apologise for her behaviour earlier. She is afraid she has caused offence by some careless remarks.'

Hardy, blushing, resumed his seat and assured Mrs Manderson that there was no offence, adding, 'I'm afraid that much of Miss Manderson's speech was rather indistinct due to her injury, so it wasn't possible to make out what she was saying.'

Mrs Manderson, accepting the small sherry offered by her husband, made herself comfortable on the sofa, and set herself to the task of being pleasant to the young man who had not only come to the aid of her younger daughter, but was clearly the object of her affections. Grudgingly she admitted to herself that the fellow was attractive and had a pleasant way with him, in spite of his lack of position. Her older daughter had recently told her that William Hardy was perfect for Dottie, and that he was gallant. Now, in denying whatever indiscretions Dottie had committed, he was proving himself to be a gentleman in character, if not in rank.

'I was so sorry to hear about your dear mother, Inspector. She was a delightful person, I'm sure she will be sorely missed by all who knew her.'

'Thank you, Mrs Manderson, I...'

'I hope you will come to dinner on Saturday evening, we would so enjoy seeing you and your charming sister again.'

This surprised him. He accepted a little diffidently, excusing his sister who was away, and adding, 'I hope Miss Manderson will be recovered by then.'

'I'm sure she shall, thanks to your prompt care and attention.' Mrs Manderson smiled at him. He reflected it was the first time he had seen her really smile. It took years off her, and he was surprised to see how young she suddenly appeared, and how very like her younger daughter.

*

Chapter Nine

'Right, what we have is this,' Maple was saying. It was Saturday morning, and he was standing in front of a schoolroom blackboard he had set upon an easel, his hands and suit jacket covered in chalk dust. He looked more like a pupil writing lines than a teacher. There was even a smudge of chalk on his chin. Nevertheless, Hardy was impressed by the work the sergeant had put into organising the main points of the robbery cases. Being organised was never Hardy's strong point. They made a good team, as their little chat with Wilfred Walter Wotherspoon three days earlier had shown.

'Help me flip her over, Bill,' Maple said. Hardy stepped forward to help turn the board over. On this side Maple had created a list of all the venues of the robberies, five of them that they knew of so far: one in Oxford at the home of a Mr Norris Smith taking place in the first week of January; one in Hitchin, Hertfordshire, at the home of

Gareth Smedley-Judd the week after the Oxford one. Next there was a gap of almost a month, then came the robbery at the other Smedley-Judd brother's home, Ian, at his home in Kensington and taking place in the middle of February. This was followed by a second robbery in Hertfordshire, in the town of Hemel Hempstead where a Mrs Emmeline Foster lived; this took place in the third week of February. Lastly there was another London-based robbery, this time in Highgate, where a Gerald Radleigh had hosted a small dinner to celebrate his elevation to the college of bishops, and which occurred while Hardy was off due to his mother's death just before the end of February.

'Very good, and now turn it back again,' Maple said. They did so, and he continued to show Hardy what he had done. 'On this side, the right-hand column is a list of all the items stolen. It's all the usual stuff you'd expect this type of criminal to go for: small, portable, easy to fence. And that's how we managed to collar Wotherspoon, he had this bracelet and earrings set from the Oxford party, and a couple of other bits and bobs, a couple of rings and a cigar-case if I remember correctly, we've got them all in the evidence room. And this section on the left is the little bit of useful information we have from the witnesses. As you can see there's not much. Basically, it amounts to: five perpetrators, all male, and a tattoo on the wrist of a tall chap. That's pretty much it. Hopefully we'll be able to add a bit more information to that.'

'It's a terrific help to have it displayed like this, so thank you Frank, that was a brilliant idea.'

Hardy said. 'How did you come up with it?'

Maple preened. 'Saw it in a report about new procedures at Interpol.'

'Interpol? Interesting. If I'm not careful, they'll be poaching you for some grand job at the Met. Now this wretched case. The thing that I keep coming back to is this,' Hardy said, 'As we already know, once everyone has been safely herded into the dining rooms, the next step is for two of the gang to hold everyone at gunpoint, and another one is stationed in the doorway to stop anyone from leaving, while the other two go off around the houses. We originally presumed that was with the intention of picking up a few more useful valuables.

'But we now know, from the maid in Hertfordshire, and from our friend the helpful Mr Wotherspoon, that although they go off, presumably to search the house, they always seem to return empty-handed. Why is that? What are they doing?' he asked. 'I feel if we can work that out, we will make some real progress.'

'Are they looking for something in particular, or just checking for hidden guests who might raise the alarm? Or else what are they doing? It don't make sense.' Maple leaned back against the blackboard, his arms folded across his chest. Their discussion continued for a few more minutes. When he eventually moved away to fetch them both a cup of tea, the back of his jacket was even more badly smudged with chalk dust and there was a clean patch on the blackboard. Gone was their meagre description of the robbers. Hardy smiled and shook his head.

As soon as Maple returned, Hardy pointed out the smudging. And the clean patch on the board. It was a good thing Maple was walking out with Janet, the maid from the Mandersons'. She'd be able to brush that suit down and have it looking smart again in no time. How he envied Frank his easy-going approach to life, not to mention the illicit union he was enjoying with the attractive young woman. So long as everything went smoothly, they should be fine. Of course, if Frank got the girl into trouble, there'd be the wrath of Mrs Manderson to face, and doubtless a hasty wedding.

Hardy began to wonder if that would be so bad. Perhaps that was the best way to do things? No one would quibble over relative stations in society, over wealth, prospects, or the suitability of the home on offer, if a child was on the way. The wedding would go ahead as quickly as possible and with the least possible fuss. The cavemen had it simpler, he thought. If only he had his own cave, he could have dragged Dottie into it weeks ago.

'Never mind about me jacket, I got some biscuits too, before that lot from Beat 17 got hold of the lot.' Maple said, his voice ringing with triumph as he sent the office door crashing back into the frame with a well-aimed kick. 'Get that down you.' He handed Hardy a cup of tea, sloping the hot liquid all over his hands and desk as he did so, causing Hardy to curse at the heat and fish out his handkerchief to mop himself and the desk top.

'You know, Frank,' Hardy said, mindful of his thoughts of a moment before, 'you need to be careful with Janet. If you get her into trouble, it won't be you who has to face Mrs Manderson, it'll be Janet. I don't envy her that one little bit.'

'It'll be fine. In any case, the worst that will happen is she loses her position a bit sooner than we'd planned.'

'You're getting married?' Hardy was more relieved than surprised.

'Talking about it. Not actually set the date yet. But you know, it's not all just about the how's-your-father. I really like her.'

Hardy smiled at him, and somewhat awkwardly patted him on the shoulder. 'I'm pleased for you both. She's a very nice girl.' He sipped his tea, grimaced at the stewed taste then turned back to the blackboard. 'One thing puzzles me.'

'Only one? There's about a hundred things what puzzles me!' Frank chuckled. He came to prop himself, cup in hand, beside the inspector. 'Go on then. What is this one thing what puzzles you?'

'How do the robbers know when the dinner party is on?'

Maple stared at Hardy then at the board, gulping his tea. 'Bleeding heck, how did we miss that? Well, they must get tipped off.'

Hardy nodded. 'Exactly. It doesn't make sense for them to just watch large houses on the off-chance. So clearly someone is passing information on to them. Most likely a servant, I should think.'

'That's a bit much. It could just as easily be one of your lot, the toffs,' Maple pointed out. 'Maybe they just wait till they get an invite.'

'They'd hardly betray their friends and family. Or risk losing their own valuables.'

'Think about it, Bill, the staff are the ones in

danger, really. Think of the footman who got coshed. The staff are the ones in the firing line, trying to help, trying to protect the families they work for. Plus, they're not likely to know the value of the stuff that's taken.'

'Hmm. You could be right. Though I think a lot of the staff would know if something was valuable or not. But I suppose one of the guests would be in a better position to know who might be invited to one of these get-togethers and what valuables they might be likely to have on them.'

'Remember Mrs Gossington's pearls—they didn't take those, she said they must of known they was paste,' Maple said.

'Yes. Yes, very true. Outside of her own home, that would probably only be known to her intimate friends. And if you think about it, a guest could quite easily pretend to give up their valuables then get them back later when the spoils are divided up. And, a guest would know the layout of the house, and possibly what other valuables might be in the residence.'

'*And*, they'd know what staff there was, and where the telephones was, and the best way to get in and out.'

They stood in silence for several minutes, deep in thought. Finally, Hardy said, 'Did anyone else say they saw a tattoo on the arm of one of the robbers?'

'No, mate. Shame, that. Could have been useful. I've asked around. None of the official tattooists have seen anything like it, or so they say, though I'll admit our description is a little hazy. But interestingly enough, one of them did say it sounded like a prison tattoo. One of the sort that the inmates do themselves.'

'Really? Interesting. See if you can find out more about that, it sounds promising. If one of our robbers has got previous form, we might be able to find out about known associates, and get the rest of the gang from that.'

'Yes sir.'

'And I'm going to make a list of the guests who attended the parties, and see if any of them crop up more than once.'

'Don't forget to check the ones who were invited but didn't turn up, Bill, it could be they thought they'd stay well clear. Might pretend to be under the weather or have another engagement.'

'Excellent point, Frank.'

'How is Miss Manderson? Janet was saying she got attacked?'

'Yes, she was mugged last night. Someone snatched her bag, and knocked her down. She's got a nasty bump and a mild concussion. Which reminds me, I must send her a card, and perhaps some flowers.'

'I hear she was all over you like a rash.'

Hardy blushed but said simply, 'You shouldn't believe everything you hear.'

'Apparently she told her mother she'd called you Darling.'

'Shut up.' Hardy smiled into his cup. 'She was fainting.'

They finished their tea in the companionable silence of a well-working partnership.

Mrs Carmichael rang indecently early to summon

Dottie to a rehearsal. Dottie explained about the mugging and her injuries, asking for some time off to recover. Slightly put out, Mrs Carmichael rearranged the appointment the following Tuesday.

'Can you be at the warehouse for three, ducks? We just need to try a few things on, get the order right, and so on. Then I could do with a word after, if you'll give me a few minutes. Plus, I've got another proposition for you from Cecil Greenwood, that film producer. He's promising you a tidy sum too. Says they were ever so impressed with you.'

Dottie agreed to be at the warehouse on time, but refused to be drawn either way about the rest. Her instinct was to turn down the film producer, no matter how much he was planning on offering her. It just couldn't compensate her for the tedium of waiting around for days on end. Her head was pounding and her whole body seemed to ache from the abrupt contact with the pavement the previous evening, but she hoped she would be feeling better by the time Tuesday came around and she had to go in to work.

Flora arrived at nine o'clock with flowers and fruit, only to find Dottie sitting at the dining table eating bacon, eggs and toast as if nothing had happened.

'I tried to make her stay in bed, but she wouldn't,' complained their mother, pouring more tea and passing a cup to Flora.

'That's a nasty bruise!' Flora said with a horrified gasp as she examined her sister's face. 'I can't believe it. I mean, it wasn't even late at night, and it's a perfectly respectable neighbourhood. I had literally just said goodbye to Dottie a minute or two earlier!'

'I wish I knew who it was,' Dottie said for the twentieth time already that day. 'I can't believe it was just an opportunistic mugging.'

'How could it be anything else?' her mother asked. Then Dottie realised Mrs Manderson knew nothing of the fabric scrap William Hardy had given her, nor of the suspicions Dottie had voiced to Flora right before the attack. But she thought better of enlightening her now, however, and said nothing, concentrating instead on her food, which she was trying to appear to relish even though the sight and smell of it made her feel sick. Her head was still pounding but if she allowed her mother to think she was less than fully recovered, she'd be bundled back to bed, and it was important for her to get out of the house to have some fresh air and some space to think, and to get some information. She couldn't bear the thought of staying at home to be fussed over and cosseted.

She finished her tea, dabbed her mouth with a napkin and shoved back her chair abruptly, saying as she did so, 'Gosh, how late it is already. Do hurry up, Flora!'

Flora, her untasted cup poised before her lips, caught and recognised the quick conspiratorial glance she had known since infancy, and set down her cup, rising and kissing her mother's cheek with every appearance of dismay. 'Goodness, yes! If we don't hurry, we'll be late!'

'But where are you going, girls?' Mrs Manderson turned in her seat to call after them; they were already halfway into the hall.

'Canterbury,' Dottie said on the spur of the moment.

'Can...?' Flora said in surprise, staring at her sister, changing it to a firmer, more assured tone mid-sentence, '...terbury. Yes of course, the cathedral tour. We mustn't miss the starting time. See you later, Mother, we shouldn't be late back.'

'Canterbury? But to go all that way, and in your condition, Florence, dear!' their mother protested, but the front door banged. They had gone. She was addressing an empty room.

'*Canterbury?*' Flora repeated as she started the car. 'We're not actually going all the way to Kent, are we?'

Dottie nodded, pain seared her temple and she grimaced, putting a hand up to gently massage the bruised place. 'Yes, sorry. It just suddenly came to me. I didn't know what else to say.'

'But *Canterbury*, Dottie. It's a hell of a distance!'

'Sorry. You don't mind, do you?'

'I suppose not. I hope you know the way.'

'Um, not really, no. It's south-east from here, if that helps.'

'It doesn't. I'll stop at the AA tea-room and buy a map. You can pay.'

'I don't have my bag. It was stolen last night, if you remember, along with my purse, my compact, my favourite lipstick, my comb, two penny stamps, and one of the handkerchiefs Aunt Sophie sent me for my birthday last year. You know, the ones where she embroidered the monogram herself.'

'How much was in the purse?'

'Six shillings and a ha'penny.'

'Hmm, that's too bad. Well, I've only got two pounds in my bag, so I hope to goodness that will do, it should be enough.'

They set off. Ten minutes later Flora repeated plaintively, 'But *Canterbury*! Dottie, how could you!'

They had a wonderful time travelling down into Kent. The roads were good, the map reliable—once they'd discovered which way round it was supposed to go—and the sun shone brightly and warmly from a clear blue sky. It was as if Spring had finally arrived. As soon as they left the busy streets of London behind, Dottie began to relax and feel better. All the way down they discussed fashion and planned changes to their wardrobes.

They made a couple of stops along the way, arriving in Canterbury itself in time for lunch. A pocket guidebook purchased at the hotel where they ate, instructed them on the sights of interest, and provided them with directions to the Cathedral museum.

The elderly gentleman who served as guide was zealous in his duty, and Dottie and Flora were both physically and mentally exhausted by the time they said goodbye to him.

But they took their afternoon tea with a sense of a job well done. Dottie had shown their guide her scrap of fabric and he had confirmed what Miss Parsons had told her. Dottie had carefully unpinned the scrap from the hem of her skirt, and was amused to see the elderly gentleman hastily avert his eyes as she did so. His cheeks were a little pink as he took the tiny piece of material from her. Flora was just relieved that the scrap hadn't been inside the stolen handbag.

It only took a few seconds for him to examine the fabric. He handed it back to Dottie, saying quickly, 'Come this way, my dear ladies.' And he bustled away leaving them to hurry after him as best they could through the groups of visitors.

He led them into an anteroom of the Cathedral. Cabinets resembling huge wardrobes covered the two long walls of the room. The guide flung open a pair of doors, and pulled out some very elderly vestments: a couple of chasubles, a cope and an alb.

'Strictly speaking these all ought to be in a museum. They are extremely old,' he told them, and to Dottie's astonishment he invited them to feel the cloth of one of the garments. It felt soft, buttery soft just like Dottie's tiny piece of cloth. The colour of the second chasuble was quite similar to Dottie's fabric. The texture too, was just like it, rubbed almost threadbare here and there, with little of the nap still remaining.

'Your piece is definitely from a similar item,' he said, 'It was common for broderers—embroiderers in today's English—to work on a ground of velvet. This could have been imported from the far east or the middle east, or from southern Europe, then worked on in this country before being sent—well, almost anywhere—all over the world. Of course, with the passage of the long years, the nap—the fluffy surface of the velvet—has more or less worn away, leaving what is in essence a mere framework of the fabric.'

So Miss Parsons had been right. Dottie was thrilled to have this confirmation. But she was still rather reluctant to reveal any more to the elderly gentleman. She certainly didn't feel able to show him the scrap of paper bearing the words *Mantle of God*. It was possible William might want her to keep it a complete secret. So she confined herself to asking simply, 'Could you possibly view this as a Godly Mantle?'

He thought for a second then nodded and smiled. 'I think you could. The priestly garments were dedicated to God's work, after all. The whole ceremony of the putting on of such garments was, and indeed still is, an act of sanctification. Think about it, ladies. An apparently ordinary gentleman—one of 'us'—comes in off the street. He will probably be wearing an ordinary suit, perhaps like mine a little elderly, a bit baggy at the knees, possibly somewhat worn at the elbows. As a priest he won't have a lovely wife,' and here he smiled at Flora, 'to take care of him and make sure his clothes are in good repair. He's just an ordinary fellow, human, fallible, flawed. He goes into the robing room, or the vestry, or wherever this is taking place, and he puts on these garments, one sacred layer upon another, and all of the best quality and in good repair. And as he does so, he is covering up the human, fallible, sinful self, and taking upon himself the divine perfection of Our Lord. His role is to breach the gap between earth and heaven. Once he is fully robed, he is God's representative on earth, no longer the down-at-heel chap who walked in off the street. So, yes my dear, the garments have great significance and importance. They are key to the success, after all, of the Church's rites and ceremonies.'

He directed their eyes to the elaborate embroidery on the back of the chasubles. Scenes from the Bible, from the lives of the saints were emblazoned across the garments, surrounded by flower and star motifs, all done in the neat, delicate stitches Miss Parsons had demonstrated. For Dottie almost the most important thing was the next piece of information he shared with them.

'The majority of broderers were women, expert, proficient, plying a respectable, and highly valued, guilded profession that paid them well and gave them position in society. Embroidery was a highly-respected career, possibly the only respectable career in those days a single woman could undertake apart from marriage or a convent life of devotion. It was a skill that enabled women to earn wages and support themselves and to receive the patronage of Earls, Kings and Popes.'

'Popes?' Dottie asked surprised. 'But we're not Catholics, we are under the sovereignty of the King and the Archbishop of Canterbury, aren't we?'

'Now, yes. Then, no. These garments were made at a time when Catholicism was our national faith. Henry the Eighth's terrible Reformation was hundreds of years in the future. Which is why these garments are so elaborate. The later Protestant faith Henry created abhorred all the embellishment that went hand-in-hand with Catholic rites and ceremonies at that time. These kinds of vestments, along with silverware, paintings, murals, rosaries, incense, rites, ceremonies and masses, all were swept away and destroyed, or their destruction was attempted. The abbeys and monasteries were by and large torn down, along with everything—and often *everyone*—within their walls. And all around the country, loyal Catholics hid as much as they could in the hope of a future return to national favour of their faith.

'Sadly, some adventurers seized these goods to make their own fortunes—not everything was turned over to the crown to fill the royal coffers and fund Henry's pursuits, and of course, his wars. Catholics who refused to recant—that is, deny their faith—would be stripped of status, wealth, land, houses, could be and often were, imprisoned, tortured, and many, many of them were executed for treason. They were heralded by those of the Faith as Martyrs. Families were divided, destroyed. These were terrible, turbulent times we are talking about. I'm certain many believers on both sides of the faith-divide thought the Day of Judgement has arrived. As a member of the Ecumenical Movement, I myself am only too thankful that we now live in more tolerant times. Many of my closest friends and colleagues are Catholic priests.'

They thanked him and said goodbye. They paused inside the museum doorway to push a few small coins into the donation box before leaving the place, their moods sober. They had plenty to think about.

'What a sweet man. A bit behind the times, but sweet,' Flora said.

'He was very knowledgeable. Though I'm not sure we're any more tolerant these days than back in the time of the Reformation. But it was absolutely worth it to come all this way and hear what he had to say,' Dottie said. 'I'm sorry I rather sprung it on you. I am jolly grateful to you for bringing me, by the way.'

'It's all right, though perhaps I should get my husband to teach you to drive as well, so that after the baby comes, you can drive *me* around. You could do with a little runabout to get you round town, darling.'

After their tea, they telephoned to their mother and to George to let them know they were on their way home, and then they were on the road again, already both exhausted from the long day, and speaking little until they reached the lights of London and home seemed almost within reach. Dottie's head ached again from her attack, and she massaged her temples to ease the pain. The swelling was a little reduced in size, for which she was thankful. But she was glad they had gone to Canterbury, she felt the knowledge they had gained had been worth it. Besides, the thought of a day in bed being nagged by her mother was enough to make her headache well worth it.

Finally, slowing the car to a halt outside the Mandersons' home, Flora said, 'I'm now absolutely certain that Dr Melville must have known what that fabric scrap was. He could hardly be who he is, I realise now, and *not* know. Could he?'

'No,' Dottie agreed in a quiet voice. 'He knew all right. The man's an out-and-out bounder. But why did he lie, Flora, that's what I keep asking myself. Why?'

*

Chapter Ten

William Hardy arrived promptly at the Mandersons' home on Saturday night. Mrs Manderson herself opened the door to him and ushered him inside, for the night had turned cold and wet, the country once more plunged back into winter. In the hall, Janet received his great-coat. As his hostess chivvied him into the drawing room, Hardy was aware of nerves, but across the room, Dottie looked up from her conversation and smiled at him.

Before he could approach her, however, a dandified young man nearby said in a loud, drawling voice, 'I say, watch out everyone, it's the fuzz. Are you here to thwart one of those dinner party robberies, constable?'

Hardy fixed him with a look of ill-disguised contempt. 'Let us hope nothing like that happens this evening,' he said.

The dandy guffawed in an affected way, and

Hardy wanted to punch him on the chin, what little there was of it. The chinless wonder went to stand very close to Dottie, in what Hardy could hardly help interpreting as a proprietorial manner. He felt as though everyone was staring at him. But Dottie shook off her guardian and came over, saying in a clear voice that reached everyone, 'I'm so pleased you were able to make it, *Inspector.*' She came to take his arm, and drew him with her to the other side of the room.

He looked at her, and saw that the bruise on her temple was well-disguised with make-up and hardly noticeable. 'How are you after your attack?' he asked softly.

She murmured, 'Fine thank you,' and then introduced him to a large old woman who was ensconced in an armchair.

'Mrs Carmichael, this is Inspector William Hardy. Inspector, this is Mrs Carmichael, I work as a mannequin at Mrs Carmichael's fashion warehouse.'

'Of course,' he said, offering his hand to the elderly woman, 'I've heard of you, Mrs Carmichael. It's a pleasure to make your acquaintance.'

'Charmed, I'm sure, ducks,' said Mrs Carmichael, giving the Inspector a very thorough top-to-toe appraisal. She patted Dottie's knee. 'Off you go, Dot, there's a good girl. This is the closest I've been to an assignation in twenty years.'

Dottie, pink-cheeked but smiling, obediently left them. Hardy was irritated to see that she was immediately engaged in conversation by the same well-set-up young man with little to boast of in the chin department. Hardy took the seat Dottie had vacated, and turned a morose expression on Mrs Carmichael.

The old woman smiled, showing good teeth, which he found somewhat surprising. 'Don't worry, Bill,' Mrs Carmichael told him, 'that chinless wonder Thurby means nothing to her. It's you she wants.'

Her directness embarrassed him, but she seemed a good sort, and like him, she was something of an outsider in this polite, well-to-do society, although unlike him it didn't seem to worry her or undermine her confidence.

'I was sorry to hear about your mother,' she continued, 'I knew her once, don't suppose she would have told you that, no reason why she should.'

'No, I'm afraid...'

'We fell out, she and I, you know. Years ago. Well before you were born. I had a bit of a thing going on with your father. Before he met her, obviously,' she hastened to add.

Hardy wasn't sure what surprised him the most, the notion of his father being the sort of man to have 'a bit of a thing' with a woman most definitely not of his own class—or indeed *any* woman—or that his father, the shrunken, ineffectual nonentity Hardy remembered, could have had any sort of appeal for women. He just couldn't marry together the memory of the man he had known with the man he must surely have been when young. Hardy shook his head. 'No, I'm afraid...' He couldn't think how to answer someone in this situation.

'Oh, he was good-looking you know, back then, and so was I. Though he wasn't a patch on you, dear boy, I don't wonder Dottie is smitten. You are the perfect foil for her dainty dark looks. I see your tie is exactly the same shade of dark red as her frock. No doubt a coincidence but very becoming to both of you. Yes, your father and I, we had a thing going on for almost a year, though his family never approved of me, of course. How could they? So then your mother came on the scene and she took him over, and she made him end it with me. I can see now she was right to do so, but at the time of course, it felt like the world had ended. I was star-struck in a way, I suppose. Thought it really would be a fairy-tale ending for me. He promised me he'd marry me, though of course, I know now they all say that. Hindsight's a wonderful thing, but it always comes that little bit too late, I find.'

Hardy couldn't think of anything to say. For a few moments, it seemed as though he and the elderly woman were isolated on their own little stage, far away from the crowds who knew nothing of their conversation. He had the strongest sense that she was about to tell him something of significance, but then their hostess announced that dinner was served, and the illusion was shattered. Obediently the guests paired up and walked through to the dining room.

The tall, well-to-do (but noticeably chinless) young man escorted Dottie in to dinner, his hand beneath her elbow in that way that made Hardy want to punch him even more. Mrs Carmichael had been commandeered by a grey-haired military type and proceeded into the dining room ahead of Hardy, rather like a ship in full sail, the silvery silk of her gown shimmering in the light.

Hardy looked to his left and noticed a tall elegant young woman directing a coy smile at him. Making a slight bow he offered her his arm, introducing himself as he did so. 'I'm William Hardy. How do you do?'

'I'm Daphne,' she told him, 'Daphne Medhurst. That's my father, Major Medhurst, in front taking in the lady in grey silk. I don't believe I've met you before?'

He found it easy enough to get into conversation with her, and seated side by side at the long table, they chatted amiably throughout the meal. Her father's eye came back to them again and again, and Hardy knew that the gentleman would make enquiries of the Mandersons to learn more about Hardy's situation and prospects.

By the end of the meal—and he wasn't quite sure how it had happened—he had arranged to take Miss Medhurst to lunch the following day.

He told himself it would be perfectly pleasant, and nothing serious on either side. She seemed a nice woman, fairly attractive, reasonably well-educated but by no means snobbish or inclined to look down on those who worked for a living. He had told her his profession and her smile never faltered. He found that he was quite looking forward to their lunch.

He glanced across the table and saw Dottie's face. His conscience pricked him when he saw the dismay, pure and unmistakable, in her eyes. Then with a mutinous set of her chin, she turned and treated Jeffrey Thurby to a brilliant smile and a loudly tinkling laugh at whatever it was—surely she hadn't even heard it—he had just said. Hardy, inexplicably furious, redoubled his efforts with Miss Medhurst.

As he stood in the hall, ready to take his leave, Dottie was coming in from saying goodnight to Jeffrey Thurby, her eyes glowing, her cheeks pink, her lips flushed and full. She had been kissed. It took everything in his power for Hardy to respond to his hostess with something approaching politeness.

'Oh, before you go, Mr Hardy,' Mrs Manderson was now saying, 'at the end of the month we are having a dinner party to celebrate Dorothy's birthday. I do hope you'll be able to join us. It's Saturday the 31st.'

Hardy took a deep breath, and ignoring the look Dottie directed at him, shook his head and with little appearance of regret, said, 'I'm so sorry, I'm afraid I am visiting my Uncle in Matlock, to spend Easter with his family, and I'm travelling up that morning.'

Mrs Manderson looked from her daughter glaring in the corner of the hall yet unable to give in to her temper and just walk away, to Hardy, clipped, barely civil, distant. Mrs Manderson felt some surprise, and was clearly disappointed as she thanked Hardy for letting her know and wished him a pleasant stay with his family, adding, 'Do remember us to your dear sister.' But he was already on the pavement and walking away.

The man Hardy dismissed as a chinless wonder was, as Dottie discovered on the front step of the house, endowed with even more determination to take liberties than any other man she'd so far encountered.

By the time she'd said goodnight and firmly shut the door on him, she felt quite hot and exhausted. And before she had the chance to speak to him, Hardy was saying goodnight to her mother and leaving the house, his grim expression telling her he was furious.

That trollop Daphne Medhurst had attached herself to him with the tenacity of a limpet and not left his side all evening. Dottie feared for Hardy's freedom. Daphne was a most notorious and determined husband-hunter. Fortune was an indifferent matter to her—she had her late mother's money, rumoured to be substantial, and her father gave her a generous allowance, according to those same rumours. But at thirty-one years of age—though only admitting to twenty-seven—time was not on Daphne's side. She needed a man, and clearly she had set her cap at William Hardy.

Dottie said goodnight to her parents and went up to bed, pleading a headache left over from her attack in the street. Not for anything would she admit that her low spirits had anything to do with a certain young policeman and the smiles he had bestowed upon another woman.

But Mrs Manderson was not fooled for a second, and was ruefully aware that her plans had gone awry. She returned to the drawing room and began to empty ashtrays, and plump cushions. She placed empty glasses on a tray. Then she went to sit on a settee near her husband's favourite chair, intent on relaxing for a few minutes before going up to bed. She took a moment to relieve her mind of its primary vexation.

'I should never have invited that fast piece Daphne Medhurst and her boring father to dinner this evening,' she told her husband. 'Daphne has spoiled everything. She is clearly determined to have Inspector Hardy, and so I shall have to find a new suitor for Dorothy. I can't leave her in that idiot Thurby's clutches.'

From behind his newspaper, Mr Manderson's only reply was a soft snore.

It was clear from her every look and word that Daphne Medhurst was enjoying his company. Not since his university days had a young woman shown so much interest in him, Hardy realised, and he ordered another glass of wine for each of them, pushing away the traitorous murmur of his thoughts, *apart from Dottie*...

Somehow, he found he was holding Daphne's hand, small and dainty in his own, and again he had to make an effort to dismiss the sense of betrayal he felt—both his own betrayal as he endeavoured to enjoy Miss Medhurst's smiles, and hers, Dottie's, as she had beamed into the eyes of that chap at dinner the night before. How Hardy wished he had taken his leave before Thurby, then he wouldn't have to think about Dottie showing the man out, and allowing him to kiss her goodnight on the step. William Hardy pushed away thoughts of Dottie in his arms, her lips against his. He was with Miss Medhurst now...

'Ouch, Billy, you're squashing my hand!' Daphne announced at that moment with her ever-present high-pitched giggle. The giggle irked him somewhat, but he told himself in time he'd get used to it, no doubt, and even come to find it endearing. He hastily apologised and released her clammy fingers. She leaned against his shoulder, and looked up into his eyes in a calculated, flirtatious manner. 'How strong you are,' she whispered, for his ears alone. He smiled politely at her, and she had to be content with that.

It seemed she was making arrangements for that evening. She was saying something about the cinema. His approval was taken for granted. Miss Medhurst was used to young men doing what she wanted so that they could enjoy her company.

'You can pick me up at seven o'clock,' she was saying, 'and quickly just pop in to meet Pops, somehow we didn't get round to that last night at the Mandersons', then we'll go on to the picture house. I can't wait to see *Deserts of Arabia*. It's supposed to be *ever so* romantic.'

He nodded. A waiter arrived with their drinks. Hardy, not normally a partaker of lunch-time alcohol, felt a little light-headed. His hand was squeezed in admonition.

'Honestly Billy, you could at least try to sound a little enthusiastic,' she chided. He hated being called Billy. He'd already told her so three times. Her response had been simply, 'Well, I like it.'

He forced a smile again. 'Sorry. I *am* looking forward to it, of course.'

'Good,' she said, and the flirty smile was back. 'Obviously in front of Pops, you mustn't kiss me or hold my hand just yet, as he's rather old-fashioned, but once we're alone of course, that would be perfectly all right. Especially in the cinema. If you know what I mean.'

He nodded. That was all that she required. Ten minutes later, she finally stopped talking, downed the last of her drink, and told him with evident reluctance that she had to leave.

He walked her home. Outside the house, she told him that because her father would be out, she didn't think Hardy should come in, '*This* time,' and she turned to face him expectantly. He hadn't planned on kissing her so soon. They had only just met, after all. But as they stood there it seemed clear she expected it, so as he said goodbye, he bent his head to kiss her lightly on the cheek. She had other ideas, however, and turned to latch her lips firmly onto his, rather shocking him by touching his mouth with the tip of her tongue.

Forced to be satisfied with his lukewarm response, she called a cheery goodbye and ran up the steps to the front door, whilst a bemused Hardy made his way to the police station and felt a considerable sense of relief on reaching his office.

Maple was there.

'Thought you were having the weekend off?' Hardy asked him. Maple looked irritated.

'I should of. But Janet was doing something and couldn't see me till tonight, and my mum nagged me that much about sitting around the house I thought it would just be easier to come in to work. You drunk?'

'A bit. Three glasses of wine at lunch.'

'Got lipstick all over your face, too. Not Miss Manderson's colour, neither.' He directed a close look at Hardy who began scrubbing at his mouth and chin with a handkerchief. Hardy decided to ignore Maple's curiosity, snapping at him instead.

'Where are we with this bloody case?'

'There's five who have been at two or more of these posh get-ups,' Maple said, and handed Hardy a piece of paper.

'I suppose that's no real surprise. These people all socialise with one another, they're all part of the same set.' Hardy read the short list. Ian and Sylvia Smedley-Judd, Gareth Smedley-Judd and Mrs Gerard were the first four. The fifth name stood out, in that he was surprised to see it there at all. 'Mrs Muriel Carmichael,' he said.

'Yes, she's some kind of fancy seamstress, I think,' Maple began to say, 'though I'm not sure why she gets invited to these posh places. That's a bit suspicious, if you ask me.'

'It's all right, Frank, I know the lady. She is the owner of Carmichael and Jennings, a fashionable warehouse of ladies' garments. Very in. And your girlfriend's mistress works there.'

'Mrs Manderson? The old dragon? She never does! Well I'll eat my hat!'

'No, you chump, not *Mrs* Manderson. *Miss Dottie Manderson*. She works at Carmichael's as a mannequin.'

'Oh yes, that does ring a bell, now you mention it. Not sure it's entirely respectable, if you ask me,' Maple added, forgetting for a moment who he was talking to, 'All these pretty young girls taking their clothes off and parading about in front of people.'

'I'm sure it's *entirely* respectable, thank you, Sergeant,' Hardy said crossly, and Maple hid a smirk behind his handkerchief as he pretended to wipe his nose. 'And more importantly, Mrs Carmichael has a lot of connections, both high and low, you might say. I chatted with her myself just last night at the Mandersons' dinner party. A nice woman, very no-nonsense. Rather inclined to be a bit blunter than is usual in polite society, but I think that's why people take to her so, she is quite a character.' In his head, Hardy replayed her great revelation, *I knew your father. For almost a year...*

Silence hung heavily on the stale air of the Inspector's office. He thought for a moment, then, reaching for his hat and coat, said, 'Come on, let's go and see her now. See if we can find out anything. And we'll arrange to see the others on Monday or as soon as convenient.'

The door was opened to the two men by Mrs Carmichael's maid-of-all-work, a thin woman with a huge beaky nose and an air of deepest gloom. She gave her name as Pamphlett, and a look followed it as if daring them to comment or laugh. They didn't dare.

Mrs Carmichael was at home, they were told, and was enjoying her tea.

'Always has it this early, half past three,' Pamphlett said with a loud sniff of her giant nose. 'She doesn't usually like to be disturbed. She might see you. Might not. Wait here.'

Here was right inside the front door. A draught came in under the front door and from around the glass of the tiny window beside it. The air in the hall was damp and chilly, which Hardy found surprising. Mould grew up the walls from the floor in the corner by the window. He felt he could smell the spores without even getting right up close. The house was a mouldering ruin, yet could have been every inch as desirable as the Mandersons' home. Surely the lady's success meant she could afford to live in comfort? Indeed, his impression of her was very much that of someone who enjoyed the finer things in life, and her business was known to be hugely profitable. So why didn't she keep her home in better order?

'You can come in,' Pamphlett said from the doorway. 'I suppose I'd better get some more cups. As if I haven't got enough to do.' She stalked off and they went into the room, Hardy tapping lightly on the door and popping his head round first, only to be waved in impatiently.

'Come in, come in, I'm sure I just heard her tell you to!' Mrs Carmichael grumbled. She looked at Maple in some surprise and turned back to address the inspector. 'I assumed that you were here to continue our chat from the Mandersons' last night, but if so you wouldn't have brought him along. Is this official business then?'

Hardy was settling himself in a chair opposite her. Maple squeezed onto the far end of the sofa upon which Mrs Carmichael lounged in a pair of the largest cherry-coloured satin pyjamas either man had ever witnessed. On her swollen feet were matching satin slippers. Hardy was no costume expert, but even he knew fashionable ladies had stopped wearing lounging pyjamas over the last few years.

Pamphlett appeared with the cups and set them

down on the tray with a clatter. Turning immediately she said over her shoulder, 'Ring if you want anythink,' and left the room.

Mrs Carmichael bid them help themselves, and the sergeant lost no time in taking a plate and adding sandwiches and an iced French fancy to it. He then poured tea for himself and his boss.

'Yes, I'd like to ask you a few questions if I may,' Hardy began. 'It's about these dinner party robberies. You were one of a small number of guests present on more than one occasion. I must confess we're still a bit stumped about these cases, and frankly we need all the help we can get. It's possible that you, having been to three of these dinners, might have seen something that could be a huge help to us.'

'You're quite the flatterer, like your father,' she said with a smile. A crocodile smile, Hardy thought. 'You know just how to get round a girl, don't you? Well I doubt if I saw anything you haven't already heard from someone else, but ask away, young man.'

'Are you a close friend of the Smedley-Judds?'

'Ian Smedley-Judd, do you mean? No not really, I wouldn't say we was close friends. But I did design dresses for Sylvia Smedley-Judd and her daughter, for the daughter's coming out ball, and her twenty-first birthday, and the party for her engagement to Lieutenant Newton-Spencer. Mrs Smedley-Judd has been coming to me for years, of course. A good client.'

'Do all your clients become your friends?'

'Not really, just a few, that's all. Most clients like to keep a distinction between their friends and their 'suppliers'. But over the years, what with taking a woman's measurements and chatting, and seeing her on every special occasion throughout her life, you gets to know people, and with a few of them, you gets to form a kind of bond. Not quite friends, but we understand each other.'

'I see,' Hardy said, and he did. It made perfect sense to him that someone in Mrs Carmichael's position could become a close acquaintance, a confidante, even an ally. As she said, not quite friends, but in some respects, even closer. 'So, you attended the party given by Mr and Mrs Ian Smedley-Judd at their home in Kensington, and also the party of a Mr Norris Smith two weeks before in Oxford.' Was it his imagination or did she seem surprised to be asked about that one? 'Then also last week, you were invited to Mrs Emmeline Foster's dinner party in Hemel Hempstead. That is correct, isn't it?'

She hesitated, clearly trying to decide what would be the best thing to say. In the end though, she agreed, adding, 'Although I wasn't able to go to Mrs Foster's owing to a bad cold.'

'Yes, so Mrs Foster said. Still you seem much better now.'

'I'm fortunate in having a good constitution,' she said, and leaned forward to take another sandwich from the plate. She bit it in half, swallowed the first piece immediately and jammed the second in right after it. The slight delay allowed her to recover her poise somewhat.

Hardy said, 'Coming back to Mr Smedley-Judd's party, did you know many of the other guests, when you got there, or was it a group of strangers?'

'I knew a fair few of the ladies, not so many of the men,' Mrs Carmichael said. She cut herself a slab of cake that almost filled her plate, and she proceeded to eat it quickly, with her fingers, clearly relishing it, and dropping crumbs all about her. 'Never could afford cake when I was a kid. Or bread too, half the time. These days, cake is pretty much all I fancy. And it's not as though I need to worry about my figure anymore.'

Hardy smiled politely. Maple took a macaroon and bit into it, groaning with pleasure, and saying, 'Whoever makes your cakes, Mrs Carmichael, is an out-and-out marvel.'

Mrs Carmichael grinned at him. 'That's Pamphlett. She's a whizz in the kitchen. Missed her calling working as a machinist for me for the last twenty years. A bit of a grouchy old stick but a heart of gold. Her first name's Anabelle, but you'll never catch her using it. Don't know why she takes such a masochistic pleasure in using that awful surname of hers.'

'Did any of the robbers seem at all familiar to you?' Hardy asked, desperately in need of getting things back on track. It was supposed to be an interview after all, and he had plans for the evening. Not that he was looking forward to the prospect of an evening in Daphne Medhurst's company. The very thought of it was enough to make him want to smash something. Mrs Carmichael laughed, however, all her chins wobbling.

'Think I could see through the wool of their balaclavas, do you? Or do you think I designed the balaclavas myself, from my new 'Robbery a la

Mode' collection?' Before he could give the defensive answer on the tip of his tongue, she laughed again and said, 'I'm just kidding you, ducks. My, but you look like your father when you're annoyed! No ducks, they didn't do nothing nor say nothing that rang a bell with me. Mostly I was just upset about my rings and my bracelets.'

Hardy stirred his tea, using the time to collect his temper and to think. Maple cleared his throat and chipped in, 'And did you notice if any of the robbers had a tattoo on his wrist at all?'

'No, I don't think...'

'Only some people have told us they caught a brief glimpse of something. It might have been the word 'duck', or something like that.'

She shook her head quite emphatically. 'No, I didn't see anything like that. Perhaps you're looking for a sailor whose been laid off, then?'

'It's possible,' Hardy said. 'We're exploring a few different ideas at the moment. Er—when the men went upstairs at the parties you attended, did you hear anything they said to one another about that? Or see what they brought down with them?'

She shook her head again. 'Can't say as I did. Sorry, Inspector. And now, if you don't mind, it's time for my nap. Got to make the most of the weekends, haven't you?'

The two policemen came away feeling discouraged.

'I don't feel like we're getting anywhere,' Maple grumbled. Hardy was inclined to agree.

'Though I got the distinct impression she wasn't being completely truthful. I'm certain she knows more.'

'Threw her a bit, us knowing about that Foster do she was invited to but never attended. Such a shame thumb-screws are out of fashion.' Maple got into the driver's seat. Hardy got in beside him, still deep in thought and without even thinking about it, began to go through his sheaf of papers again.

'Ian Smedley-Judd,' Hardy said, 'Let's take a drive round there and see if we can find out anything. Someone has to know something, surely. Sooner or later we're going to find out what that is, I really believe it. This Smedley-Judd was invited to four of the parties, that we know about, and actually attended three, including his own and his brother's of course. If anyone can help us, he can.'

'Probably him what done it,' Maple said with a laugh. 'If this was a book, it would be the last person you thought of, and in this case the last person to think of would be the host of the party.'

'It's always a lot easier in books than in real life,' Hardy complained.

'At least we've had our tea,' Maple observed with satisfaction. 'Did that old bird really know your family then? Sounded like she knew your old man pretty well.'

'A bit too damned well,' was Hardy's terse response.

In less than half an hour, they halted the car outside the Smedley-Judds', and Hardy only had two and a half hours until he was due to arrive at Daphne Medhurst's home to escort her to the cinema. Their conversation with Mr Smedley-Judd was unlikely to take more than an hour at the absolute limit, which meant there was nothing to keep Hardy from his assignation with Miss

Medhurst. He was still not looking forward to the evening. Why on earth had he let her talk him into it? On balance, he felt he'd rather go to the dentist.

Mr Smedley-Judd was not at home, the butler informed them, but Mrs Smedley-Judd was in the drawing room and was happy to see them. Or at least, as it transpired, she was happy to see Maple.

Hardy had noticed before Maple had this effect on ladies of a certain age. His big size and schoolboy looks made them view him as a large, hungry child needing to be mothered. Consequently, as soon as the policemen sat down, she rang for tea and began to tell Maple he reminded her of her nephew Michael, her younger sister's boy.

Hardy had a brainwave. Leaving Maple to charm as much information as he could from the delightful Mrs Smedley-Judd, Hardy made his way along the hall to the back stairs and down into the kitchen, where he made the acquaintance of the cook and showed he too could turn on the charm with the lady in charge of that domain, and he coaxed out of her a cup of tea, with a large slab of cherry cake precariously balanced in the saucer.

Hardy reminded the cook of her former mistress's elder son, it appeared. 'Always in my kitchen, he was, when he was down from Eton or wherever, telling me he was *starving*,' she said with a laugh. 'You young fellows don't eat half as much as you should.'

He asked her if she'd mind telling him a bit about the night of the robbery. 'I know you've already been through it all,' he said, 'and believe me, I'm very sorry to have to take you through it all again, but I think my sergeant and I have missed something. Perhaps if you and I put our heads together, we might come up with something useful.'

By now he had all seven of the regular staff gathered about him. They were warm, they were welcoming, with none of the suspicion or dislike of the police he often encountered. They could see that, in spite of his cut-glass accent, he was one of them—his cuffs were fraying, his shoes down at the heels, his jacket elbows were wearing thin.

They had quite a lot to tell him.

Yes, they said, they had all heard a car. The sound had come from the rear alleyway which led to the mews. There were only ever three cars garaged in the mews. The Alleyns', who were away at present in the north, and they had taken their car with them. Mrs Henderson from the house at the end of the street, who was too poorly to go out in her car. And the sound hadn't come from Mr Smedley-Judd's own car, as that was locked away in the garage as it was most days and evenings.

'He doesn't use it much when they're in town,' said the butler. 'Mostly he sends for it if we go down to Hertfordshire, or if they go away for Christmas or the summer holidays.'

The young footman, certainly no more than twenty or twenty-one, had little to contribute about his attack. His back had been turned—a fact that Hardy remembered from the statements—as he had been in the butler's pantry, attempting to telephone for the police.

'Hit me from behind, the blighter,' said the

footman, and Hardy dutifully examined the site of the injury, the swelling now greatly diminished, on the side of the young man's head, completely hidden by his thick mane of dark hair.

'Still, we did pretty well out of it all round,' the butler Morris chimed in.

'Indeed? How so?'

'The youngster had five pounds from Mr Smedley-Judd, on account of how he tried to help out by calling the police, only to get clouted for his trouble. And all of us got a rise in our wages, due to his gratitude for our loyalty, and out of his concern that we might give notice. True enough, people sometimes leave a place if there's a robbery or some such, but what I say is,' said Morris, settling back in his seat with the air of a sage dispensing wisdom to an eager group of acolytes, 'what I say is, we're the lucky ones, 'cos we've been done, ain't we? It's all the other places what wants to look out—you never know who might be next.'

Hardy allowed an admiring pause to follow this pronouncement before asking, 'I don't suppose any of you remembers anything about the men, do you? I mean, one could hardly expect you to, it was all so frightening, and everything happened so quickly.'

No one said anything. They exchanged looks and shrugs. For a moment Hardy thought his enquiries were over, but he noticed the little between-maid glancing back and forth and fidgeting.

Hardy said to the girl, 'Have you thought of something?'

She was nervous, and glanced at Mr Morris as if for permission to speak. The butler seemed to consider for a moment then inclined his head slowly, and the girl's relief was obvious. Clearly Morris enjoyed a traditional butler's status in the household.

She spoke in a soft, childish voice, her words stumbling over each other. Hardy judged her age to be fourteen or fifteen, and she was a shy little thing, unused to being the centre of attention.

'Well, I'm not saying it's anything for definite, but I did just notice this one thing, and it mightn't mean anything, and I don't want to get anyone into trouble, nor myself neither, as I wouldn't not never dream usually of saying nothing...'

She paused for breath and Hardy, mentally reviewing what she'd said and realising she hadn't said anything yet, smiled at her and said, 'No of course you wouldn't, but it is everyone's duty to help the police as much as they can in cases such as this.'

She blushed beetroot red and nodded.

'So, if there is anything, even something very small, something that seemed a bit odd, or you noticed, just tell me and I'll decide whether or not it's important.'

'But what if it gets the master into trouble?'

'Why on earth should it, girl?' Morris said sharply, and in the corner by the stove, the parlour-maid was heard to say, 'Tell the truth and shame the devil, that's what I was always taught as a girl.'

Still blushing furiously, the between-maid hung her head.

'What's your name?' Hardy asked her.

'Ellen, sir. Ellen Miller.'

'Well Ellen, just tell me what it was you saw, and let me worry about what it means. I promise you won't get into any trouble.'

She bit her lip, and he was unsure if she would speak at all. Then in a rush, she blurted out, 'It was the bag, sir. And I know I wasn't supposed to be in there, but the door was open and I wanted so badly to get a look at the Holy Mother, she's so beautiful.'

Mr Morris wasn't pleased. 'Ellen Miller, I told you last time! You had no right...'

She burst into tears. 'I know, Mr Morris, I know. But I just wanted a quick look, that's all. She's so beautiful. I didn't think it would do no harm!' She ran from the room.

Hardy felt annoyed. He said to Morris, 'Why did you...' but then gave it up. He sat back. 'Does anyone know what she's talking about?'

They all looked at each other. He felt certain they knew. If he wasn't firm now, they would conceal that knowledge. He needed to know what they knew.

'You must tell me. Anything you know could be crucial to this case. It could prevent other robberies. Even other injuries. Next time, a footman or butler might not get away with a nasty bump on the head. It could be far worse.'

Mr Morris cleared his throat. It seemed he was to be their spokesman.

'The girl's talking about Mr Smedley-Judd's collection. It's in the room next to his study. Mr Smedley-Judd is a dedicated collector of religious art.'

Hardy felt as though a bell rang in his brain. He

found he was holding his breath. Morris continued, 'None of us is allowed into the room. Mr Smedley-Judd keeps the door locked as some of the items are very old and delicate, and some are very valuable. But well, he sometimes forgets to lock it, I suppose. Ellen was brought up in a convent, she's an orphan—she's quite fond of some of the things she used to see in the church. It seems she has taken the opportunity of popping into the room for a look around.'

'What kind of art is it?' Hardy asked. Morris shrugged.

'Well, you know. Pictures, statues, candlesticks, chalices and such. Gloomy stuff for the most part. Not that I'm a religious man myself, but I suppose if you are, well, no doubt it means more.'

There were one or two nods of agreement. But no one seemed to know anything more. Hardy asked the housekeeper to take him up to Ellen's room to talk to her.

They found the girl sitting on the floor beside her bed, no longer crying, though the tears still marked tracks down her cheeks. She was holding a rosary and praying softly.

Although the door was open, and she was a junior servant, Hardy knocked on the door and waited on the landing until she invited him to enter.

He sat on the floor next to her. 'So you grew up in an orphanage?' he asked. She nodded.

'Yes, but the nuns were kind to me.'

'And you like to see the statues and so on.'

'I like to see the Virgin Mary. She looks so kind. And she knows how hard things can be. I ask her to help me, like the nuns taught me. They told me she's sort of everyone's mother, not just the Baby Jesus's.'

'I'm sure that's true,' Hardy said. 'I lost my mother recently.' He had felt all right at first, had been going to say more, but suddenly the sense of loss hit him again and his voice wavered, and he couldn't continue. Ellen patted his hand. After a pause he said, 'So what was this about a bag?'

She bit her lip again. The housekeeper, seated on the opposite bed, no doubt belonging to the other maid, leaned forward and said, 'It's all right, Ellen. You can tell the inspector.'

'Well it was there in the room, under the little side-table just inside the door. It's the table what has got the big chalice-cup thing on it. I just thought it was odd, that's all.'

'What kind of bag?'

'A black leather one, like a doctor's.'

'And are you saying it's not usually in there?'

'I've never seen it before. But it was the same kind of bag and I just thought...'

He shook his head, not understanding. 'The same as what?'

'The ones what the robbers had. I saw it. I'm sure—at least, I'm sort of sure—it's the same one. It's got a bit of fluff caught in the loop where the handle's attached to the bag. A bit of green thread stuff, like it's got snagged on something. It's just a tiny little piece, but I saw it straight away.'

Hardy regarded the girl. There was no doubt in his mind that she was telling the truth. He turned to the housekeeper.

'If I send a policeman over to take this down in a

statement, will you see to it that no one else knows about it? I want you to keep this information strictly to yourselves. Don't talk about it with the other staff or even the Smedley-Judds. This could be vital information.'

They promised him solemnly not to breathe a word, Ellen gripping her rosary tightly as she did so.

'Do you have a key to this collection room?' Hardy asked the housekeeper. She shook her head.

'Only Mr Smedley-Judd has that. I'm sorry, Inspector.'

Hardy nodded, then thanked them and went back downstairs. Maple was waiting in the hall, his face still bearing a liberal scattering of crumbs.

'Ready, Guv—er, Bill?'

'Just a moment. I need a quick word with Mrs Smedley-Judd. Is she still in there?'

'Yes.'

'Stay here, Frank, and don't let anyone in. I'll only be a moment.' He tapped on the drawing room door and put his head round. 'Sorry to trouble you again, Mrs Smedley-Judd. May I just ask, do you have a key to Mr Smedley-Judd's art collection room? I'd very much like to quickly check something in there if it's not too much trouble.'

If she was surprised, she hid it well, yet Hardy was convinced she *was* surprised. That, and possibly alarmed. She immediately offered him an apologetic smile and shook her head.

'I'm sorry, Inspector. Only my husband has a key to that room, and as you know, he isn't at home at the moment. Perhaps you wouldn't mind returning another day? It might be best to arrange a specific time with him so you can be sure not to miss him.'

'Of course, Mrs Smedley-Judd, that's no trouble at all. Well, thank you very much for your time and for the tea, of course. Good day.'

They got in the car and Hardy told Maple what he had learned.

'Cor lumme,' Maple said. Hardy agreed.

'It's certainly very interesting.'

They returned to the police station. Whilst Maple dispatched a constable to the Smedley-Judds' to take the statement from the maid, Hardy wrote up his notes. He paused to look at his watch. He had a little less than an hour and a half before he had to be at Miss Medhurst's. Plenty of time to go home, have a wash and a shave and change his clothes before going to meet her. He just didn't feel like moving.

'So did you find out anything from Mrs Smedley-Judd?' he asked Maple.

'Apart from the fact that I'm the spit of her favourite nephew? Not really.'

*

Chapter Eleven

As it was, he arrived home a full hour before he was due to meet Daphne, but he was reluctant to get ready to go out. He sat in the kitchen in a daydream, thinking too much about too many different things. If his mother had been there, no doubt he could have confided some of what he was feeling to her. It struck him yet again how very silent the house was without her. How he wished she could have lived long enough to enjoy the greater comfort his improved income would have afforded them, after all their recent years of hardship and worry.

He made a pot of tea, but had no sooner poured out a cup than he remembered something he had neglected to do, and was forced to make a hurried visit to the Manderson home. He had something on his mind.

He rang the bell at twenty minutes past six. Janet answered. He had known Dottie would not answer the door, knowing they would all be getting ready for dinner, but he couldn't help the pang of disappointment he felt at not seeing her.

'I'm so sorry, Janet, I know it's a dreadful time of day to call. I wonder if Mr or Mrs Manderson could spare me just a couple of minutes?' She was helping him off with his coat, his hat already on the hallstand.

'Don't worry about it. I'll go and check, Mr Hardy. One of them will probably be able to see you,' she said and opened the door to the drawing room, indicating he should wait in there.

He felt a sense of shock on entering the room and seeing Dottie seated on the sofa on the far side, a book in her hand, her hair shining and smooth under the beam of the electric light. She wore a rather fetching navy dress with a white collar, both colours suiting her delicate complexion as well as her lovely figure. She looked up and slowly blushed pink when she saw him. He crossed the room to shake her hand, horribly uncomfortable at arriving unannounced, yet his heart was pounding and he felt elated just to see her.

'Good evening, Will—er, Inspector Hardy. Are we expecting you? I'm afraid I'm dining at Flora's this evening. They're calling for me any time now.'

He was staring, but couldn't help himself. He stammered an apology then added in a more measured tone, 'Um, no, I'm afraid I called on the off-chance of speaking with your father or mother. I confess I completely forgot what time it was.' Liar, said his conscience, and her eyes said the same. Huge eyes. Deep, velvety soft brown eyes.

More like pools, drawing him in, making him forget...

'Inspector! Janet tells me you need a quick word about something?' Mrs Manderson, as forbidding as usual, spoke from the doorway. He turned to offer her a slight bow, not quite sure how to proceed. It occurred to him now he had come on a fool's errand. Instinct told him she would not listen to his request.

She only gave him half her attention as she attempted to fix a corsage to her shoulder. Dottie crossed the room to help her mother with the pin. Standing side by side, he couldn't help thinking how alike they were, and yet how different. Dottie was taller by some four or five inches, and far more slender than her mother. Dottie was softer and gentler in manner, and yet, who knew? Perhaps Mrs Manderson had also been soft, girlish, gentle and shy once upon a time. Now she was a formidable woman, forceful, domineering, confidently in command of her household. And her plans would not be thwarted.

Nerves made him rush his request and he didn't present his argument in the best manner, but she began to shake her head almost immediately, though she allowed him to ramble on, and she didn't stop shaking it until he drifted into silence. Then she said, 'I cannot possibly cancel our plans. The party invitations have already gone out. The food has been ordered. Several guests have already accepted. It is going ahead. That's the end of the matter.'

'But Mother...' Dottie began. Mrs Manderson held up a hand.

'Nonsense, Dorothy. And now, I must finish getting ready for dinner. Good evening, Inspector.'

Mrs Manderson swept out of the room, with the air of one carrying all before her. Dottie watched her mother with a mingled expression of embarrassment and admiration.

'Golly,' she said.

'Quite,' Hardy responded.

'I'm so sorry...' She shot him a fraught look.

'It's my fault. I knew she'd say no, and I can't say I blame her. I just felt I had to... Never mind, forget about it. Look, I must go or I'm going to be late. Please give my regards to your sister. Enjoy your dinner, and don't let this upset you.'

'Where are you going?'

'To the cinema. To see that wretched *Desert* thing.'

She knew immediately what he meant, and was upset. She treated him to a cool, distancing look that could have come from her mother. 'I see. Well, give my regards to Miss Medhurst. I hope she enjoys the film.' With that, she swept from the room.

'Golly,' said Hardy, though privately he said a great deal more.

Dinner at Flora and George's that evening got off to a tricky start. Dottie arrived upset and angry, and was immediately closeted in her sister's morning room whilst she let off steam. Flora looked on in amusement.

'Dottie, darling! Do calm down. It's only the pictures.'

'You know what Daphne's like at the pictures!'

Dottie stormed. 'As soon as the lights go down, she'll be all over him. He won't stand a chance!'

Flora was trying not to laugh but it wasn't easy. The very thought of Hardy as the helpless innocent victim of Daphne Medhurst's amorous intentions filled her head with ludicrous images. Half-laughing, half-serious, she held out her hand to her sister, pushing her back down onto the seat.

'Dottie! Be sensible. Put yourself in his position. Would he behave like this over your dinner with Dr Melville? I hardly think so.'

Dottie appeared to consider this for a moment or two then burst out with, 'But that wasn't in the dark! And anyway, he doesn't even know about Melville. Does he?'

'I doubt it. But even if he did...'

Dottie sighed and sank back against the cushions. She ran frantic fingers through her hair, making it stand out in such a way that Flora felt inclined to pass her a mirror.

'I suppose,' Dottie admitted, 'that I'm making a bit of a fuss. But honestly Flora, Daphne Medhurst... Once she gets him in her clutches...'

'I'm sure your favourite police inspector can defend his own virtue without your help,' Flora pointed out.

Dottie had been on the point of saying that he wasn't her favourite police inspector, but saw from Flora's expression that she wasn't taken in for a moment. Dottie sighed again, and in a small voice, she said, 'I just don't like to think of her kissing him.'

Flora leaned back beside her and patted her knee. 'I know Dottie, but after all, it's just a couple of kisses. Surely you can spare her a couple of kisses when you'll have him all to yourself forever?'

Blushing, Dottie hotly declared not only that it could never happen, but that she certainly didn't want it to. Laughing, Flora pulled her to her feet.

'Come on, you. My poor husband is waiting for his dinner.'

Things started to go awry from the moment he arrived late at the Medhursts' home. He had not changed out of the rather sober suit he wore for work. Daphne gave him a pointed look and a sniff of disapproval. He told her that it was because he had been busy with work and had run out of time. Obviously he couldn't tell her he hadn't felt like making an effort.

Then when they finally came out of the picture-house that Sunday evening following the tedious offering that was *Deserts of Arabia*, Hardy and Miss Medhurst were no longer on speaking terms.

As they waited to cross the road with the rest of the cinema's clientèle, Hardy attempted a last effort at gallantry by offering her his arm. Her response was to tut loudly and half turn away, leaving a wide gap between them that was rapidly filled by others who didn't realise they were together. The onset of the rain brought out the umbrellas, and soon Hardy lost sight of his companion amidst the streams of people pushing and scurrying to get out of the weather and get home.

When he reached the other side of the road, Hardy paused and turned to look about for her—

she ought to be easy to spot, tall and slender, in her smart, bright peacock-blue coat, the matching hat barely covering her bright, certainly dyed he admitted now, auburn waves.

He couldn't see her. He felt annoyed, and was tempted to simply give up and go home. But he had not been brought up to act in such an ungentlemanly way, and having satisfied himself she was not on his side of the street, he crossed back again to the cinema side and continued to look about for her. A taxi left the nearby rank and drove off, but he couldn't see who was inside. After several minutes of scouring the rapidly thinning crowds, he was forced to conclude she had gone. Swearing under his breath, he debated once more what to do.

He was still tempted to just go home, but decided to walk to her house, if only to have the pleasure of giving her a piece of his mind when he saw her.

From her position in the back of the cinema entrance hall, Daphne Medhurst smirked to see Hardy so put about. Serve him right, she thought. Boring old stick, younger than her, not that you'd know it, he was so old-fashioned. A girl wanted a bit of fun. At their age they ought to be past all that politeness and arm's-length stuff. She had shocked him with her boldness, she knew that. But if you liked a chap—or thought you did, she reflected now somewhat ruefully—why not let him know, that was how she saw it. No good waiting until you were married then finding out you'd got yourself lumbered with a monk or a woman-hater. She wanted a red-blooded man who knew what he wanted and wasn't afraid to take it. She leaned a little to her right, and could see Hardy walking off down the road.

Behind Daphne, further back in the gloomier part of the foyer, a man watched her from behind a newspaper. Clearly the girl had had a spat with the copper and had given him the push, which made things much easier for him. Very much easier. He folded the newspaper and made his way towards her.

'Surely you haven't been stood up, a gorgeous armful like you?'

Daphne turned to look at the man who addressed her. She had been going to give him a set-down but thought better of it when she took a good look at him. A tall, good-looking man, grinning admiringly at her like that. And he was clearly well-to-do, his accent could cut glass and his suit was definitely bespoke.

She gave him a rueful look. 'Apparently, he didn't think so,' she said, dropping her eyelashes and giving him that sly glance upwards that men liked so much.

'Well his loss, I'd say, and a chance for someone else to convince you there are still some red-blooded men left in the world.' He held out his arm.

She hesitated for a few seconds. But he'd used the same words back at her that she'd thought herself, and the smile he gave her was flattering.

He leaned towards her and in a stage whisper said, 'Come on, let's paint the town red, sweetheart!'

She laughed then, and took his offered arm. 'Oh,

go on then.'

They went out and down the steps into the now-deserted street. William Hardy was nowhere to be seen.

She wasn't there. That much was plain the second Hardy got to the house. Major Medhurst, clearly confused as to why his daughter's escort should arrive back without her, stood back to allow the young man into the house. He invited him to wait in the little sitting room where there was a roaring fire and a chess game in progress.

The Major had no partner, he was playing both sides by the simple expedient of turning the board around after each move. He invited Hardy to sit. Hardy, agitated, sat, albeit on the edge of the chair. He didn't know quite what to do. Neither did he want to alarm the older man.

'Had a tiff, I suppose?' the Major suggested. Hardy cleared his throat and admitted it was so.

'Easily done, with the ladies,' the Major said, very much along the lines of explaining the strange behaviour of an exotic species. 'Trouble with us chaps, always putting our foot in it.'

'Er, yes, indeed,' Hardy agreed, adding, 'Then we got separated in the crowd outside the picture-house. I didn't see which way Miss Medhurst went. I waited for a few moments, then I realised she must have come home. At least, I thought perhaps...'

The Major nodded, seeming completely unconcerned, and said, 'Well, no doubt she'll be back shortly. Play a game of chess while you wait, then when she gets home, I'll leave you to make it up with her.'

They began to play. Or rather, Hardy, unable to concentrate on the game already in progress, allowed his queen to be captured almost immediately.

'I'd been playing for over two hours,' the Major commented.

Hardy apologised, adding, 'I really think Miss Medhurst should be back by now.'

'Nonsense, dear boy. No doubt met up with some girlfriends and gone for a late supper at someone's house.'

Hardy stared doubtfully at the Major. 'Would she do that?'

'Oh yes, always bumping into girls she was at school with, that sort of thing. Large circle of friends. Not out of the ordinary for her to come home in the early hours. I never worry about her. You know what girls are like with time-keeping.'

Hardy bit his lip, trying to decide what to do. The Major waved the brandy decanter at him, but Hardy declined. He made up his mind and got to his feet.

'I'm sorry, Major, I'm afraid I really do have to leave. It's almost midnight and I've got to be up early for work in the morning.'

The Major clicked his tongue. 'My God, yes, I know what that's like. Up at the crack of dawn. Reveille. No bugle to get you up out of bed though, I'll be bound.'

Hardy forced a smile and tried to sound hearty. 'No indeed, an ordinary alarm clock for me! Well, thank you for your hospitality. Er... I'm very sorry, once again for the unfortunate...'

'Not at all, not at all. Ladies, eh? 'Leave 'em alone, and they'll come home, bringing their tails behind them', that's what we used to say. Young fillies, what? Like to keep us fellows on our toes, keep us guessing. Well, goodnight, young man, goodnight.'

Outside in the street, a light frost made every surface glisten. The street was dark. It was empty. Of Daphne Medhurst there was no sign. Hardy was seriously discomposed. With his sense of duty unfulfilled, he made his way home, alternately angry with himself and angry with her for the position she'd put him in.

He saw no one resembling her on his journey. Once he reached his house, he left his coat in the hall and went immediately to the telephone. He put a call through to the Medhursts', waiting a full two minutes for the Major to answer.

'No, she's not here yet,' the old gentleman replied to Hardy's question, 'But I expect her momentarily.'

'Will you telephone or please ask your daughter to telephone me as soon as she arrives home, it would set my mind at rest. It doesn't matter how late it is.'

The old man assured Hardy he would do so. Hardy slept in a chair in the sitting room, in case the telephone bell should ring.

Finally at a quarter past six in the morning, the telephone rang.

As Hardy stood looking down at the dead body of Daphne Medhurst half an hour later, he was aware for the first time of what it was to feel a cold fury.

The alleyway where her body had been dumped was littered with rubbish and stank. She had been deposited in a bricked-up doorway. No care had been taken to straighten her clothes. Her humiliation was complete in death. Her dress was bunched up, revealing pudgy white thighs above darned stockings. Her undergarments, in contrast with the smart outer wear, had evidently like the stockings, seen better days. Clearly the rumours about her wealthy status were unfounded. Her hat lay on the ground. Someone had stepped on it and crushed the crown.

He felt protective of her, a strange, belated sensation given the way he'd felt as they left the picture house the previous evening. He leaned over to pull her dress straight and neat to her knees. Over his shoulder he said to Maple, 'Ask the doctor if she's been interfered with, or violated at all.' Even as Maple nodded and made a note, Hardy thought to himself, I can't believe I'm asking that about a woman I took to the pictures. Then something struck him. 'Where's her bag?' Only now had he noticed it was missing.

Maple shrugged and cast about him helplessly. 'Perhaps she didn't have a bag with her,' he said.

'Of course she did, women never go anywhere without their bag. I want it found. Send some men to knock on doors, we need to know if anyone saw or heard anything. I know there aren't many residences just here, so they might not get much, but we've got to try.'

'Sir.'

The strand of beads she had worn when he last saw her had been snapped. Small red beads lay all over the alleyway. A young beat constable almost fell over as his boot slid on one. He cursed and kicked it aside. 'Hey!' Hardy yelled at the youngster. 'I want all those beads picked up and put in an envelope.' He knew they weren't likely to be important to the case, but in any case he wanted it done. Luckily few were foolish enough to challenge a detective inspector, especially one in a bad mood early on a Monday morning.

'Yes sir, straight away,' the lad responded immediately.

The doctor arrived with his assistant, and between them they quickly erected a small screen to shield the cold remains of Daphne Medhurst from the public. Hardy was glad they did so, he did not know how much longer he could stand there and look at her corpse. He had seen enough dead bodies in his short police career, some of them horribly mutilated, some of them in advanced stages of decomposition, but never had his involvement felt so personal. He gladly stepped back from the scene, allowing the doctor to begin his preliminary examination.

Maple stepped back with him, and in a low voice said, 'You obviously knew her, Bill. Is there anything you think I should know?'

'Got any cigarettes?' William Hardy asked him. Maple handed one over, greatly surprised.

'Never seen you smoke,' he observed. As a reply Hardy struck a match, lit the cigarette and took a long slow drag, leaning back against the building wall, his eyes closed, his faced turned up towards the thin morning sunshine. After a moment he said,

'I took her out last night. I met her at the Mandersons' dinner on Saturday night, I suppose I thought I quite liked her, though I wouldn't have spent any more time with her. On closer acquaintance, she wasn't really my type. Rather too free and easy, a bit too pushy. I had lunch with her yesterday, and before I knew what was happening, I was committed to taking her out last night. She wanted to go to the pictures. That new Arabian romantic thing.'

He exchanged a look with Maple, who tried to stifle a laugh. 'Don't see you in the back row, snogging and trying to cop a feel.' Catching sight of Hardy's face, he hastened to apologise. 'Sorry sir. Didn't mean to be irreverent. Just—you know—a sudden mental picture of what courting couples usually get up to in the cinema.'

Hardy couldn't help a short laugh. 'It's all right. No, I'm afraid we fell out. I lacked enthusiasm for the young lady's charms, I'm afraid. It feels horrible saying this about her but she was a bit, er...'

'Cheap?' suggested the ever-helpful sergeant. Hardy shook his head.

'We shouldn't say such things, and after all, I hardly knew her... She's dead, the poor woman.' He threw down the cigarette butt and ground it under his heel. 'And now I've got to tell her father. Poor blighter.'

'Want me to come along?'

'No. I want you to go the picture-house, the one on the Avenue, see if anyone there noticed her leaving. Obviously she met up with someone, somehow, somewhere. I lost sight of her at the kerb outside the place. See if there are any pubs between the picture-house and here, she might have met someone in a pub, or outside. It was closing time, someone may have seen something.' He sighed deeply. 'Right then...see you back at the office.'

Clearly there was something in Hardy's appearance that warned Major Medhurst that his visitor was no longer a prospective suitor but a police officer bearing bad news. Medhurst disappeared back into the house on seeing Hardy, leaving him standing at the open front door.

Hardy stepped into the house, and closed the door behind him. In doing so, his fancy was that he had shut out the noise of the outside world and entered a house already in mourning, even though the grim news had yet to be delivered. The house felt hushed, as if waiting.

Hardy went into the sitting room and found the Major there, standing by the window looking out, his thin shoulders heaving with the weight of his grief. There seemed nothing to say. Hardy's very presence told him everything. Hardy stood in the doorway and wondered what to do next.

'How?'

Hardy cleared his throat, and said softly, 'I'm afraid it appears she was hit over the head.'

Medhurst nodded. After a pause he said, 'These little hats the girls all wear nowadays, no protection.'

'No indeed,' Hardy replied, belatedly remembering to remove his own hat. He took a seat. The chessboard had been set up again, a match was already in progress. No doubt a new game had been started after he had taken his leave the previous evening.

'When can I see her?' Hardy was startled when Major Medhurst spoke suddenly right beside him. Tears ran unchecked down the man's face. He was wringing his hands, his fingers restless and trembling.

'Not today,' Hardy said. He shook his head gently as he said it. Didn't want to tell the man it would take time, that the pathologist would have to cut her open first, that her body had to be scrutinised and taken apart, the last shreds of her character torn away by the procedures of investigation.

'I must. I must see her. I must see my little girl.' Medhurst collapsed sobbing into the armchair. He swept his hand out and sent the chessboard crashing to the floor, pieces scattering. A bishop went underneath the chair, Hardy noted, and a pawn broke in two as the elderly gentleman stepped on it with a tatty bedroom slipper.

Hardy still had no idea what to say. In Medhurst's place, he would no doubt feel exactly the same. He remained silent and waited for the sobs to subside.

*

Chapter Twelve

'What on earth is Mother up to at the moment?' Dottie asked her father over lunch the next day. 'She's hardly ever here. She's always rushing off.'

'I know,' said her father, and his tone indicated he wasn't too worried about the situation. 'Some new charity or welfare thing, I don't doubt. You know how she's always got the bit between her teeth about some cause or other. This one's with your friend Mrs Gerard.'

'Hmm.' Dottie picked at her food, she had no appetite at the moment. She sighed too, and loudly.

Her father watched her closely for a while and then, with uncharacteristic insight he said, 'Something on your mind, dear?'

'It's just this terrible thing about Daphne. Janet had it from Sergeant Maple this morning, as you know they are walking out together. No doubt it's still supposed to be kept quiet, but he seems to tell

her rather a lot of secret police business. But...
poor Daphne. I mean, I never really liked her,
but...'

'I know, dear. However, I can't pretend I liked
the girl. Rather fast, I always thought. No doubt
that's not what you youngsters call it these days.'

'Hmm.'

'And she was trying to be fast with your young
fellow, from what I can make out,' Mr Manderson
ventured cautiously, still watching his daughter
closely over the edge of his newspaper. She
recoiled slightly at his words, which told him all he
wanted to know. He reached out to pat her hand.
'Don't fret, my love, he'll be back.'

'I don't care what he does!' she declared, shoving
back her chair with a crash and running from the
room. He heard her run up the stairs, across the
landing and into her room. Above his head there
came an almighty crash as she slammed the door
with all her might. The whole house seemed to
shake with the force of it.

Alone at the dining table, Herbert Manderson
pushed away his empty plate and, setting aside his
newspaper, reached for the domed dessert dish,
his mouth already watering. Lifting the lid, he
found nothing inside apart from a note from his
wife. *'No Dessert, Herbert—You Are On A Diet!'*
This was all heavily underlined to press home her
point. He set down the lid rather loudly. Herbert
Manderson felt an urge to copy his daughter and
shove back his chair and run upstairs, slamming
doors as he went.

Instead he went to his study and settled himself
at his desk with a whisky and a box of biscuits. He

reflected on his younger daughter's behaviour. Mentally he began to calculate the likely cost of a wedding for her. 'Not this year,' he told himself, 'so definitely next.' He made some notes in his diary.

After the business of the meeting of the Daughters of Esther was over and dealt with, and refreshments were being enjoyed, Mrs Manderson found herself seated beside the leader of the group. It was clear the woman had something on her mind, which she quickly laid out for Mrs Manderson, ending with,

'My dear Mrs Manderson, I hope you know I would never ordinarily ask you to do such a thing, but as the saying goes, 'desperate times call for desperate measures'.'

Mrs Manderson clutched her cup and saucer tightly and regarded her companion thoughtfully. In her mind, she was beginning to put together several seemingly insignificant occurrences which, taken as one, assumed a greater importance. With the practise of many long years, she quickly controlled the anger she felt. She said nothing; her eyes remained steadily fixed on the woman opposite her.

Clearly sensing what she took to be an inner resistance, Mrs Manderson's companion tried a new tactic: a direct plea. She set down her cup and saucer and leaned forward, dropping her voice to a confidential pitch.

'Mrs Manderson, may I be frank with you? We are both women of the world, we know what matters in life, and what may be termed 'set dressing'. I know your daughter's welfare is of the first importance to you, as it would be to me, in your situation. This is a circumstance where we can help one another. Allow me to take this worry from your shoulders, and in return you have the power to relieve my mind considerably. I need that scrap of material, it may prove to be very important.'

'You said earlier,' Mrs Manderson replied, 'that your agents had tried twice to acquire this item you need, and without success. How did you even know my daughter had this–this thing?'

'Your daughter showed it to a friend, who being a very loyal friend, told me what she had seen. I recognised immediately that it was something of significance.'

'Mrs Gerard, do you imagine I can succeed where he—or should I say, they—have failed?'

'A mother can always exercise authority over her child...'

There was a lengthy pause. Finally, Mrs Manderson asked, trying but not entirely succeeding in keeping her voice neutral, 'And was it one of your 'agents' who hit her, knocked her to the ground, left my daughter injured and defenceless? In the street? Was that part of your 'enquiries', as you put it?'

Her companion was wise enough to realise this was a make-or-break situation. She assumed a pained expression, and leaned forward once more, this time to pat Mrs Manderson's hand. 'My dear Mrs Manderson, Lavinia, if I may, words cannot...I can't lie to you. It *was* one of my agents who was responsible. I'm *truly* sorry for what happened. It was *never* part of our plan to allow any harm to come to dear Dottie, pardon me, to Dorothy, in any form. He admitted to me that he tugged a little firmly at the bag, and that she fell and bumped her head on the pavement. He panicked, it's true, I'm afraid, and he fled instead of summoning help. He said he assumed the passers-by on the street would help her. And believe me, no one regrets more than I... and we were *so* relieved to find that her injuries were mercifully slight. This is another reason why perhaps your own intervention in the matter is so desirable.'

Mrs Manderson's only reply was a tight nod of her head, and with that her companion had to be content.

Mrs Manderson went to sit beside a vast figure swathed, like herself, like all of them, in black wool.

'My dear Muriel,' Mrs Manderson said softly, 'I hope you weren't surprised or inconvenienced by Dorothy's absence from the warehouse recently. But really it's hardly unexpected, considering.'

Mrs Carmichael regarded Mrs Manderson from the shadows beneath her capacious hood. 'I don't know what you mean,' she said in her habitually blunt manner. 'What happened to Dottie?'

'She was attacked in the street. She'd just been having tea with Flora at Lyons'. In fact, in many ways, I'm thankful that it was Dorothy who was attacked. I dread to think what might have been the outcome if it had been Flora... and in her delicate condition.' She allowed her voice to fall away and waited for Mrs Carmichael to sip her tea and consider.

'Are you saying Dottie was deliberately targeted

by an attacker?'

'Oh, I think it's quite clear she was singled out, don't you? I'm sure no real harm was intended, but when a young woman's bag is snatched, the young woman in question is bound to put up a fight, isn't she? These girls today have so much spirit. Not like in our day when we just meekly handed over anything we were told to.'

'Someone snatched Dottie's bag?'

'Indeed.'

'What did they want?'

'Well, it couldn't have been money, she never carries a lot about with her. The police haven't yet recovered the bag.'

'Sounds like a pointless crime.'

'And yet we know, don't we, that there could have been a real point to it. A very *small, scrap* of a point. It seems she showed something to a friend, and that person told someone else,' Mrs Manderson, copying her companion, also sipped her tea. 'I think I shall be resigning my position here. One likes to do one's bit to assist the unfortunate, but in doing so one expects, even relies upon, the loyal support of one's sisters in the organisation.'

'Of course,' said Mrs Carmichael. She said no more. She was looking across the room at another figure. Her voice sounded thoughtful. Mrs Manderson felt she had achieved her aim, and murmuring pleasantries, she withdrew.

'Muriel Carmichael here,' said Mrs Carmichael with little pretence at patience. 'Yes, I know it's very late. I don't care about that, tell Mrs Gerard that I want to speak with her. If she doesn't contact me immediately, I shall have no choice but to go to the police and tell them everything I know. I can't have my own friends being attacked in the street and injured. Not to mention the inconvenience to my business when they can't come to work because of those injuries. I'm not going to stand for it. We're supposed to be doing good, not attacking people. It wasn't supposed to be like this. So you can tell her from me, I'm don't want to be involved any longer. It's all gone too far.'

She slammed the receiver down, feeling better for letting off a little steam. It would do Mrs Gerard—and the others—good to know they couldn't have things all their own way. Especially not now, not after this.

At the other end, the butler had been on the point of asking her to wait whilst he went to fetch Mrs Gerard, but Mrs Carmichael, Muriel, as he remembered her from their young days, hadn't given him the chance.

He hung up the telephone and went to the drawing room. He knocked once on the door and went straight in. Mrs Gerard was seated at her writing table by the window. She was already dressed for bed but had come back downstairs to make a few notes in large spidery writing on a long, yellowed sheet of paper. Her notes were scattered about the page, linked by carefully ruled lines. He ahemmed politely, and waited while she blotted her page. She turned to him.

'What is it, Aitchison?'

'Mrs Carmichael telephoned, madam.'

She nodded. 'And?'

'She was greatly agitated, madam. She spoke of talking to the police.' He then proceeded to repeat everything Muriel Carmichael had said before slamming her receiver down.

When he finished speaking, Mrs Gerard was pale, and her mouth set in a firm, straight line. She said nothing immediately, and Aitchison waited patiently whilst she mulled it over. At length she said, 'Kindly telephone to my nephew and tell him I'd like him to join me for tea tomorrow afternoon.'

Aitchison nodded and withdrew. Mrs Gerard opened the drawer of her desk and took out her rosary. She bowed her head in prayer.

That Tuesday morning, Hardy arrived back at the police station, exhausted and grim. Maple and a good many more officers were still out. There was a message on Hardy's desk saying that the chief superintendent wanted to speak with him. Hardy groaned inwardly but went straight upstairs.

His interview with his superior officer was mercifully short. A mere fifteen minutes later, having assured Chief Superintendent Smithers repeatedly that everything was being done to find the culprit, he returned to his office and shut the door, hoping that would keep everyone out.

He sat in silence for several minutes. His thoughts went round and round in his head. Every avenue of thought, every remembrance of the crime scene, of the evening before the murder when Daphne was very much alive, it was all played and replayed in his mind. Was it a simple mugging gone wrong? Or was there more to it than that? He should have stayed with her... And time and again his reasoning came back to one single thought: where was Daphne Medhurst's handbag?

Hardy stared into space. Only a sheer effort of will restrained him from leaning forward and burying his head in his hands. What a mess it had all turned into, he thought. He was no further forward on the robberies, and he hardly knew how to begin the investigation into Daphne Medhurst's murder. There were papers everywhere: reports, interviews, memoranda to remind himself what he needed to do, what to look into or find out about, and for the moment he had no idea how to sort out any of it in order to make some headway. A certain proverb about woods and trees came to mind.

On top of everything, even though he knew, absolutely knew, deep down that he was not to blame, he could not shake off the sense of guilt he felt over Daphne's death. He felt it was the result of some terrible failure on his part to deliver her safely home to her father.

Would she still be alive if he had been a little more giving, a little less strait-laced during their evening out? He felt like a prudish spinster now. He had told Maple all about it, and had seen how his friend tried to disguise his smile. Hardy felt humiliated, and even ridiculous for his missish response to Daphne's overtures, but couldn't see any way he could have responded differently. He hadn't been attracted to her, had no desire to be in any way intimate with her. And he wasn't the sort of man to indulge in careless, meaningless sex. But certainly they shouldn't have fallen out. Not that they had exchanged angry words, but fall out they had certainly done, with that cold angry silence stretching between them. If they had left the picture-house talking and laughing as other couples had done, arm-in-arm, he could have taken her to supper then seen her home afterwards. And she would still be alive.

The thought of her death reminded him of his mother. Since her funeral he'd had little time to think of her. He had not even replied to his sister's letter. Nor his uncle's. He really must make more of an effort. And tomorrow, he should, he really wanted to, go to the cemetery and lay some fresh flowers on his mother's grave.

He felt bowed down by the weight of all these worries on his shoulders, and yet the one that pressed hardest and heaviest upon him was the one he could least bear to think about. Her expression! So cold, so clearly angry, and so, so very like her mother's stern, forbidding countenance. Would Dottie Manderson ever be his friend again?

It was late afternoon at *Carmichael and Jennings: Exclusive Modes for Discerning Ladies*. 'Come in, Dot, do, my dear.' Mrs Carmichael, looking vaster than ever, was already at her desk, her shoes discarded just inside the office door. The rehearsal was over and Dottie was presenting herself at the office as requested.

'I'm glad to see you looking so well after your attack last week. That bruise'll soon go.' Mrs Carmichael motioned for Dottie to take a seat. She offered sherry which Dottie declined as always.

Mrs Carmichael poured herself a generous glassful and leaned back, glass in hand, and regarded Dottie. She decided it would be best just to get to the point.

'Do you remember that tiny piece of material you showed me a while back?'

Dottie nodded. She was immediately on her guard, Mrs Carmichael noticed.

'Do you still have it? It didn't mean much at the time, but somehow I just couldn't get it out of my mind, so I asked a few friends what they thought it could be. It turns out it could be something quite interesting. They told me what to look for. I'd love another quick look at it, if I may?'

Dottie's eyes were fixed firmly on her. For the first time in their two-year acquaintance, Mrs Carmichael felt the core of stubbornness, that quiet, yet determined 'something' in Dottie that would not be budged. She knew, before Dottie couched her polite refusal, that it was no good.

'I'm so sorry, Mrs Carmichael, but I'm afraid I don't have it anymore. It didn't seem important so I just threw it away.'

The girl stammered over the word 'threw' and Mrs Carmichael knew it was a lie. But there was nothing to be gained in pressing her. She simply sat back and took another long swallow of her sherry, then topped up the glass and changed the subject. Really, she reflected with a sense of irony, if the whole of the item had been given into Dottie's safe-keeping, it couldn't have been more closely guarded. If this was how she was with just a tiny piece of the hem...

The following morning began very early in Inspector Hardy's office.

'How did the robbers get to the Smedley-Judds', d'you think, Guv?'

Hardy sighed. What Maple had just asked raised two problems in Hardy's mind. The first was his annoyance over Maple's new tendency to keep calling him Guv, like a character out of some cheap novel. The second was that the sergeant, leaning beside him against the desk, and staring at the board, had just asked an incredibly insightful question.

'Why didn't we think of that before? You're a genius, Frank, and I am a prize idiot.'

'The way I see it,' said Maple as if Hardy had not spoken, 'If it was me I wouldn't want to risk walking, even if I didn't have far to go. Especially once I'd got the loot to carry.'

'Me either. Of course they wouldn't. There's no knowing how quickly the police might arrive, or someone, several people even, might be bold enough to give chase.'

'Or daft enough.'

'Or daft enough. In spite of the weapons. So they'd *need* to have transport.'

'Yes Guv.'

Hardy sighed again. 'Frank...'

'The other thing what's bothering me, sort of the same thing, really...'

'Yes?'

'They'd have to have transport to get to Hemel Hempstead and to Hitchin. Even Oxford's not exactly right on the doorstep.'

'True.'

'So that means they've got to be free to come and go. Not working long hours for instance, or got someone keeping an eye on them. Not working somewhere where they'll be missed.'

'Not watching the kids,' Hardy added. Maple directed a look of scorn at his boss.

'They're all blokes. They're not going to be minding the kids.'

'They might,' Hardy said. 'Working class women often work in the evening, and they go out as soon as their husbands get home from work. So, once the husbands come in, they have to watch the children.'

Maple's scorn heightened. He laughed and shook his head. 'Don't be daft, Bill. No self-respecting bloke is going to be stuck looking after the kids. That's women's work.'

Hardy said nothing, but privately thought his idea was sound. The robbers were men who had the freedom and the means to travel around to commit their crimes.

'And you're assuming they're working class again. Most of them wouldn't even have their own car. Only your lot can afford to run a car. In any case, they couldn't use their own cars, it'd be too risky. What if they was seen? If you like, I'll check up on car thefts around the time of the robberies, see if I can find out anything that seems relevant. But I don't think it'll get us anywhere. Bill?'

But Hardy was deep in thought, apparently staring at the board, yet not seeing what was in front of him. He was mentally going through information, processing what they knew, puzzling and sifting.

Maple was gone for half an hour and returned looking disappointed. The piece of paper in his hand held just one incidence of car theft on or about the time of one of the robberies. He held it out to Hardy, who ignored it, saying instead, 'What does Wotherspoon's son-in-law do for a living?'

'What, young Cedric? Well he's a...' Maple halted as his thoughts caught up with his mouth. He grinned at Hardy. 'Guv, Bill, mate, you're a bloody marvel! Cedric is a cab driver.'

Hardy nodded, satisfied. 'Thought so. What shall we do first, have another chat with Wotherspoon, or pick up Cedric?'

'Wotherspoon. And if you like, I'll get a uniform to bring in Cedric. That will save us a lot of running around. But first, let's go and get some lunch at the pub.'

'You go, I'm not hungry.' Hardy turned and moved around his desk to sit in his chair. He certainly looked fed-up, Maple thought, then he remembered Daphne Medhurst.

'Bill?' he began. This time Hardy heard him and looked up. Maple said, 'I'm really sorry about the young lady, Bill.'

'Don't worry about me. I'm more angry than grief-stricken. I'd only seen her a couple of times, and as I said, we weren't suited.' He broke off. This was all old ground, and he drew the line at taking away her character now she was dead by saying anything about her behaviour. His mother's admonition of 'If you can't say something nice, don't say anything at all,' was too well-ingrained to allow him to be too truthful about Daphne. Instead he softly added, 'But whatever she was, she didn't deserve to die in an alley.'

There was a moment's silence, then Maple said, 'She was quite tall and slim, wasn't she?'

'Yes.'

'A bit like Miss Dottie.'

'I suppose so, though there's the world of difference between the two, and Miss Manderson's hair is dark brown, not Daphne's auburn colour. And Dottie is at least two inches taller than Daphne was.'

'Yes, but if you didn't see the two of them together, you mightn't notice that. I suppose most of us chaps go for the same kind of girl.'

'What's that supposed to mean?' Hardy's tone was sharper than he intended. Not that Maple minded. He simply shrugged.

'All I'm saying is, you, like all us blokes, like the same thing. You like 'em tall and slender and dark. Whereas I like 'em a bit shorter and rounder and softer and fairer. You like a woman what's tall like you, to make you more of a match. I'm as tall as you but it doesn't worry me that Janet's a bit of a titch. Plus, I like a girl with a bit of meat on her.' His hands carved the approximate outline of a figure eight in the air.

Hardy said nothing. His thoughts were racing. He felt as though something had slotted into place in his mind. Two parts, previously separate, had come together to form one, larger part of the same picture.

'Are you saying...?'

'All I'm saying is, what if the attack on Daphne...'

'...Medhurst was actually intended for Dottie Manderson? For God's sake man, why are we hanging around?'

Hardy was out of his chair and wrenching open the door, grabbing his coat and hat at the same time. Maple heard his racing feet pounding the corridor, and in a rather more leisurely manner, he got to his feet. He strolled to the door, turned out the light and ambled towards the front desk. Hardy was already on his way back, all frantic action and frustration. 'Come on, for God's sake, Frank...!'

'Er, Bill...?' Maple called. Hardy halted.

'What?'

'Where are we going?'

'To the Mandersons', of course!'

'Why?'

'Why what?' Hardy looked as if he couldn't believe his ears. He was on the point of losing his temper. He stood there, breathing hard, and clenching his fists.

'Why are we going to the Mandersons'? To begin with, I doubt Miss Dottie will be at home, and then again, what are you going to do? Tell her someone is trying to kill her?'

Hardy stared at him, floundering, like a fish lying on the bank taking its last few gasps of air. 'Well...'

'No, Guv,' Maple said firmly, 'We need to talk to Wotherspoon and Cedric. We need to look at both these two cases from a new angle.'

'Miss Medhurst's death is nothing to do with the robberies!' Hardy yelled, but mid-sentence he began to question that. He fell silent and thought for a moment. What if it wasn't just the two cases of Daphne's death and Dottie's mugging that were connected, but also the robberies? What if all his three crimes were actually one? But why? How?

'You need a beer, Guv,' Maple said, and pulling Hardy by the arm, he led him outside and down the street to their favourite lunchtime haunt.

As they went inside, Hardy said with feeling, 'Please stop calling me Guv.'

'At the moment, I feel like calling you quite a few other names. And there's you pretending you're not mad about Dottie Manderson.'

*

Chapter Thirteen

'And then what happened?' Hardy asked, smiling at the telephone receiver as his sister told him all her news. He raised an eyebrow at her reply and then laughed. She was enjoying herself now she was beginning to recover from the shock of losing their mother. She was being pampered and spoilt by their aunt and uncle, and it was doing her the world of good. It made him happy to hear her sounding almost like her old self, full of all the places she had been and the people she had met. When the call ended, he felt reassured. It was a weight off his mind to know she and their younger brother were safe and happy.

As soon as he'd finished speaking to Eleanor, he asked the operator to put through a call to his married sister Celia, then he talked with her for ten minutes, mainly about her baby and the latest thing the little one had learned to do. From her surprise at his questions and her excited comments, William suspected he showed far more interest in the child than the child's own father. The telephone was a large expense, but one he didn't regret for a moment. At least the Met contributed towards the cost, as the telephone was the primary means of contacting him for work purposes.

Satisfied that his family were all well, and furnished with everyone's news, he sat at the kitchen table with a fresh pot of tea. It was so quiet in the house, but he refused to give in to the urge to visualise his mother at the head of the table, telling him to wrap up warmly or asking what time he'd be in for dinner. Equally, he couldn't allow himself to picture Dottie there either. He felt in a kind of no man's land, in limbo, neither single nor married, but waiting, as always, for something to happen.

He put on the radio, and concentrated on drinking his tea. His thoughts always came back to Dottie, he realised. Was he in love with her, or was he simply obsessed? Every woman he met, he compared to her. He thought about her continually, night and day. Especially night, he admitted to himself. How different she was to all the women he came across both socially and professionally, even compared with the woman he had been engaged to just four years earlier, and thought he was madly in love with. That had been nothing to how he felt about Dottie. How different Dottie was to Daphne Medhurst, for example. He briefly entertained a daydream of taking Dottie to the cinema. If she had initiated the embrace that Daphne had wanted, he knew he'd have had no difficulty whatsoever responding. If only he had the chance...

He poured another cup of tea. Still thinking, in his mind he pictured Dottie, and also Daphne. Although he was a police officer, he didn't believe in capital punishment, if asked he'd probably say he believed life was sacred. Daphne, flighty, artificial and shallow, had not deserved to die. Someone had to pay for what they had done to her, and it was his job to make sure they did so.

He was forced to conclude that Maple was right, there was a superficial similarity between the two women, especially if one only saw them at night. 'And if someone saw them with me,' he added as the sudden realisation hit him. A cold feeling seemed to settle somewhere inside.

It began to seem entirely possible, even probable, that Daphne been killed by mistake. Mistaken for Dottie. Dottie herself had also been attacked. Dottie's home had been broken into, her room searched. It was Dottie, not Daphne, who was being watched, stalked, attacked. Dottie. Who was about to have a dinner party to celebrate her birthday.

Hardy's tea was growing cold. He sat there in the kitchen, the radio whispering softly to itself, the embers of the fire dying away.

Dottie.

But why?

'No Mother, I'm sorry but I can't! How did you even...?'

'Dorothy, I don't know why you're being so tiresome about this. Please just give me this bit of

cloth or whatever it is. Clearly it's putting you—
and all of us, my dear—in danger. I will keep it safe
and out of harm's way.'

'Mother, I can't...'

'Dorothy, for goodness' sake, for once in your
life, just do as I ask!' Her mother's voice rose
sharply, but even now, as Dottie watched her
mother's face, she could see she wasn't angry,
although her precise emotion was hard to gauge.
Dottie was about to shake her head, and to venture
a fuller explanation, but her mother simply threw
up her hands and stormed out of the room.

The newspaper dropped on the other side of the
room, and her father quirked an eyebrow at his
daughter. 'What was all that about?'

'Just some bit of stuff Inspector Hardy gave me.
He wanted me to try to find out what it was.'

'And did you?'

'Yes.'

'And why won't you give it to your mother?'

'I've got to give it back to the inspector. I can't
give it to anyone else because it's part of an
investigation. I suppose I should have told her
that.'

There was a pause. Then he said, 'And why does
your mother want it?'

'I've no idea.'

'Hmm.'

'It's not like her to give up so easily, though.'
Dottie commented. The newspaper was
repositioned. There was no response from behind
it.

Dottie frowned. Everyone seemed to know about
the tiny scrap. And everyone seemed to want it.

She felt angry that someone was trying to use her mother to get it from her.

Dinner was long over in the Manderson household, and Mr and Mrs Manderson retired to the drawing room to sit by the fire. Spring was still not quite upon them, and the evening was typically damp and chilly for London. They sat side by side on the sofa nearest the fire, and, because they were alone, Mrs Manderson leaned into her husband and he placed an arm about her shoulders and settled his cheek on her hair. He thought how like the early days of their marriage it was, just the two of them, and the firelight. Sometimes he missed those days.

His wife continued the same conversation that had vexed her throughout dinner. 'I just can't decide what to do for the best, Herbert. I hardly like to cancel this dinner party at this late stage, but what if the inspector is right?'

'Hmm.'

'Herbert? Are you attending?'

'Hmm,' he said again, and placed a kiss carefully on her forehead. She treated him to a playful slap.

'Behave yourself and listen to what I'm saying.'

'I am listening,' he protested, nevertheless risking another quick kiss. 'You've said the same thing for the last hour and a half. And I've told you at least five times, we need to think about it and make a decision in the morning.'

She was biting her lip, lost in thought. He said, 'And what was all that fuss about some piece of fabric?'

But she just looked at him and shook her head.

'It's nothing, just a favour someone asked me to do. But coming back to this party, what if we don't cancel, and these—these gunmen break in? Suppose someone is hurt? And we've already had one break-in, I really don't care to have another.'

'No dear, of course not,' Herbert Manderson sighed, got up and went in search of a newspaper.

Meanwhile, Dottie was out with Flora and George and a group of friends at a rather rowdy dance at a ballroom. Flora had decided to sit this dance out, and Dottie sat with her and they watched the band and the couples on the dancefloor. Flora was enjoying Dottie's latest gossip, which led after a number of twists to James Melville. 'Dr Melville has a tattoo? I can hardly believe it.'

'He puts make-up on some kind of mark on his arm to hide it, though sometimes it gets rubbed off,' Dottie told her. 'I think it must be a tattoo, if it was just a birthmark, why worry? It's on his wrist, so it's hardly ever going to be seen. And it's not very big, so again, I think it can't be just a birthmark. No one would trouble to hide something like that.

'I see what you mean,' Flora said. 'Perhaps there's some strange explanation, though a tattoo seems the likeliest. But no respectable person has a tattoo, not unless they're a retired sea captain.'

'I think that might be why he hides it. Think how all the stuffy people at the museum would react if they knew. It's terribly avant-garde. Mother said she thought he seemed Bohemian. I thought he was just boring.' Dottie took a sip of her cocktail, grimaced at the taste and pushed the glass away.

'Ugh,' she said, shaking her head, her dark curls bouncing as she did so. Flora took in Dottie's slim figure in the close-fitting pale gold silk-satin dress, and the negligent dancing slipper just bouncing on the tip of her toes as she jiggled it to the music. Flora said crossly,

'You make me feel positively geriatric, sitting there so slender and chic. How dare you!'

Dottie grinned. 'You'll be back to your normal alluring self in a few months, then you'll be making George wild with jealousy as all the men flock to sit by your side and hold your hand, or line up to dance a tango with you.'

'I wish! I bet it will take me simply ages to shift all this weight. I have rather made a pig of myself now that I've got an excuse to indulge.' Flora looked at Dottie. 'What's wrong, dear? Is it William? You look so forlorn whenever I mention his name. Are you really so enamoured of him?'

Dottie coloured, and fiddled with a cocktail stirrer, concentrating fiercely on her upside-down reflection in its gleaming bowl. 'Of course not! However I need to see him, to give him back his scrap of fabric and tell him what we found out about it. I'll phone him in the morning. It seems like I hardly ever see him, he's so busy all the time. And, I suppose he's still taken up with grieving for Daphne Medhurst. I mean, I'm terribly sorry about what happened to her, but I never liked her one little bit. Still, poor Major Medhurst, he must be devastated. He's going to go and live with his sister in Southsea, Father was telling us this morning. But if *she*, Daphne, were still with us, I'm sure William would never escape her clutches, she was so determined to land him.'

Flora couldn't help raising her eyebrows at Dottie's bitter tone. Her sister's face was a picture of absolute misery. Flora quickly said, 'I'm sure it was nothing serious. I mean, they hardly knew each other. And you know, I don't think it would have lasted five minutes, I really don't think she was the type of girl to 'land him' as you so eloquently put it.'

Dottie said nothing, clearly not convinced. Flora, a little more worldly than her younger sister, was only too aware that even the nicest, most intelligent of men were all too easily led astray by the feminine wiles of a really determined husband-hunter. Daphne Medhurst had, sadly, fallen neatly into this category. But he had been lucky, and escaped before things progressed too far and she snared him. Flora fervently hoped he would not get lured in again so easily next time.

'Have you seen any more of Jeffrey Thurby?' Flora asked.

Dottie shook her head. 'He's a fool,' she said crisply, 'I can barely tolerate him for half an hour, let alone a whole evening. And he has more than a passing resemblance to an octopus.'

'Too many hands?'

'It's not funny, Flora.' Dottie said, still cross. Her eyes became wide and anxious. She leaned across the table and said in an earnest, panicking voice, 'Flora, what if I'm left on the shelf?'

Whatever she had expected in response, it wasn't Flora's abrupt guffaw of laughter coming in the middle of a break in the music. Heads turned all around the ballroom.

'You never take me seriously,' Dottie said crossly.

The next morning, Dottie was arguing with her mother. She knew she wasn't going to win, but felt she owed it to herself to at least make an effort to resist the tide that seemed to carry everything along in its wake. Just call me Canute, she thought. Outwardly, she smiled politely at her mother.

'I know you invited him because of me, Mother, but surely you realise he's boring, rude and that we didn't exactly part on the best of terms? I certainly have no desire to ever see Dr Melville again.'

'What I know, young lady, is that he's a respectable gentleman with an interesting career and good prospects at a well-respected, world-renowned British institution. Not only that, but for some inexplicable reason, he clearly likes you very much, because he has called twice a day for the last ten days. You owe him the courtesy of hospitality.'

Dottie, knowing in her heart it was useless, nevertheless was preparing a further salvo when the telephone rang. She waited with bated breath to see if it was anyone for her. However, almost immediately Janet came hurrying upstairs to tell Mrs Manderson that Mrs Gerard was on the line.

'I told her you were dressing, ma'am, but she said it was important and that she'd only take up a minute of your time.'

Mrs Manderson, seeming rather distracted, hurried away without another word.

'Odd,' said Dottie to Janet, 'I didn't think Mother and Mrs Gerard were on telephoning terms.'

'She's rung quite a few times lately. Mrs Manderson is helping Mrs Gerard with her charity work. Not sure what it is, though.'

'Golly,' Dottie said, 'Mother and her charitable works. Well, that certainly explains why she's always out at the moment, and why she always looks so flustered. Oh, I'm so annoyed about that wretched Dr Melville. I suppose there's no chance his invitation might get lost?'

Janet laughed, and turned to go back downstairs. 'No chance, Miss Dottie, I'm afraid your mother put them in the post herself yesterday morning.'

'Damn and blast it,' said Dottie.

'So Dr Melville *has* been invited to tea?' Mrs Gerard queried. Mrs Manderson nodded, even though her partner in the telephone conversation couldn't see it. Belatedly she added,

'He has. In fact, I've already had his acceptance. Although I should say my daughter is not at all happy about it. Oh, you needn't worry, I've overruled her, as I always do in these kinds of matters. But I'm surprised to hear you say how deeply attached he is to her. *She* tells me that he and she didn't particularly...' She let the thought fall away, too tired to try to think of an apt rephrasing of Dorothy's furious, 'I simply can't stand the sight of that wretched man!' Tact also held her back from upsetting her friend by revealing exactly what her daughter had said about the young man. She seemed to recall the phrase 'He could bore for Britain in the Berlin Olympics!' came into the discussion somewhere. She herself had thought him very suitable. More so, perhaps, than the young policeman. Of course she saw now that she should have spoken to Florence about it. Florence would certainly know if Dorothy genuinely disliked Dr Melville, or if she was simply being contrary. At first Mrs Manderson had suspected the latter, but now she wasn't so sure.

'Hmm. Well I'm sure the dear boy will soon get her to change her mind. I'd like you to arrange to leave them alone for a few minutes, just to give him a chance to tell her how he feels. You don't object to that, do you? I can assure you he has only the greatest respect for dear Dottie...'

When Mrs Manderson came away from the telephone, she felt uneasy. She couldn't exactly say why she did. There had been nothing in either what Mrs Gerard had said nor what she had requested that Mrs Manderson could take exception to, or that could account for the unpleasant sensation that lurked somewhere behind her shoulder. But coming so soon after the mugging... She shook her head. She was just being foolish.

So Young Melville wanted to speak to Dorothy in private, did he? Well that could only mean a proposal. A bit soon, in her opinion, they hardly knew each other. But still, there was no reason for her to forbid him to speak. If Dorothy was so set against him, she was old enough to tell him to his face. And certainly forthright enough, when pushed. Dorothy was nothing if not forthright. Her mother's instinct told her Dorothy would definitely refuse him.

Lavinia Manderson made her way to her

husband's study. It would greatly relieve her mind to tell him about Dr Melville. On the very slim chance that Dorothy might accept the young fellow, she felt it would be useful if her father had at least an inkling of what was going on.

She tapped lightly on the door, and went in immediately. He was at his desk, and glanced up, smiling, as soon as he saw her. Mrs Manderson shut the door behind her, and turned the key in the lock. She crossed the room.

He raised his eyebrows. 'What's the matter?' He pushed his chair back, and his wife came around the desk and sat on his lap. He put his arms around her and kissed her neck. She leaned back against him, heaved a great sigh and said, 'Oh Herbert darling, these girls! Such a worry.'

He laughed. 'What has Dottie been getting up to now?'

'It's not so much what she's been up to as what she hasn't. As you know, my friend Mrs Gerard...'

'Not that old bat!'

'Herbert really!' Lavinia swatted his hand away as he attempted to disarrange her neat curls. 'And you can stop that, too. I only came in here to tell you about Dorothy and that Dr Melville.'

Herbert Manderson, greatly resembling his daughter, rolled his eyes.

'Mrs Gerard tells me that he is completely smitten with Dottie. As you know, I've invited him to tea at Mrs Gerard's request. Now she's asked that I might ensure they are left alone for a few minutes, so that he can tell Dottie how he feels. I believe he may propose. I'm not absolutely certain, but I believe he may...' her voice faltered. The sense of unease prevailed. Her husband stared at her, frowning.

'And just how does our daughter feel about the young chap? I rather got the impression...'

'Hmm, well I'm afraid that may be where Melville's plans come unstuck. She just told me ten minutes ago that he was boring and rude.'

'I seem to remember that doesn't necessarily mean one is going to be refused.' His voice was warm. He kissed her cheek, lingering to breathe in her scent.

'Herbert, behave yourself!' Mrs Manderson said with something suspiciously like a giggle. Her daughters would not have recognised this girlish woman as their mother. She slapped him playfully on the arm. 'And I never, *ever* said that you were boring. Rude, yes. You were very rude, my dear. I don't know why my father didn't forbid you to call.'

'He knew true love when he saw it, I suppose.'

'Or perhaps he simply realised you were in desperate need of reform. Well, that's all I wanted to say. I thought you ought to know. I don't know why, I'm just rather...Oh I don't know, I'm so on edge about this whole thing. Really, having daughters is such a responsibility.'

'You don't need to worry about Dottie, she will find her own man. Or perhaps I should say, she has already found her own man.'

'After he walked out with Major Medhurst's fast daughter? I think it's all over with Inspector Hardy.'

'Oh that!' Mr Manderson laughed. 'It didn't last two minutes. Sorry for Daphne and all that, but she didn't have what it takes. It was never going to last any time at all. You only have to look at the fellow to see his mind's already made up on Dottie. Give him some time to get over the loss of his mother, then we'll have him here again for dinner. And this time there will be no *femme fatales* to lure him from Dottie.'

'He hasn't got sixpence to his name,' Lavinia objected.

'*I* didn't have sixpence to *my* name,' Herbert pointed out. She kissed him on the nose. She got to her feet and patted her hair carefully into place.

'*You* had potential,' she said, 'and besides, I had my grandfather's fortune.'

'Pride, darling,' he said and reaching for her hand, he kissed it. He pulled his chair back up to the desk and took up his pen. 'Young men have pride. They don't want to depend on their wives.'

'Yes, true.' She went to the door, unlocked it and opened it. From the doorway, she turned and blew him a kiss then went out, closing the door behind her. Mr Manderson set down his pen once more and sat staring at the door, a smile on his face.

'I'm a lucky devil.'

*

Chapter Fourteen

Dr Melville took his seat in the armchair opposite Dottie, but even if she had liked him, she had other things on her mind. Her mother had not asked her about the scrap of material again, and Dottie had not had a chance to explain about needing to give it back to William. She didn't know whether her parents had discussed the matter privately, that was a possibility. But what worried Dottie was how her mother even knew about it, and she covertly watched her mother as she greeted and seated the guests.

There was an underlying edge, Dottie realised. Her mother was very tense. It had nothing to do with the occasion: here she was completely in her element as hostess. Something else had happened to upset her mother.

Dr Melville, feeling neglected, contrived to accidentally bump Dottie's knee with his own, and when he apologised, she could hardly avoid looking at him and reassuring him with a quick smile to cover her frown. He smiled back, clearly relieved. Really, a little voice in her head said, he was so very handsome. Perhaps he wasn't really rude and boring. Had he simply been a little nervous when he had taken her to dinner? Shy? She thought about this as she passed around sandwiches and tea. But no, she dismissed the idea almost as soon as it was born. He was not the man for her. But then who else was there? William Hardy's face came to her in a flash, but she quashed the elation she felt. No, he had been involved with Daphne Medhurst and was no doubt still grief-stricken.

She shook her head to clear it of the pointless fantasy and made a determined attempt to attend to the conversation. On her left, Mrs Gerard was accepting a miniature savoury from Mrs Manderson, and opposite her, James Melville had already disposed of four sandwiches without waiting for anyone else to begin eating. He ate without apparent enjoyment but with a determination Dottie had once seen at the homeless refuge when she had helped out in a soup kitchen down by the docks. She looked at him closely, wondering what she really knew about him.

'Dr Melville, could I trouble you to draw that curtain across? I'm quite being blinded by this unexpected sunshine.' As he got up to pull the curtain across, Mrs Manderson turned to Mrs Gerard. 'It's such a shame to block it out when we've had so much dreary weather, but I really can't see a thing.'

Murmurs of agreement went round the little circle and a fifteen minute conversation about the weather ensued. Dottie glanced up to watch Melville, noting as he stretched that he had a thin figure beneath his coat, an insignificant behind, no shoulders or chest to speak of, and unusually long arms, with thin bony wrists and the hands she had noticed on first meeting him, so large, yet so delicate. She saw once again the round, slightly darker brown patch that stood out against the rest of his pale skin on the inside of his wrist. She could make out something that looked like a letter D.

An hour later, Dottie regarded James Melville with loathing. He was wiping his nose, blood blotching alarmingly on the white linen of his handkerchief.

It was all her mother's fault, Dottie decided. Why on earth should she have imagined Dottie would welcome a proposal of marriage from James Melville when she hadn't even wanted him to come to tea? And how could her mother have colluded with Melville, knowing the misery he was intent on inflicting?

The moment her mother had taken Mrs Gerard and the other guests out to look at the garden, leaving Melville alone with Dottie in a very pointed manner, Dottie had known what was about to happen. With a sinking heart, and more than a little exasperation she had tried to head him off, but like the arrogant Mr Collins in Jane Austen's classic work, he had insisted on having his say.

However, nothing could have prepared her for the impassioned way he had launched himself at her, clutching at her legs from his position on his knees before her. She was more annoyed than upset or offended. She was very puzzled by his sudden amorousness, given that he hadn't even attempted to kiss her goodnight when he'd brought her home after the dinner they'd had the previous week. He had barely even taken the trouble to bid her goodnight, yet now here he was latching onto the hem of her dress as if his very life depended on it.

Dottie did what any well-brought-up lady would do. She lifted her knee suddenly and violently in his direction. Melville fell back onto the carpet, taking half her skirt hem with him. He whacked his head on the coffee table, sending cups, spoons, plates, teapots, and sugar basins flying across the floor, then slammed back onto the carpet, stupefied. He stared at her with unmistakable hatred, blood pouring from his nose.

'What the hell?' he shouted, groping for a napkin to replace his handkerchief which was soaked. Dottie would have liked to ask him the same question. At this point Mrs Manderson returned with her guests, a polite hostess smile on her face, until she surveyed the scene.

Dottie took one look at the debris strewn about her, the bloodied would-be beau at her feet, and her mother's astonished face, and did the only thing she could do. She gathered her torn skirts and ran out into the hall and up the stairs to the sanctuary of her bedroom. Pushing past Mrs Gerard, Dottie couldn't help noticing the odd expression the older woman fixed on her. But it wasn't until she'd been calmly in her room for several minutes that she was able to discern what it meant. It was nothing short of the deepest anger.

Dottie slumped down on her bed. What a disaster a simple afternoon tea had turned into. She bit her lip. In her mind's eye she saw again his look of outrage and bewilderment as her knee unexpectedly impacted with his nose, and the force of it had thrown him back onto that rather uninteresting bottom. She would not laugh. Rather wildly she wondered if she should drag her chest of drawers across the door in case Dr Melville—or anyone else—including her mother, should try to come in to remonstrate with her.

She quickly changed her skirt, remembering to remove the pin and the scrap of fabric from the torn hem of the skirt she'd taken off and put them into the hem of the new skirt. As she did so, in her mind's eye she saw again the earlier scene: Melville fawning at her knees on the floor. His ludicrous, and, she realised now, completely fake marriage proposal. Now she seemed to see the scene as it really was. The back of his hand had been bleeding, which had nothing to do with the slamming of her knee into his nose. It was bleeding before that. He had scratched his hand on the pin on her skirt hem. He had been trying to get the fabric piece.

She felt even more outraged, and a little bit afraid. How close he had come to getting the scrap. 'Serve him right if I'd accepted his stinking proposal,' she told herself, hugging herself to keep from shivering.

From downstairs there was the sound of voices then the front door slammed. Covertly she observed Dr Melville and Mrs Gerard together descend the steps to the street. They paused in conversation for several minutes, Dr Melville still attempting to staunch the bleeding.

How odd, Dottie thought. She hadn't realised how well Melville and Mrs Gerard knew each other. Their demeanours were not at all those of casual acquaintances commiserating over an eventful tea, or an unsuccessful proposal. Their heads were bent close together, in spite of his injury and their conversation appeared quiet and hurried. He was shaking his head to something Mrs Gerard had asked him. Her hand was on his arm. She glanced back at the house, and Dottie drew back still further behind the curtain, even though she knew they couldn't possibly see her.

Just then two other guests came out of the house, and Dottie watched as Mrs Gerard and Dr Melville stepped apart a little and turned to nod and smile banalities at the other two who moved off to their own car, leaving Dr Melville and Mrs Gerard to hurry away together. By leaning out of the window as far as she could, Dottie saw that they walked to the end of the road, then hailed a cab and they both got in together and drove away.

Clearly, then, they were far better acquainted than was generally known.

Blissfully unaware of the eventful afternoon tea at the Mandersons', William Hardy was at home with his feet up on the coffee table in the little sitting room, and a small glass of whisky in his hand. He had come home early, taking his work with him. He felt certain it was going to be a long evening so decided he might as well get comfortable. He was reading witness statements.

How many times he had read through them already, he didn't know, but although he had initially sat down with them half an hour earlier, with no other expectation than that something, anything, might strike him, now he was aware of a growing sense of excitement.

A small detail had struck him, and a further small detail had followed that, and now, he was convinced he had an important clue in his hands.

This was the part of his job he liked, he realised. So often, especially of late, he had wrestled with the notion that he was not suited to his career, but at moments like this, he knew beyond doubt that he was doing what he was not only gifted at, but that he loved. It was this that he loved, this bringing together of small details to create a credible, even pleasing, picture of events.

And it had just happened again. He got out his notebook and began to write.

An hour later he knocked on the Mandersons' front door. Janet opened it, and through her association with Frank Maple, saw a friend standing there, not just a visitor. She grinned at him and stepped back for him to enter.

'Oh my Gawd, Mr Hardy, you'll never guess what!'

He gave her a questioning look, but said nothing.

'Mrs Manderson's in a terrible fury. Miss Dottie's had a proposal from that rather dishy Dr Melville, and she only went and punched him on the nose! Blood and crockery everywhere, the tables overturned, and Miss Dottie in her room, scared to come down, I should think!'

She paused for breath. The inspector, usually so correct in his behaviour, was openly gawping at her, torn between laughter and trying to remain polite. Finally recollecting that he was in fact, a visitor, Janet said, 'Oh, I'm so sorry, sir. Do you want me to take your coat? Are you expected?'

'Er, no. And no. I just called on the off-chance. It—it was Miss Manderson I hoped to see.'

'If I was you, I'd take her out for a while. The drawing room is a complete mess and Mrs M is in the morning room, and in the worst mood. I'm not sure she'd be very welcoming...'

'Perhaps you could ask Miss Manderson if she'd do me the honour...'

But Janet was already halfway up the stairs, calling back over her shoulder, 'Half a mo!'

Hardy waited, full of intense feelings that had nothing to do with what he now regarded as a break in the case. He hoped neither of Dottie's parents would come out. He didn't feel like being polite and making small-talk. He heard the sound of hurrying feet and glanced up, expecting to see Janet returning, but it was Dottie herself.

She grabbed her coat, grabbed his arm, and ran him out of the door and down the steps. He felt light-hearted, as if they were playing truant from their lessons. They were halfway along the street, laughing, before she stopped to put on her coat. He took it from her and held it so she could slip her hand into the sleeve.

'Did Janet tell you what happened?'

'Only very briefly. Am I to congratulate you?'

'On making an unholy mess and infuriating my

mother? Yes.' She turned to look into his face, her
eyes laughing into his. That was the moment he
knew what he felt for her was truly love and not
some mere obsession. He toyed with the idea of
dropping to his knees right there in the street to
beg for her hand, but felt she'd probably had
enough of marriage proposals for one day. Instead
he contented himself with straightening the back
of her collar and offering her his arm.

'Sounds like you need to escape for a while.
Tea?'

'It's almost six o'clock.'

'An early dinner, then?'

'All right. Thank you. I feel so naughty, running
out of the house like that. But really, it's better to
let Mother cool down a bit before attempting to
explain. Though I'm afraid even when she knows
what happened, she still won't forgive me.'

They found a seat in a small restaurant, right at
the back, away from the windows and a bunch of
noisy, already-tipsy students. Hardy ordered their
food, and a drink each, then he sat back, suddenly
aware that he was actually, finally, out with her.
She watched him closely, her hazel eyes steady and
grave.

'So, why did you come to rescue me?' she asked.
He began to tell her about his small details and
watched as her eyes grew round like those of a
child listening to a thrilling adventure story. She
immediately picked up on the things he thought
were significant, yet she made him feel he had
been intelligent in seeing the clues. She was able to
confirm his suspicions.

William watched in amusement as Dottie leaned

forward and rolled back the hem of her skirt. She pulled out a dressmaker's pin that was there, dumping the pin in the ashtray on the table. She put the scrap of material in his hand. Uncurling his fingers, he saw the tiny scrap he had originally entrusted to her so many weeks earlier, it seemed like the distant past.

She straightened her skirt, which he reluctantly admitted was better for his blood pressure, though he had greatly enjoyed the sight of her slender legs, long but shapely, encased in the fine thread of her stockings, far finer than those his sister wore. He wondered idly how much it cost her father to keep Dottie Manderson in clothes and stockings and other necessary items. With a sense of dismay, he realised it was likely to be well beyond the pocket of a police inspector.

She was staring at him, and he realised she had spoken and was waiting for his response. He had no idea what she had said, and felt compelled to admit it.

'I said,' she repeated, 'that it would be safer for you to keep this, as I'm beginning to think it's behind all the trouble I've been having.'

Really, she was thinking, flash these men a bit of knee or ankle and they go completely to pieces! Was it really so hard to leer at a girl's legs *and* listen to what she was saying *and* come up with a sensible response? He was a little flushed, she noted, and his pupils were dilated. He seemed flustered and had forgotten how to behave in public. He had definitely gone to pieces. On the other hand, it was rather nice to know that even though she was almost the ripe old age of twenty—

no longer a child, but a mature *woman*—that she still had the ability to knock a chap for six. Also, she added to herself, it was nice to know William's professionalism could slip a little now and then.

'Hmm,' was all he said. He took out his tatty leather wallet and carefully placed the scrap between two pound notes to keep it flat and safe.

She began to tell him everything Flora and she had discovered in Canterbury. He listened with flattering intensity, without once interrupting, and when she had finished, he simply nodded and said, 'Y-es, it's all starting to make sense. That is very interesting.'

But rather than elaborate on this, or tell her what he was thinking, he turned to her and reached across the table to take her hand.

Wild imaginings raced through her mind. Was he about to propose? Surely not, he couldn't, surely... idiot, she told herself, of course he wasn't. But nevertheless, she was aware of an acute pang of disappointment when he said, 'Look here...'

'What? Why are you looking so serious? Don't you ever smile?'

He smiled then. She was entranced. How rarely she had seen him smile. His teeth were nice, white and even, and his often rather chilly blue eyes were suddenly warm and bright. The corners of both eyes and mouth lifted, the eyes crinkling at the edges. She smiled back, and he, in return, was also entranced.

'That's better,' she said, tearing her eyes away after what felt like an eternity. Her hands were not quite steady so she folded them in her lap. 'Now what was it you were going to say?'

'Just that I really don't like the idea of this dinner party of yours going ahead. I'm very concerned...'

Her smile faded. 'I am too, but my mother insists. I could take to my bed and pretend I was sick—believe me, I've thought about it—but she wouldn't allow it. She's made up her mind I'm afraid, so we're rather stuck with it.'

'Now look,' he said, and the eyes were chilly again. He was angry but not with her, and she knew it was only because he was worried.

She patted his hand. 'I know, William, dear, but there it is. As you will soon discover, you simply can't argue with my mother. I'm sure everything will be all right. You'll have it all figured out by then, I know you will. Everything will be quite all right. Surely we're not the only people having a big dinner party? Besides, we're no match socially for the likes of the previous victims mentioned in the papers.'

But in her heart, she wasn't quite as sure as she'd sounded.

Seeing that she was getting upset, he changed the subject. 'Have you noticed that Catholicism keeps cropping up?' He kept his voice low, afraid of causing offence to anyone seated nearby.

'Not especially.' She frowned at him, thinking. 'But then, we're not Catholics, we're very much Anglican, which is just the same, if you ask me.'

'We are too. And yes, it's all much of a muchness in my view. But for some... I suspect Ian Smedley-Judd is a Catholic—there's a crucifix hanging up in his study. And he collects religious art.'

'That doesn't necessarily mean... And anyway,

what if he is?'

'Exactly. What if he is?' Hardy thought for a moment then continued. 'Right after my father died—and we lost our home, my family and I were looking for temporary lodgings until we knew more about our situation, the kind of home we could afford to rent, that sort of thing. I remember a good few of the lodging houses I went to had signs in the front window. 'No Blacks, No Jews, No Catholics'. And a whole list of other things people couldn't be or have. No children. No dock workers. No Irish. No unemployed. Makes you wonder who they *did* take. There is still so much prejudice about, even today. Some of it is directed at Catholics.'

'My grandmother used to refuse to take on Catholic servants. I have no idea why. She had a 'thing' about them. That's how my mother put it, anyway. You and I would call it prejudice, or bigotry, now. But it's still very common. I had dinner with a young man once and my mother said, 'You needn't think you can marry him, you know, he's a Papist.' Honestly, in this day and age! I mean, surely we were all Catholics once? Before Henry and his blasted Reformation.'

He nodded. He was about to mention the Irish situation, but she said, 'Mrs Gerard once told me she had a great uncle who was excommunicated by the Pope. 'My grandparents never mentioned him again,' was what she told me. The shame was felt throughout the family. Some of her ancestors were even executed. So obviously she is a Catholic, and a very committed one. Do you think this is relevant to the robberies?'

'I'm not sure, but certainly there's something suggestive in it. I think all our dinner party hosts and hostesses were Catholic.'

'What sort of religious art does Smedley-Judd collect?' she asked, coming back to what he'd said.

'No idea. I haven't been able to get into his little secret room to look at it.'

'What if it's something connected with that little scrap of cloth?'

'Just what I was thinking myself. But how? And why?'

'You told me the scrap of cloth was amongst Archie Dunne's effects when he died. Where did he get it anyway?'

He stared at her. 'I'd give a week's wages to know the answer to that one. Got any ideas?'

She shook her head. Her hair curled about her ears. He wanted to touch it, push it back, stroke her cheek. He folded his arms and leaned back. She said, 'Not really, I can only guess it came from his wife. Was the handwriting on the paper his?'

'I don't know. What do you mean, from his wife?'

She shrugged. 'Well, how many young men go about with bits of cloth on their person? It was wrapped up as if it was something important. Which clearly it is, with what we now know, and the mugging and even the robbery at my house. So how did he get it and why did he keep it? Most men, most women too, would look at it and think it was just rubbish and throw it away. So he, or whoever wrote that note it was wrapped in, clearly knew exactly what it was, and were keeping it for some specific purpose. I don't know much about

Archie, but no one's suggested he was any kind of expert in ancient relics.'

'And Susan was?'

'Susan came from a proud old, very wealthy, very *Catholic* family. And they come from Hertfordshire, where there was a lot of anti-Catholic violence during the Reformation and for years afterwards. I can far more easily imagine her family having something of that sort than Archie. His family are all what my mother calls *nouveaux riches*.'

'Hmm. Mine would have called it that too, come to think of it. Well that's certainly given me something to think about. It could link in with my robberies.'

They said goodbye outside. He wanted to kiss her, she was absolutely sure, and as they ended up with a kind of hybrid handshake-hug, she longed to be in his arms and held safe. She walked home feeling cold, with a growing sense of dread deep inside. How she wanted to cancel the wretched dinner party.

*

Chapter Fifteen

'What a shame Diana isn't here,' George said, setting the tray of drinks down on the garden table. 'I can't believe it's turned out so nice today. Spring has well and truly sprung.' He peered at the jugs on the tray. 'Let me see, a classic mint julep or daiquiri? Or something of my own invention? Flora, my love?'

'Mint julep, of course,' she said, stretching out her glass. 'I don't know why but since the baby started, I just can't drink daiquiris like I used to. And I don't advise anyone to try George's own concoction. It's lethal.'

'George, really!' said her mother sternly.

Changing the subject hastily, Flora said, referring back to George's comment, 'Everyone's here except poor Diana. How perfectly rotten to get pneumonia at this time of year. It has been quite damp lately, hasn't it?'

Mr and Mrs Manderson both received a tall glass

bearing a strange assortment of fruit pieces and curling strips of peel.

'Is there any actual drink in this?' Mr Manderson peered into his glass.

A few feet away, and awkwardly propped in a deckchair for the first time in her life, George's mother, Mrs Cynthia Dulaisne Gascoigne, commented that drinks nowadays seemed to be far more about appearance than the quality of the refreshment they offered. She added, 'Yes, poor dear Diana. You know, George, what a martyr your sister is to her chest. She has been *so* ill this past winter, first with bronchitis and then it turned to pneumonia, and really we were so anxious about her, weren't we, Piers?'

'Hmm,' said Piers Gascoigne de la Gascoigne.

'Of course, she's over the worst of it now, but *so*, so weak and run down,' Mrs Gascoigne continued brightly; she paused to take a sip of her drink, grimaced and set it aside. 'The doctor *absolutely* insisted that she needed to right away for a full three months, he said, didn't he, Piers, she needs to *completely* relax and convalesce.'

'Hmm,' repeated her husband, and Dottie felt that he really sounded as if he didn't care a fig for his daughter's wellbeing.

'So where has she gone?' Dottie asked. Mrs Gascoigne was frowning at her husband, but turned a bright smile on Dottie, and Flora beside her.

'Oh! To Scarborough. Yes, the healthy seaside air. She's gone to stay with her old nanny. So suitable, and of course the old lady is an absolute treasure and was so thrilled to have Diana, for as long as it takes her to fully recover her strength.'

'She could have come here,' Flora pointed out. Mrs Gascoigne, with the skill of the true socialite, managed to turn a gasp of dismay into a light tinkling laugh.

'Oh no, dear, quite unsuitable. The traffic, the pollution. No, she needed to go to the coast, I'm afraid. And in any case, she could still have some remnant of infection which could so easily be passed to you. And through you to Precious Baby.'

Dottie felt nauseated by Flora's mother-in-law's gushing way of talking. Thank goodness she only had to put up with them once or twice a year. And as if Mrs Gascoigne wasn't bad enough, her husband was an absolute pig. No manners, no conversation, and clearly he couldn't care less for his own family members. How very sensible Flora was to have insisted on remaining in London when she and George had married, thus avoiding George's family for the greater part of the year. And how wisely she ignored the worst excesses of the in-laws' behaviour. Not for the first time, Dottie felt she had a lot to learn about diplomacy from her sister.

It felt like a very long Good Friday, and Dottie wished it over and then it would be her birthday and the day of her party.

Around her conversations rose and fell, whilst Dottie stared into space and thought about William Hardy's warning. Should they really have cancelled? Her mother had been adamant that they shouldn't. But what if something terrible happened?

She shivered.

'Cold, Dorothy?' her mother immediately enquired. Before Dottie had a chance to respond, her mother was on her feet.

'George, dear, we're going back into the house. It's growing cooler, and I can't risk Dorothy or myself catching a chill, not with the party tomorrow.'

George had little option but to gallantly assist them to carry their belongings and glasses and plates into the house, Greeley his butler and Cissie the maid running to help.

The evening dragged by, with Flora and George, Mrs Manderson and Mrs Gascoigne carrying the weight of the conversation, and Mr Manderson and Mr Gascoigne contributing little, and Dottie, practically bored to death, nodding here and there, and thinking alternately about William Hardy and her party.

The morning of the party brought rain.

When Dottie came down to breakfast, a year older but feeling as petulant as a five-year-old due to the weather, there was a stack of cards and envelopes beside her plate.

She began to read the cards, making an effort to smile and thank her parents for their good wishes and their own birthday card to her. Her father presented her with a little jeweller's box, and kissed her cheek.

'Happy birthday, my darling. We hope you will like these.'

She pulled off the pink ribbons and opened the box. Tiny sapphires set in gold twinkled at her from the pale velvet bed. She gasped, and for a few seconds was frozen in position, then with trembling fingers she took the earrings from their case, and one at a time, put them on. Her mother handed her a small mirror.

'Oh, they're beautiful, thank you! Thank you both so much!' She leapt up to give them both a hug, noting that her mother seemed surprised but pleased by her reaction.

'I'm glad you like them,' her father said, 'and if you're a good girl, you'll get a matching bracelet for your twenty-first.'

'Oh I shall be good, I promise,' she said with a laugh. 'I'll put them back in the box for now, but I'll wear them tonight.'

When she went back to reading her cards, at the bottom of the pile she found one in an envelope addressed by what at first seemed an unfamiliar hand and bearing a Derbyshire postmark. But when she opened the envelope and took out the card to read the greeting, she felt she had known the writing all along. It read, *'To dear Miss Manderson, with sincere good wishes for a very happy birthday, yours truly, William Hardy.'*

She didn't know, of course, how long he had agonised over the choice of words, unable to say what he really wanted, yet unwilling to be completely conventional and bland. He had practised on a separate sheet of paper over and over again until he simply gave up and wrote the only thing he felt he could say. *Yours. Truly.*

But the simple sentiment lit a glow in her heart that carried her on through the long, anxious day and into the evening, and the arrival of the first guests.

Though in spite of Hardy's words, Dottie was on edge the whole day, and it was never more clearly brought home to her than when she fumbled as she attempted to fasten her necklace with fingers that trembled and refused to work the tiny clasp.

For practically the whole day she'd been telling herself they had been fools to ignore William's concerns and go ahead with the party. Yet her common sense asserted itself, making her feel it was ridiculous to think that they—of all the households hosting dinner parties across the vast expanse of London—should be singled out as targets by the robbers.

Still a tiny voice insisted that it was going to happen. It was with great trepidation that she went downstairs to greet her father's business associate, Sir Montague Montague, the first guest to arrive, as always—and the last to leave.

She accepted his whiskery kiss on the cheek and his hearty good wishes for her birthday, exclaimed with delight over the gift he gave her, wrapped neatly and tied up with tartan ribbon, no doubt by his mother as usual. As she unwrapped it, and smiled, and thanked him sincerely for the lovely scarf ring with a sleek black-enamelled cat on the front, she seemed to be in two halves. One half was functioning conventionally, smiling, chatting, just as she should. The other half of her seemed to be standing in a corner, watching each new arrival with large terrified eyes, wringing her hands and wishing that William was there.

The acid test, if it could be so called, came when they all moved into the dining room for dinner.

There were twenty of them in all, including Dottie, her parents, Flora and George, and the table had been extended as was customary on such occasions.

The doors to the drawing room had been pushed back to create more space, and the little orchestra her father had hired for the evening had set themselves up in there. The furniture had been pushed back against the walls, or removed altogether, and the carpets rolled back to create an impromptu dancefloor for later in the evening. As the guests took their seats and began to chatter and laugh, the orchestra struck up a soft waltz.

Every time the door opened, Dottie's eyes turned that way, her heart seemingly in her mouth. She knew, absolutely knew, that it was only a matter of time. Mrs Gerard whispered something to her neighbour and left the room. After the incident with Melville at the afternoon tea, Dottie felt a slight reserve had grown between herself and Mrs Gerard, whom she now thought of primarily as her mother's friend. Dottie thought Mrs Gerard would be likely to miss her appetiser if she didn't hurry back, but the lady always left it rather late to pop to the convenience whenever she was out to dinner.

They had borrowed Flora and George's maid Cissie and their butler Greeley to assist at the table as the Mandersons' had only a small staff of women. Mrs Manderson was still old-fashioned enough to believe that a truly important occasion warranted the additional gravitas that could only be supplied by a man-servant, and it didn't matter a jot that all their guests knew that he was the

Gascoignes' butler.

The door opened, and Dottie felt as though everything within her halted. But then she saw it was just Janet coming in and she relaxed once more.

Frank Maple was hugely enjoying himself down in the kitchen of the Mandersons' residence. Hardy's instructions to him had been to keep his eyes open and be ready for anything. He was making sure he complied with his boss's wishes by keeping his eyes either on Janet's pleasing form, or the food the cook was passing to him to 'try'.

Opposite him, young beat copper Danny Paige was learning as much as he could from Sergeant Maple, who had opened his mind to hitherto unrealised possibilities. Maple had been on the beat for more than ten years before his promotion just before Christmas. Danny felt he could get a lot out of this evening—and not just the free food or the pleasure of being in a nice warm kitchen instead of out walking the beat in the chilly rain of the last day of March.

'Get your great feet out of the way, will you, Frank Maple!' Janet said, squeezing past him with two large baskets of hot bread rolls. She nudged him with her hip as she went by, and he had to remind himself he was still on duty and not give in to the temptation to slap her on the bottom.

Margie, the young between-maid, who had stayed on that evening to 'oblige', cast a shy smile at Danny, who blushed to the roots of his hair but still managed a shy smile in return. Cook caught the two and smiled to herself, shaking her head indulgently at the prospect of young love.

'See Danny,' Maple was saying, 'when you're on the beat, it's vital to get to know the staff in all the houses on your patch. That way, if anythink happens, they already knows they can trust you, and they tell you stuff you can't find out no other way. It's vital,' he added again, mainly because he liked the sound of it. Danny nodded earnestly, and made a mental note. Then Margie went by and he forgot everything Maple had said.

They could hear Cissie talking to someone in the rear lobby, then she came into the kitchen. 'They're ready, Mr Greeley,' she said, and Greeley set aside his newspaper, got up and yawned and stretched and fastened his waistcoat. He waited a second whilst Cook gave the silver tureen a last wipe to get rid of a smear of soup on the rim, then he picked it up and left the kitchen. Margie followed behind him with a tray of chilled meats, and Cissie brought up the rear. Dinner had begun.

Dottie saw it was just Janet coming into the dining room carrying baskets of bread rolls. She relaxed back into her chair and turned to reply to M'Dear Monty. He was halfway through one of his interminable—and grisly—shooting anecdotes. But a sudden gasp from further along the table claimed her attention, and everyone at that moment appeared to freeze in their places.

Dottie turned back to look towards the door, knowing exactly what she would see, not that it was any less frightening. A man had come in right behind Janet, shoving her ahead of him so that she stumbled and bread rolls tipped out of one of the baskets and bounced under the table. The gunman seemed not to notice that he stepped on one, crushing it beneath his heavy boot. He held a small black gun.

Then Dottie realised there were two more men—also holding guns—standing in the doorway, and beyond them, two others stood at the foot of the stairs in the shadows of the hall. Above the frightened commotion, from the centre of the room she heard a man's voice say loudly, 'This is a robbery. No one will be harmed if you do as you are told. Everyone to the far end of the room. Now!' He was standing on a chair, looking around at everyone.

The robbers' appearance struck her as frighteningly alien. It wasn't just the boots and rough clothes they wore, unfitting for an evening dinner and dance, or even their weapons, but it was the knitted masks they wore over their faces. Their heads were completely covered apart from the eyes, which peered out from two small round holes in the masks. Four of the men held firearms, small black pistols that looked as if they were just plastic, almost like a child's toys and yet, Dottie knew beyond doubt, perfectly lethal.

As no one moved, the ringleader waved his pistol above his head in a menacing manner and shouted, 'I said, *now!*'

With shrieks and gasps, the guests pushed back their chairs and began to hurry across the room to stand in front of the window overlooking the rear garden. A few male guests appeared ready to attempt to take on the robbers, but a pistol levelled at their chests soon persuaded them to fall into line.

'And you lot,' the man said, jerking his pistol in the direction of the band who sat petrified in their seats in the corner of the drawing room. As one, they laid aside their bows, sheets of music and instruments, walking over the improvised dancefloor and across the room to join the party guests. At the same time, the dining room door opened again, and the remaining staff were marched in by the two men from the hall: Greeley carrying a huge, steaming soup tureen, Cook still clutching a dripping wooden spoon, Cissie with Margie and her platter of meats, with a shamefaced Sergeant Maple and Constable Paige bringing up the rear. The staff set down their burdens and came to stand beside Mr and Mrs Manderson, and Dottie saw that Janet held the hand of the weeping young tweenie Margie who was barely fifteen, and at that moment looked closer to eleven.

Once the guests were all herded by the window, one of the men came to stand in front of them, his weapon trained on the crowd. The man on the chair stepped down. He signalled to the unarmed man who brought over a pair of leather doctors' bags. Another man placed himself in the doorway, his gun trained on the group. Dottie thought she saw the two from the hall go upstairs, but it was dark out there now, and she couldn't be sure. They were gone for what seemed like an eternity, and she prayed they would not happen upon poor Mrs Gerard and frighten her or hurt her in any way. Eventually they returned, mercifully without the old lady, who was clearly still sensibly hidden in the W.C. The men had nothing in their hands, and even their pockets sat neat and flat against the material of their jackets. So what had they been doing, Dottie puzzled.

'Now this is what's going to happen,' the first man said, 'you are all going to hand over your valuables. No one will try to be a hero, heroes don't live very long. Make no mistake, we will shoot anyone who doesn't do as he—*or she*—is told. Don't try and hide anything, we shall shoot you. Don't try and stop us, we shall shoot you. Am I making myself perfectly clear, ladies and gentlemen? You are to co-operate with us fully if you want to live a long and happy life.'

Two of the robbers then took a doctor's bag each in addition to the guns they carried. They then forced each guest in turn to remove their jewels and other valuables, and place them in the bags. Dottie could see one or two gentlemen were becoming angry and heated, protective of their womenfolk. Surely sooner or later, one of them would lose his head and do something rash? Dottie felt her stomach lurch with fear and her breaths were coming in rapid little gasps. One of the robbers was coming nearer, laughing to himself. Dottie caught the sound of it and hated him for revelling in the terror he and his cohorts inflicted.

Flora was first, and Dottie felt a tense moment of horror as she watched Flora with trembling hands peel off her bracelets, her wedding and engagement rings, the ring their parents had given her for her twenty-first birthday, and the dainty little eternity ring George had given her for their first anniversary—not merely jewellery but memories and emotions—then she pulled off her earrings and dropped them into the bag the robber held out in front of her. George added his signet ring, his watch, silver cigar case and his wallet then stepped back to put his arm around Flora's shoulder and draw her close against him, his eyes smouldering with impotent rage. Flora put her arms around his waist and hid her face against his shoulder.

It was like being stripped bare.

Lady Fraser, that poised, glittering socialite, was once more a gauche, shivering ingenue, standing there in front of Dottie wearing just her shoes and a simple frock—that no doubt cost the earth—for all the world like she was naked but for a petticoat, her long and lovely hair cascading about her shoulders now that she had no combs or tiara to hold it on top of her head.

Montague Montague was relieved of his silver-filigree cigar case, and the heavy gold ring that had been given to his father for his twenty-first birthday, some fifty years ago before coming to Monty on his father's death. The robber took forty pounds in treasury notes that he found neatly folded in the inside pocket of Monty's evening coat. They left him standing there, his monocle dangling loose from his waistcoat, a look of deepest misery etched on his usually amiable face.

Then, 'Your necklace, if you please, Miss.'

This was addressed to Dottie. And suddenly furious, Dottie couldn't help retorting, 'I don't know why you said please, it's not as though I have any choice in the matter.'

His blue eyes flashed with temper and he moved

a little closer, placing the cold muzzle of the pistol at her throat. 'Oh, but you do have a choice, my dear young lady. Feel free to decline at any time,' he told her softly. There was a long pause. Dottie, almost too scared to move, was convinced she would be sick, or faint. A hard jab from the pistol recalled her to what she was supposed to do, and her fingers trembled on the clasp for the second time that night as she began to undo her necklace. He laughed at her terror, whilst she heard a number of ladies gasp and at the same time, her father's voice came to her, 'You swine!' and he took a step forward, but was held back by one of his guests. Over the gunman's shoulder she could see her mother's face, frozen in fear, a white mask that made her almost unrecognisable. The Reverend Trent whispered an earnest prayer, his lips moving, his hands folded in front of his chest.

The man held out the bag and Dottie dropped the necklace in, hearing the soft clink as it landed on top of the other valuables: poor old Monty's ring and banknotes. Mrs Fry's pearls, Lady Fraser's diamond brooch with the matching earrings, Mr Fry's antique watch that had been in his family for four generations and which had so delighted Dottie when she was a little girl and he used to come to afternoon tea and she'd sit on his knee to play with his watch. All there in the bag, still warm from the heads, throats, bosoms, the fingers and the pockets of their owners.

The robber prodded her again with the pistol. 'Now the ring and that rather charming bracelet, and your lovely earrings,' he rasped. Trembling, she pulled off the ring and holding her hand out over the mouth of the bag, allowed the ring to fall inside. She tried to undo the catch of her bracelet, but her fingers were stiff and she couldn't seem to make them work. The robber grew impatient and transferring his gun to the same hand as the bag, he snatched at the bracelet, wrenching it from her arm and it too was thrown into the bag, although several small gold beads dropped and rolled across the floor. One became a tiny glint of light next to the heel of Montague Montague's shoe. She carefully unhooked the new earrings given to her only that morning—a lifetime ago—by her parents. She dropped the earrings into the bag with everything else.

The robber half-turned away from Dottie then reached up to snatch a silver and pearl hair-ornament from Dottie's hair, and held it up to look at in the lamplight. His sleeve rode up as he held it. There was a mark on the inside of his wrist, not quite covered by a small patch of make-up. Dottie gasped. He turned to lock eyes with her, then following her eyes, he saw what she had seen. For Dottie it was as if the world and everything it contained had stopped still for a second. Her mind struggled to understand what she had seen, and the gunman in the centre of the room, the ringleader, looked across at his colleague and Dottie. 'What's up?' he demanded.

Dottie breathed again, trembling from head to foot, and gave the smallest pleading shake of her head. What would he...?

'What is it?' the ringleader insisted.

There was another long pause then the man with the bag gave himself a slight shake, and said, with his unmistakable accent, 'Nothing. I just thought for a moment she was going to faint.'

The ringleader laughed. 'Let her faint, spoiled brat. Get on with it.' And the robber moved on to the next couple, who were already hastening to pull off their valuables and hold them out.

Finally, they had gone around the whole room. Even Sergeant Maple had had to give up a watch and chain and coins to the value of almost a pound. Danny Paige, standing there in his uniform, blending in about as well as a lighthouse on a dark night, had given up a small cigarette case and a silver St Christopher charm on a thin chain.

'All right,' the ringleader shouted, 'everyone down on the floor. Count to two hundred before any of you move, or you'll live to regret it. But not for long,' he added with a chuckle.

Danny Paige saw his chance. In a flash he grabbed the still-steaming soup tureen off the table and flung it at the ringleader, flooring the man in one swift motion and sending soup splashing up the wall and over the floor. But behind him, a robber levelled his pistol and with only the merest hesitation, fire three shots in rapid succession full into the young policeman's back. Margie screamed and buried her face in Janet's neck, and Flora, without even a murmur, slid to the floor in a dead faint. Dottie broke out in sobs, and Maple uttered a howl of rage.

But it was all to no avail. One robber helped up the ringleader, whilst the other three, rushing to the front of the room, trained their guns once more on the crowd, and the rebellion was squashed.

'As I said,' the ringleader snarled, not needing to raise his voice in the shocked hush of the room, 'get on the floor. Now. Count to two hundred, or there will be even more that will never rise up again.'

As the guests all lay on the floor, some of the ladies being helped by those around them, some of the ladies, in spite of the threatening situation, being careful of their gowns, the robbers began to retreat to the doorway. The door slammed shut. The first two bold men immediately got to their feet, and a shot rang out in the hall and everyone screamed and fell flat on the floor again.

Silence fell on the room. After a few moments, heads began to lift again, and M'Dear Monty, whom Dottie would forever remember for this brave deed, got to his feet and went to the door. A lady gasped, 'No!' but he grasped the handle and eased the door open. Seeing nothing to alarm him, he went out into the hallway with Dottie's father following him. Inside the room, it felt as though everyone held their breath. Maple and the Reverend Trent bent over the lifeless body of Danny Paige.

Presently the words came back to them from her father, 'It's all clear. They've gone. I'm phoning the police.'

Suddenly everyone was up and talking loudly. Some men, ashamed now of having been cowed, talked loudly about what they would do when they got their hands on the devils who had perpetrated the crime. Hanging was too good for them, was the common consensus. Dottie, clinging numbly to her mother, was horribly afraid she was going to be sick. She ran from the room and only just made it to the bathroom in time.

When she came out, Janet was there. 'Are you all right Miss? I've put Miss Flora into your room to lie down, Mr Gascoigne was worried about her colour. And Mr Manderson says the police is on their way. And Cook is putting on the kettle to make tea for everyone, though Mr Gascoigne and Sir Montague is handing out whisky to the gents, and some of the ladies too, I don't doubt. Is there anything you want me to do?'

'Yes,' said Dottie, 'Stay with Flora, make sure she's all right. I'm going downstairs.'

'Oh Miss, are you sure you should? What if they was to come back?'

'They won't,' Dottie said, 'they've got what they came for.' She could see the body of the young constable, a tablecloth already draped over him, and Maple still sitting beside him on the floor, his head in his hands. Tears started in her eyes.

Glancing up, she saw Mrs Gerard at the top of the stairs, peering over the banister. The old lady's face was grave. Dottie ran up to take her shaking hand and help the woman back down the stairs.

Half an hour later, another uniformed constable opened the Mandersons' front door to the detectives. Mr Manderson's library was placed at their disposal, and almost immediately, once Janet had set down the tray of coffee and sandwiches on a side table next to Mr Manderson's largely untouched collection of the works of Walter Scott, they began to bring in the guests, two at a time, to take statements.

Her parents were the first to be seen. Dottie was still shaken and upset, but wanted to keep busy so she made herself useful in the kitchen with Cook and Janet, cutting sandwiches and making more coffee, whilst Margie ran in and out with plates and cups and the like. Hopefully with the resilience of youth, Dottie thought, Margie would recover from the ordeal, but for now, she wouldn't stop talking about what had happened.

'Ooh Miss,' she said, her eyes gleaming with yet more tears, 'when he held that gun to your throat, I thought you was a goner for sure. Like that poor young fellow...'

Dottie's eyes widened, and the image of it sprang from her memory like an ambush.

Seeing Dottie blanch, Cook snapped at the youngster, 'Margie, for the dear Gawd's sake, get these sarnies upstairs before people starve to death.' When the girl had gone, Cook came to put a hand on Dottie's arm. 'She don't mean any harm, Miss Dottie.'

But Margie, thus spoken to, simply ran from the room in a fresh flood of tears.

'It's all right, she's too young to know how to deal with it.' Dottie managed a faltering smile at Cook who patted her arm. Dottie turned to collect a couple of plates, and carried them up the short few steps to the drawing room, where everyone was gathered, the dining room having been closed off. Anything to keep moving, to stop herself from thinking about it. A wave of nausea came over her, and at the turn of the stairs she had to pause and take some deep breaths until the feeling went away. By the time she reached the drawing room, she was composed once more and she took some time to help Janet pass around the food and the coffee and generally ensure the guests were kept busy and felt looked after.

Another twenty minutes went by before Dottie was summoned. She felt rather nervous and paused outside the door to pat her hair into place and straighten her gown. The constable who was acting as both messenger and usher glanced at her as if wondering why she was hesitating, but then the door was open and she was being shown in, and a nice older gentleman in a dark blue suit was getting to his feet, holding out his hand to her and saying, 'Do come in, Miss Manderson, I gather you've had a rather disastrous birthday party this evening.' The understatement was delivered with a gentle smile and her first thought was, 'He's rather sweet, like an uncle or an old friend of Father's,' and her second thought was, 'I'd forgotten it was my birthday.' She said this to the detective who nodded and replied,

'No doubt not what you'd expected of the evening. I'm Chief Inspector Barrie, and I'm standing in for Inspector Hardy while he's away for the Easter holidays. I'd like to ask you a few questions about anything you might have noticed. I hope you don't mind, all this has been rather trying for you and I expect you're a good deal shaken up.'

But his initial avuncular chatty manner soon disappeared and he took her over and over her statement about the events of the evening, leaving her exhausted and tearful. It was as if he thought it was her fault the robbery had occurred, which chimed exactly with her own self-recriminations, as she thought of all the opportunities they had had to cancel the wretched party.

Eventually all their guests had been permitted to leave, the musicians had been paid twice over as compensation for the perils they had faced, and the Gascoignes' staff had been sent home to Mortlake Gardens, whilst the Mandersons' own staff were sitting in the warm kitchen, too tired to discuss the evening any further, and having one last hot drink before retiring for the night.

Dottie and her parents, along with Sergeant Maple, stood silently in the hall, watching as the body of the young constable was carried outside and driven away. Dottie's mother, not usually given to such gestures, had patted Maple's arm and told him he shouldn't blame himself. Though they knew he would continue to do so, because as he said to Dottie, 'What am I going to tell Bill when he comes back?' She shook her head. She had no idea what she was going to tell him either.

*

Chapter Sixteen

William Hardy had completely forgotten there was such a thing in the world as leisure, and he couldn't shake the slightly guilty sense of indulgence he felt at not being at work. An evening walk along the river with his family, followed by a concert at the bandstand had been a wonderful distraction.

A terse interview with his superiors had left William in no doubt as to the official view of him taking three days off in the middle of an investigation, but he had remained uncharacteristically stubborn, citing the need to deal with his late mother's legal affairs and to spend some time with his grieving siblings. A reluctant agreement had been forthcoming, and so here he was, listening to an open-air concert in a small Derbyshire country town.

He had started the day with a late breakfast of huge proportions, and had watched the younger members of the family, gathered at his uncle's home especially for the holiday, as they foraged for Easter eggs around the house and grounds.

Although eggs were not traditionally hunted until Easter Sunday, his uncle had taken great pains to explain to the children that they had special permission from the King to hunt for them on Saturday as the King knew they were going to be sailing with Aunt Cassie's brother and his wife for the Caribbean on Easter Monday and had to be in Liverpool the night before. The adults had exchanged sly, conspiratorial smiles over this announcement. Edward, now fifteen, had been sceptical but was still young enough to be persuaded to join in the fun.

Even Eleanor had taken part, under the guise of 'helping' the smaller children as she too professed to be too old for such nonsense. William smiled as he heard his brother exclaiming more than once that something 'Jolly well wasn't fair'. He heard Eleanor laughing too, and he was struck by how happy she was, and how refreshed, by this visit to Derbyshire.

His aunt and uncle joined him at the garden door as he watched the game.

'Bill, we really need to speak to you about Eleanor,' his uncle said.

William turned. 'I'm so grateful to you, Uncle Joe. It's been an age since I've seen her so light-hearted. She's completely transformed.'

'It's our pleasure. We're just glad to be able to help.'

'Bill, dear, we have reason to believe that a young cousin of my brother-in-law is interested in

Eleanor. Romantically, I mean.' His aunt said. Hardy mentally meandered through the relationships.

'She's only just eighteen,' he cautioned.

'Well, yes, but...'

'And how old is this fellow?'

'He's twenty-four. And of a good family. A nice boy, not brash, not bullying. His father owns the mill at the other end of town. They're Quakers, but that's not a problem, is it? Better than being a drinker.'

'Yes indeed.' Hardy turned back to look out at the foragers; his brother's further indignant exclamations reached his ears.

'The thing is, Bill, she's happy here. And she has prospects. We'd like her to stay with us if you'll allow it.' His aunt came and put her hand through his arm, and stood beside him looking out into the grounds.

'I'm very grateful to you both,' he repeated, 'but I have a duty...'

His uncle held up a hand. 'Don't say that. It's been a pleasure to have her here—and young Edward. And if you can manage to care for yourself in London, we'd like to keep her with us. She already seems very attached to this young fellow, and we'll keep an eye on the situation, you can be sure of that.'

'Do you know if she has any provision under the terms of your mother's will? It would be as well to clarify the situation, in preparation for the future,' his aunt asked.

William sighed. 'It's not a lot, I'm afraid. The investments haven't done very well, and Mother's income has suffered as a result. Mother left her money jointly between Edward and Eleanor...'

'Nothing to you or Celia?' his Aunt Cassie asked, and he could tell she was a little shocked. He smiled.

'I am to administer Edward's money until he is twenty-one. And I assume Mother felt that Celia's husband could support her well enough.' He hesitated, then, wanting to be completely frank, he said, 'Edward's money is being used to pay towards his school fees, but due to Mother's losses, it only covers about half the cost. By the time he is twenty-one, I'm not sure there'll be anything left. As it is, Eleanor will only have about £120 a year.'

'Oh dear,' was his aunt's sorrowful reply. 'Still, I suppose it's better than nothing.'

He knew it was a disappointing figure, but there was nothing he could do about it. He sincerely hoped that Eleanor's young man was not depending upon marrying a rich wife.

The rest of the day was spent in relaxation, games and eating good food. After dinner, the ones who were departing for foreign shores early the next morning said their goodbyes and went home. William, Eleanor and Edward spent a leisurely evening with their aunt and uncle in the drawing room, talking of memories and old friends. It was a warm, lazy evening, and William couldn't remember how long it had been since he'd been so relaxed. When the ladies and Edward had gone up to bed, Uncle Joe invited William to take a nightcap with him in his office. Sitting in a worn leather armchair, William seized the opportunity to ask his uncle if he'd ever heard mention of a Muriel Carmichael in connection with his father. Joe Allsopp handed William a crystal tumbler containing a small measure of whisky, then turned to tidy the drinks tray. William—thinking like a policeman—was convinced his uncle was giving himself thinking time.

At length Joe said, 'Well, you're a grown man. I'm sure as a policeman you know more than I about the weaknesses of men. In those days, with your father it was women.' He halted, then shook his head and said, 'Actually that's not quite fair. I loved my sister—still do, though she's left us—but I can't pretend she was an easy woman back then. When Garry was rich, they were both so different. I suppose I wasn't surprised to find that Garfield sought comfort elsewhere.'

Joe came to sit opposite William on a wide, battered sofa. William nodded, thinking back to what Mrs Carmichael had told him. 'But I thought he knew her *before* he met Mother. At least, that was the impression I formed.'

'Who told you about it?'

'She did.'

Joe was a good deal surprised. 'Muriel Carmichael's still around? I see.' He nodded to himself. He sighed, 'Well, yes, it started well before they met. Then your mother came on the scene, a match was fixed up between both of the fathers. And somehow, your mother got to hear about this seamstress. She even went to see her. 'Keep your hands off my fiancé', or words to that effect. Your father promised to give Muriel up. His father had threatened to cut him off. But...well...'

'He started seeing her again?' William hazarded. His uncle nodded.

There was a silence as each of them pondered and tried to decide how much to say or to conceal. After several minutes, and casting a quick glance over his shoulder as if for eavesdroppers, his uncle said, in a low, confidential voice, 'Look here, Bill. The thing is, looking back now, I realise your father really loved this girl. Class-wise they were no match, that's true. But he was—oh, he was a different man with her—and by all accounts she had quite the head for business.'

'Indeed,' William said. 'She's been hugely successful.'

'You know her quite well then?'

'Yes.'

'Still a looker?'

'Not really, no, but she is an impressive woman, Very impressive. One wouldn't want to underestimate her.'

'See here, Bill,' Joe said, 'I said to him at the time, forget what your father says, forget about Isabel. My sister and I loved her, but like I said, a devil of a woman to live with, one imagines. Sorry, Bill, no disrespect to your mother. Oh, I know I should have stuck up for her, but I believed I was doing the right thing. I told him, 'If you love this woman and she's everything you say she is, marry her and tell the family to go hang.' He drained his glass and got up to pour another.

'But he didn't, clearly.'

'No, I'm sorry to say this, Bill, but your father was something of a moral coward. And he was never truly happy with your mother. And, quite obviously, as we now know he had *no* head for business.' He sank down on the sofa again with a sigh, shaking his head at the memories. 'He would have been so happy with that Muriel girl. But he had no backbone, your father.'

'What about me?' William asked suddenly. He hadn't intended to ask such a question, but it was out now. His uncle turned to look at him.

'What do you...?'

'Do you think I have a backbone?'

'Well, haven't you?' His uncle asked. It was William's turn to sigh and shake his head. He said no more, so after a moment his uncle said, 'Eleanor said something about a Miss Manderson.'

William could feel himself blushing. His uncle laughed softly and clapped him on the shoulder. 'So it's all true! Well, I'm very glad to hear it, Bill, very glad. Is it too soon to offer my congratulations?'

'Very much so. Her parents will never allow her to marry a mere policeman.'

'You're a mere policeman now, but who knows what's to come...Well, well. So that's why you're so determined to stay in London.' He clinked his glass against William's. 'To love.'

William couldn't help a wry laugh as he repeated the toast.

His uncle said, 'Manderson. Anything to do with Herbert Manderson?'

William, surprised, nodded. Joe said, 'I was at college with him. Nice fellow, bit of a bumbler, but nice. Not a bean to his name when he married that saucy little piece, I can tell you.'

William almost choked on his drink on hearing

Lavinia Manderson referred to in such terms. But his interest was definitely piqued. '*No* money?'

'Not a bean...'

'Interesting. What about her parents?'

'Oh, dead against it, obviously. But she had enough backbone for the two of them, and refused to give him up.' Joe cast a sly look at William. 'Does this daughter have a backbone?'

William smiled into his drink. 'Oh yes. Enough for two, and to spare.'

It had been agreed the whole family would attend the Easter Sunday service at the little church in the village nearby. If the weather was fine, they would walk the half mile, and if rain threatened, they would drive.

He slept late, after a long dreamless sleep had claimed him, and when he awoke in a large, well-decorated room, in a large, comfortable bed, it took him some time to remember where he was.

Yes, he thought, this was far better for Eleanor, and even for Edward, than the little rented house in London, with its threadbare carpets, thin, elderly blankets, and damp patches on the walls. At some point he would tell his uncle and aunt that he wanted to accept their offer, and see if he could come to some arrangement with them. He didn't want the financial burden of caring for his siblings to fall completely on their shoulders.

It rained the next morning, so they did in fact go to church in the car, their uncle driving them himself, as he did not keep a chauffeur. As they sat in the cool dimness of the little country church, waiting for the service to begin, Eleanor put her arm through his and whispered, 'So, Bill, have you seen anything of Miss Manderson lately?'

He smiled and nodded, but there was no time to tell her anything more. The vicar appeared, and summoned the congregation to stand and sing the first hymn. Eleanor squeezed his arm and smiled back, then raised her clear voice in song.

With half his mind occupied in thinking about the robberies, Hardy felt more like an observer of the service than a participant. The vicar, in his special Easter robes, went through the service as laid down by the church many, many years before, speaking the words that had been spoken time and again by others before him, and that would, no doubt, issue forth the length and breadth of the country, all the preordained phrases falling upon the ears of the needy, the lost, the saved and the faithful. William thought about the rites and services the vicar performed.

On the journey back to the house, his uncle said, 'Can you believe that the Reverend Barker and I used to scrump apples together when we were lads? Many's the time one or other of us got a good hiding for the scrapes and mischief we got into. Not that you'd know it to look at him now, in his grand vestments, looking so Godly and important. Amazing what a difference a dog-collar can make!' For the second time, William thought about what Dottie had told him about the function of religious vestments.

The next morning, the headlines in the newspapers on the breakfast table proclaimed, *'Another dinner-party robbery in London: gunshots fired: one dead.'*

Hardy, white with fear, dropped his knife and ran for the telephone at once. Within an hour he was on his way back to London and Dottie Manderson.

Chief Inspector Barrie bumped into him in the corridor at the police station the next morning. 'Ah, the very fellow! Glad you're back, and not before time. Look here Hardy, can you pick up those robberies again? There was another one two nights ago while you were away, you might have seen the news headlines. Unfortunately, I've just been told I'm being seconded to this political scandal. You know, the one involving the prime minister's daughter and that foreign prince. Strictly hush-hush, you know the sort of thing. All the case notes are on my desk. If there's anything else you need, just leave me a note, I'll be in and out...'

Hardy was struck by how pale she was, and there were deep circles beneath her eyes. If only he could put his arms around her and tell her everything would be all right. Unfortunately, he wasn't able to do any of that in front of her parents or Sergeant Maple. He did the next best thing.

'Please do sit down, Miss Manderson. I just need to ask you a few more questions, I'm afraid. I'll try not to take too long about it. Would you like anything to drink? Perhaps Mrs Manderson wouldn't mind if Sergeant Maple rang for some tea?'

Dottie smiled, 'You needn't worry. I'm quite all right, though it's been so awful. That poor young constable.'

'In that case, let's get started. I know you've already told Chief Inspector Barrie all this, but could you just tell me again, in your own words, what happened. And if any of you remember anything else, please feel free to add it in.'

And so for the next hour and a half, she and her parents went back over the events of that night. He didn't write anything down, he just listened. And Dottie remembered how, when he had first come to speak to her after the death of Archie Dunne back in November, she had found it so odd, even unprofessional, that he didn't make notes. Now she knew it was just that he liked to pay full attention to what he was being told. Frank Maple made notes on Hardy's behalf.

She told him about the tattoo on the arm of the man who had held a gun on her. His eyes gleamed with triumph as she told him about it. She had the impression it was significant. She wondered if perhaps someone else had seen it at one of the other robberies? Then she told him about the make-up on Melville's arm that she'd noticed at the disastrous tea party, and her theory that he used make-up to disguise the tattoo. She told him how some weeks before, when Melville had reached in front of her at the restaurant, she'd seen part of the tattoo then. Belatedly she realised he hadn't known about the dinner with Melville, and he quirked an eyebrow at her, causing her to blush, but he said nothing.

'So you believe it was Dr Melville who held the gun on you at your party?'

'Yes, I'm convinced it was him.'

'You're absolutely certain?'

'Yes, because of the tattoo, which I'd already seen before. And his eyes. And the accent. I recognised his voice when he spoke to me. And he tried to protect me from the other man by saying he thought I had been about to faint. I think he was afraid the other man might shoot me if he thought I'd recognised Melville.'

'And was it Melville who shot the young policeman?'

'No, it was one of the other men.'

'You're certain?'

'I am. But I didn't recognise any of them at all.'

'Thank you, Miss Manderson, you've been a great help. I appreciate you giving up your time to speak to me today. I'm so very sorry your party went so badly wrong.' He got up to leave, shook hands with her father and practically bowed to her mother, then Dottie walked him and Maple out to the front door, though Maple made an excuse and hurried down to the kitchen, presumably to snatch a few minutes with Janet.

Dottie put her hand on William's arm. 'I didn't kiss him.'

He turned to look at her, the door was half-open, letting in a cold draught. 'I'm sorry?'

She bit her lip. 'Melville. When he took me to dinner. I didn't—I didn't kiss him.'

He smiled and leaned so close she thought he was going to kiss her. 'Good,' he said softly, and kissed her cheek. Then he ran down the steps and he was gone.

Dottie smiled for almost the first time in the three days since she'd turned twenty years of age.

'Good,' she repeated.

It was later that same day. During a visit to her sister and brother-in-law's, Dottie came in slowly from the hall and sat down. Flora, now fully recovered from the robbery, and George exchanged a look. It seemed as though Dottie was in a dream.

'Dottie?' George said in his usual hearty way. 'Anything wrong, dear?'

She looked up, frowning, and shook her head. 'No. But... well I've just had an interesting chat with Cissie. It's just something she said...' Her voice trailed off. In her head, mental jigsaw pieces were slotting together. Surely not? Surely...

'What did ...?' Flora began but Dottie held up her hand.

'I'm sorry, I must just pop down and see Cissie again. If I'm right, I think William might want to speak with her.'

'Certainly, but...' Flora's words fell on deaf ears. Dottie was already out of the drawing room and heading down the back stairs to the kitchen. 'I could have rung for Cissie, she needn't have gone down there herself,' she commented to her husband then went back to trying to unpick the row of knitting that had gone wrong.

There was a light on in William Hardy's house. The soft glow of it showed through the transom window above the front door as Dottie came up the steps and took hold of the heavy black-painted knocker. The sound of it was like the last trump awakening the dead for judgement.

A moment later and the door was opened by the man himself, in his shirtsleeves and no tie. He looked both disconcerted and pleased to see her, but before he could invite her in, or utter any kind of greeting, she'd pushed past him and was halfway to the kitchen. By the time he'd shut the door and returned, she was already filling the kettle, her coat thrown over the back of one of the chairs.

He watched her for a moment, standing leaning back against the dresser, his arms folded across his chest. His face wore an amused expression, though his eyes weren't giving too much away.

She set the kettle on the stove, wrestled with getting the stove to light, then cast about her for cups and spoons. For a well-born young lady, she had a practical bent he liked.

'And you can take that smug expression off your face, for starters,' she told him, trying hard not to laugh. 'I'm not here to see you, I just need to tell you something relevant to your investigation.'

She found the cups, and rinsed a teaspoon under the tap. Not finding a towel to dry it on, because he hadn't remembered to wash any, she made use of the hem of her sleeve. She avoided looking at him as long as possible, but finally, there wasn't anything else left to do. She turned large wondering eyes on him.

'Come here,' he said.

'Don't boss me about! Just because you're a man, you think you can order me about. And anyway, I'm not coming over there.'

'Why not?'

'Because if I do, you'll kiss me, obviously. And I

know how men get when a woman gets within kissing distance.'

'And how is that, exactly?'

She floundered. But she'd wrestled with enough amorous young men on the doorsteps of houses, the dimly-lit boxes of theatres, the dancefloors of hotels and restaurants of Britain to know she was right. 'Well, you know. They get 'all unnecessary', as Janet would say.'

He laughed then. 'And Janet is probably an expert in that field after walking out with Frank Maple for the last six weeks or so.'

'I wouldn't mind if they did any actual walking out,' Dottie grumbled, 'And how Mother hasn't caught them, I'll never know. From what I can make out, they spend all their time indoors.' She glared at the stove. Why didn't that wretched kettle boil?

He'd crossed the room without her hearing him. Standing behind her, he put his arms about her, and dropped his head to nuzzle her neck. Her eyes fluttered closed as her head tilted back to lean against him.

A few moments later Hardy sighed. 'Hmm, you're right. I'm definitely feeling all unnecessary.' With great reluctance, he let her go and went to sit down at the table, anything to put a little distance between them. Papers strewed the table's surface; he had been going through all the statements yet again.

She wasn't sure whether she was glad or not by the distance he put between them. She probably ought not to have come in the first place, knowing they would be alone in the house together. The kettle finally boiled. The tea caddy yielded barely enough tea for their drinks. Dottie carried the cups over and set them down on the one small clear patch of the table-top. 'Have you eaten?' Since his mother had died and his sister had gone away to stay with their uncle, it was her constant concern that he was not eating properly.

He had to think about it, which didn't bode well. 'Er, no, not as such.'

'I knew it!' She went to look in the pantry. From inside, her voice sounded hollow and echoing. 'There's nothing in here except two jars of jam and half a bag of flour. You haven't even got any more *tea*! What on earth have you been living on?'

He shrugged. Not that she could see that. She shut the door and came back, one hand on her hip, the other reaching for her coat. 'Do you want to eat first or talk shop?'

He hesitated. 'Look, I can't really...'

'Good lord!' she said, 'I mean, everyone knows policemen are badly paid, but I had no idea it was this bad. I'll take you out for dinner, and I will pay. You can swallow your male pride for once.'

Common sense prevailed, and after a moment he nodded. 'It's just that there have been rather a lot of extra expenses of late. I'm not usually quite so...'

'Of course not,' she said, keen to reassure him. 'And it will get easier over time. You've only had your promotion a couple of months ago.' She stared at him. He wasn't sure what she meant by it. He stayed where he was, staring back at her. At length, her tone something between exasperation and amusement, she said, 'Well, William, go and change your shirt and put on a jacket and tie. I'm not going out in public with you looking like that.'

He did as he was told, running upstairs, filled with excitement. His second evening out with her! He felt embarrassed by the idea of her paying, but he had to admit she was right. He did need to eat, and he couldn't afford it. But once things got back to normal—whatever that was—he could pay her back and take on his proper role as the breadwinner. It was only one dinner, after all, there was no need to make quite so much of it.

Downstairs in the kitchen, Dottie was writing out a shopping list. She would give it to Janet later, and make sure the items were obtained for him. He could come and collect them himself, that would give her the excuse of seeing him again. She'd need to remember to tell her mother he was coming to dinner the next evening.

He was downstairs again ten minutes later, clean, tidy, hastily shaved and looking buoyant. It was a look she recognised, again from all the dinner dates and drinks parties she'd attended in the company of the opposite sex. It was the look of a male getting ready to take liberties. She smiled and shook her head. Men were so predictable. She had gathered up his papers into a neat pile. 'Shall we bring these with us, or can I trust you to behave yourself if I come back with you after dinner?'

'I promise to behave,' he told her solemnly. 'Scout's honour.'

She gave him a withering look. 'You were never in the boy scouts.'

They were still arguing about it as they walked into the little restaurant around the corner.

They ate quickly and didn't linger. Back in his kitchen, Dottie was ready to get down to business.

'With all the guests invited to my party, we had to borrow Cissie and Greeley from Flora, you know, to help out.'

He nodded, not really seeing where this was going.

She came to sit beside him at the table. He felt comfortable with her so close, and when she leaned her head against his shoulder, it felt only natural to put his arm round her and hold her close to his side. He kissed her hair.

'Pay attention!' She swatted his knee. 'This afternoon, at Flora's for our baby-knitting group of two, I popped downstairs to the lavatory there, it's really the one for the servants, but it's a bit closer than going upstairs. And then Cissie told me that on the night of my party, just as we all went in to dinner, Mrs Gerard had asked her to direct her to it.

'Mrs Gerard told Cissie that her knee was playing up, she has arthritis, you know. Mrs Gerard said she couldn't manage the stairs, so she wanted to quickly pop to the servants' lavatory which you probably don't know is right next to the back door. Cissie said Mrs Gerard was most insistent that no one should know, as it embarrassed her to admit to feeling her age. Cissie said she didn't say anything before because she felt sorry for the old lady. Actually, I saw her go out, and I guessed where she was going. She's rather renowned for her untimely visits to the W.C.'

If Dottie had held any doubts at all about either the relevance or the importance of this information, these were immediately dispelled by William leaping to his feet and rummaging through his heap of papers. After a minute he found what he was looking for; he pulled out a statement and began to read it through, his eyes scanning the lines rapidly until he found the right part.

'Look at this,' he said, and thrust the page at her, sitting beside her once more.

'What is it?'

'A witness statement. The guest was someone present at the dinner party of a Mr Gareth Smedley-Judd, at his home in Hitchin, Hertfordshire, a little more than six weeks ago.'

'I'm assuming there was a robbery there too?'

'There was.'

'Any relation to Ian Smedley-Judd?'

'His baby brother.'

Dottie smiled. 'How unfortunate to have two robberies in one family and just a few weeks apart.'

'Isn't it?'

She began to read. He watched her closely as she did so. Her hair fell forward to curl about her face. He had to resist the urge to brush it back, to stroke her hair and feel the silky strands between his fingers.

'Is this...' she looked up, a frown making a crease between her brows. 'Is this a *pattern*?' she asked. 'Is this how they do it?'

He nodded slowly. 'I think it could well be. I'll bet it's not the same person every time. It can't be, because your Mrs Gerard wasn't at this particular one, though she was at one or two of the others. But here, you see, what this witness says about another lady who was there.'

Before he could continue, she read, "Mrs Smedley-Judd was, luckily enough, in the bathroom the whole time, so she was the only one of us who wasn't robbed, and didn't have a gun pointed at her. I was just concerned they might search the house and find her.' But that's exactly what... oh no, it couldn't be! Not Mrs Gerard! She's our *friend*! I was so worried the robbers would find her and hurt her, or take her jewellery, and yet all along...' Tears filled her eyes.

He stopped resisting, and swept her into his arms to hold her tight, hugging her fiercely and sneaking a sly kiss onto her cheek. 'Dottie! Don't be upset!'

She kept her face pressed into his shoulder. They sat like that in the silence of the kitchen for some time, until, pushing him gently away, she went upstairs to the bathroom to wash her face and repair her make-up.

When she got back, he was busy at the sink, washing their cups and saucers. The spell was broken. She didn't know whether to be glad or sorry, but it was for the best, she knew that. How easy it would be to just let go of responsibility and abandon herself to his arms, especially now that there was no one else in the house to intrude on their privacy.

On returning to the kitchen, her first words were, 'I'm afraid I must go now,' and she said it rather formally. And only when she'd said it did she realise he was speaking too.

'I really think it would be best if I walked you home,' he was saying.

And on a rather shaky breath she laughed and said, 'My mother would never approve of me being here alone with you in the evening.'

She put on her coat. He fetched his own on the way to the door, and they walked through the streets of London, hand in hand, and on the steps of her house, he contented himself with a quick kiss on her cheek before wishing her goodnight. He watched her safely inside then went back home. His heart was light. He felt like singing, not a sensation he was prone to. William Hardy was well and truly in love.

*

Chapter Seventeen

'How many pearl necklaces does Mrs Gerard own?' Hardy asked. The maid had been nervously twisting the edge of her apron between her fingers, but when she heard his question, her nerves left her, and she relaxed immediately. She treated him to a scornful look.

'Why just the one, of course. Don't you know how much *real* pearls cost? And a lady such as Mrs Gerard, she ain't going to have no truck with artificial ones.' She rolled her eyes.

'No, I don't suppose...'

'Why, she'd never hear the end of it if she did, and never be able to hold up her head in public again for the shame of it, poor love.'

'Indeed. Well, I just wanted to check...'

'The very *idea*...'

He held up his hand to prevent a further onslaught. 'Please.' He made a note in his notebook. 'And has Mrs Gerard had her pearls damaged or replaced, or has there been any time in the last three months or so when they weren't available for her to wear?'

The maid thought about it. 'Well, the catch was loose a while back. That would be about the middle of February, I remember as she only came back from abroad just a day or two before. She couldn't wear them for a week or so, as they'd gone for the catch to be mended. And then, almost as soon as they came back, she broke the string and they had to go off to be restrung, and so again, she was without them for a week or so.'

'Did you have to send them off for the catch to be mended? Or did Mr Aitchison do that?'

'Oh no, Mrs Gerard attended to it herself. She doesn't mind doing little things like that.'

He took her through the dates, and was elated to find they matched the dates of two of the robberies, the Ian Smedley-Judd one in Kensington, and the robbery a week later in Hemel Hempstead at Mrs Foster's. Next he asked, 'And did you see her break the string? I expect you had to help her pick up the beads. It's always so hard to find them all, isn't it, they roll all over the place.'

She didn't even need to think about it, just shook her head and came straight back with, 'No, her nephew was here. He got them all up for her. I offered to count them to make sure they was all there, but she said they'd already done it.'

'Her nephew? The honourable Cyril Penterman?' Hardy hated the sight of Cyril Penterman, after his brief flirtation with Dottie before Christmas.

'What? No, he's in New York with his new wife. No, the other nephew.'

'Ah,' said Hardy, feigning realisation. 'The short, dark-haired gentleman?'

The maid laughed. 'Er, no! Some detective you are, Inspector. Her nephew Mr James. He's as tall and fair as Mr Cyril, but oh so good-looking, like a Hollywood film star. And with that lovely Scottish accent. He's ever so classy. All the girls are mad about him.'

'Ah, my mistake. I imagine Dr Melville visits often?' He was holding his breath. If the maid corrected him now, his conjectures would be wholly without foundation.

She didn't. Giving just a slight nod of agreement, she continued, 'All the time. In and out several times a week, he is, but then, she's so fond of him, and it does her good to see him, otherwise she'd be quite lonely.'

'I expect he's wonderful company for her. Did he go with her to Mrs Foster's in Hemel Hempstead? A few weeks ago, that was?'

'Yes, I think so. Oh yes, he did, definitely. They drove there together in Mrs Gerard's car, he was doing the driving though, and I remember she told him to make sure he looked it up in the AA book to be sure he knew the way. 'I don't want to miss my dinner,' she said. She makes me laugh the way she goes on at him. Like a music hall act they are, sometimes.'

Hardy smiled and thanked the maid. As he left the house by the servants' door, he felt the thrill of knowing his case was all coming together at last. He had spotted the discrepancy, Dottie had confirmed it, though of course, he hadn't mentioned any names. But now it was clear. The pearl necklace, bracelet and earrings Mrs Gerard had were her only set. Even the very wealthy wouldn't have large quantities of pearl sets of jewellery. So how had she managed to have three identical sets stolen at the parties she attended? By pretending they were broken, of course, and gone for mending.

Muriel Carmichael was sleeping. Her large form was comfortably swaddled up beneath her blankets and an ancient counterpane made by her own fair hands as a young girl learning her craft. It adorned her bed more as a trophy than a practical ward against the cold night air.

Every night when she pulled back the counterpane to get into bed, she felt the old thrill of achievement and victory over her inauspicious beginnings. On the three occasions every year when the counterpane was sent to the Chinese laundry for specialist cleaning, the upset to Muriel Carmichael's routine made it difficult for her to sleep. And the following day she snapped and grumbled at everyone who crossed her path, from Pamphlett her maid to the mannequins at the warehouse. Then, on the return of her counterpane, her usual jovial mood, like her routine, would be restored.

As Muriel Carmichael slept, snoring softly in her warm nest, a long thin stick was inserted between the two panes of the front room window downstairs and the flimsy catch pushed aside. The stick—a broken garden cane—was withdrawn and dropped on the ground and after a short pause the lower window pane was slowly and gently raised.

It squeaked slightly in the frame, but no one seemed to hear the sound. After another short pause, the window was pushed upwards again until a large space, sufficient for a man to pass through, was achieved.

The figure was clad all in black to blend into the shadows and escape the notice of any insomniacs or night workers out and about in that part of London at three o'clock in the morning. He put one foot over the sill, found a secure footing on a long low wooden chest inside, and quickly slipped into the house.

He'd made no sound at all apart from that one small squeak of the window. He felt pleased with himself. He made a good crook—efficient, daring and with not a moment wasted. Turning, he carefully lowered the window again. This time the window made no sound at all.

He crossed the room. He knew the layout of the house, having visited on more than one occasion, and besides, his eyes had quickly adjusted to the low level of light coming in from the street.

From the bottom of the stairs, he could hear the sound of her snoring. Smiling to himself he picked up the vase from the hall stand and carried it up the stairs with him.

At the top, he went over to her door, and looked inside. It was darker here, but after just a few seconds he could see the gleaming white pillow and make out the head covered in tiny prickly curlers, the generous form of her making a large mound under the bedclothes. He knocked the bed frame with his knee, just enough to disturb her, and her snoring hitched and paused. He sprinted silently on rubber-soled feet back to the head of the stairs, lobbed the vase down to smash on the floor below, then smartly stepped back into the shadows as the woman, just in her nightgown, came hurrying from her room, shouting, 'Who's there?' He'd known she wouldn't remain timidly quaking under her blankets until morning.

It was the work of a moment to step forward and plant both hands into her back and shove with all his might. She didn't even turn, had no suspicion he was there. She plummeted downwards in the dark, too surprised even to scream, sleep-addled and unable to fathom what had happened.

She crashed into the hall stand. There was an earsplitting sound of glass, wood and bone splintering and snapping, then silence. But no human sound. She had said nothing since that first, challenging, 'Who's there?'

Upstairs the maid was already getting out of bed and hurrying across the hall. He stepped back behind the door of the guest bedroom, as she snapped on the light and ran down the stairs, screaming at the sight of Mrs Carmichael's prone figure. Pamphlett, her hair plaited in a severe braid down her back, her nightgown concealed beneath a gentleman's burgundy silk smoking jacket of huge proportions, threw herself on her knees beside her mistress's body, uncaring of the pool of blood coming from the wound on the old woman's head. She felt for a pulse, found none, and whispered a short prayer. She dashed the tears from her eyes and went into the back parlour to ring for the priest and then the ambulance, in that order.

While she was gone, he hastened down the stairs, stepped exultantly over the body of the one who had threatened his freedom. He was out of the front room window within a minute and safely down the road and away. Elated, he cheered to himself. It was done.

It was still dark when Hardy arrived at Mrs Carmichael's house. A number of neighbours were either standing in the street, or peering from behind curtains and blinds. Several uniformed constables were in the street in front of the house to make sure no one got too close.

Pamphlett was sitting on a dining chair in the middle of the street, being comforted by a neighbour with her hair in curlers and holding a bottle of gin.

Hardy had already been briefed by Maple in the car on the way there. He felt a deep sense of anger. Dottie would be devastated, he knew, she had been so fond of the old girl. And he himself had been hoping, once his workload had lightened, for a further conversation with Mrs Carmichael about his father. Now that would never happen, and her knowledge and her secrets would go with her to the grave.

But now it seemed unlikely that this was just a simple domestic accident. True, many of the sudden deaths that occurred every day could be attributed to accidents, misadventures or carelessness either in or around the home. But from what Pamphlett had said, he couldn't help but feel it was suggestive...not conclusive, though, just... Was there anything to reinforce the possibility it was not an accident?

He found it almost immediately. Pamphlett had repeated her story of the squeaking front room window, and the unsecured catch. He took a look for himself, and found the catch was indeed pushed back. Using his own handkerchief and Maple's too to avoid obliterating any fingerprints, he lifted the lower sash, and it rose easily enough with only a soft squeak, just as Pamphlett had said. Not enough to wake the street, but loud enough if you were lying in your bed half-asleep. Probably during the daytime hustle and bustle no one would even notice the sound, but in the dead of a fine night the sound would carry. He had no doubt the sound would carry within the house and be heard clearly by people already awake.

Then he spotted the short length of bamboo cane. He carefully picked it up with his handkerchief and passed it to Maple, who held out a large envelope to receive it.

'Get that looked at, Frank. There's just a chance we might get a print off it if he didn't wear gloves, the main part of the stem is so smooth and shiny, it makes an ideal surface. It's the perfect tool to push back the catch on the lower sash—it slides up between the two panes very neatly. When the fingerprint fellow gets here, get him to take a look at the window frame too, would you? Especially on the inside. You never know, we might be lucky.'

Maple hurried away to call the fingerprint department at the Yard. As he went he called over his shoulder, 'When you go inside, watch yourself. They said there's broken glass everywhere inside the door, and it's sharp enough to cut right through your boot-leather.'

Thus cautioned, Hardy went into the house. He'd known, of course, that Mrs Carmichael's body was still there in the hall. And by now he'd seen a number of corpses, but it always gave him an initial jolt when he first saw the victim lying where they had fallen in death. This occasion was no exception. And for the second time in less than a fortnight he was looking down at the dead body of someone he had known in life.

The medical examiner was on the point of leaving. He was putting his things away in his black bag. Just like the one the maid Ellen had mentioned, Hardy reminded himself. He exchanged a 'Good evening' with the doctor, even though it was in fact fast approaching breakfast-time. Maple came in as the doctor went out and tipped his hat.

'The fingerprint chappie will be here in about half an hour. Apparently, it's been a busy night. The other bods have already been called out to other crimes, so we've got to hang on for someone else to cover. He's just having a spot of porridge before leaving home,' Maple told Hardy, adding, 'He's Scottish, so that probably accounts for it. I don't think I could face porridge on an empty stomach myself.'

'A bowl of hot porridge would do me a treat right now,' Hardy said, aware of the early spring pre-dawn chill eating through his coat and jacket and settling in his bones. 'I suppose you're a bacon and eggs bloke.'

'And kidneys. You can't beat fried kidneys to set you up for the day. And Janet does fried bread a treat too.'

'I'm not sure I needed to know that,' Hardy said. 'But I assume she's just fattening you up for an early heart attack and a nice fat police pension.'

'Have a heart, mate. A bloke's got to eat.'

Hardy stood as close to the foot of the stairs as possible, in view of the fact that Mrs Carmichael's own feet were in the way. 'And get something to cover the poor woman,' he snapped, suddenly angry at how carelessly she had been covered. 'Give the woman some dignity.'

Maple hurried away to get the tablecloth from the dining room table, and he draped it over Mrs Carmichael's body.

'What d'you think?' he asked Hardy, waving a hand wide at the scene.

'I think she was pushed,' said Hardy. He turned to go up the stairs. Maple followed. Hardy went into the bedroom, saw the covers pushed back.

'She heard a noise, but I was wrong, it couldn't have been the noise of the window, or she'd have caught him as he came up the stairs. So she heard some other noise, and she got out of bed. She didn't bother with her dressing-gown or her bedroom slippers. So, she was in a hurry, then. She heard something, and she rushed out to see what it was.'

He went back into the hallway, carefully skirting the top of the stairs, not easy in the dim narrow space. The door leading to the attic floor stood open. Next to that was the little guest bedroom. That door also stood wide open. Hardy went in, careful not to touch anything.

'Can you get the fingerprint chappie to look at

this panel of the door, and the one on the other side as well. I think our fellow came in here to wait for Mrs Carmichael to come out, then he'd be perfectly placed to pop out and shove her straight down the stairs. It would take no time at all. So whatever noise she heard him make, he made it deliberately, to lure her out. He came here to kill her, not to rob the house.'

Back on the landing, he stood looking down the stairs. It was all coming together in his head. 'If the man came up from the front room, he'd have gone past the hall stand. That vase—that's how he got her out here. He collected that on his way past, and threw it down the stairs from up here. That's why the top of the vase is right up there by the front door. He threw it with all his strength. There's no possible way she could have fallen down the stairs and smashed into the hall stand in such a way that the top of the vase could break off and end up right by the front door, a good twelve feet away, in front of her. She was murdered.'

His sergeant nodded in understanding; it took someone with Hardy's own special way of looking at things to bring the crime to life. That was what he admired about Hardy, he was an instinctive investigator. 'Now all we need to know is why,' Maple said.

Hardy sighed. That was the difficult bit.

'Oh no, not Mrs Carmichael!' Dottie wailed. 'How terrible! Oh, poor Mrs Carmichael!'

The initial shock over, Dottie subsided, and sat. Silent tears rolled down her cheeks. Their mother also seemed shocked to hear of the death. Flora was vaguely aware of surprise. Surely her mother hadn't known Mrs Carmichael half so well as Dottie, and yet she seemed so very upset.

Hardy had rung the Gascoignes to ask them to break the news for him. 'I'm very sorry to impose, but I need to ask a favour of you. I'm afraid Mrs Carmichael was killed last night, and I need someone to tell Dottie. I can't get away for a while yet, and I don't want her to find out by seeing it in the newspaper, I know how fond of the old lady Dottie is, or rather, was,' he'd said, and George had wholeheartedly agreed with him. He and Flora had gone to the Mandersons' first thing in the morning to break the news.

Now as Flora sat watching her sister and her mother, she decided there was little to choose between them in terms of their response to the news.

'It was supposed to look like an accident,' Flora said. 'At least, according to William it was.'

'Then why is William involved?' Mrs Manderson asked, and it was only later that Flora realised her mother had used his first name. 'Surely he is investigating these robberies?'

'William seems to think there may be a connection as Mrs Carmichael was a guest at some of the homes where there was a robbery. He said he thought she knew something she hadn't told him.'

Tears were still rolling down Dottie's cheeks. 'But what about the warehouse? What about the orders? What about the mannequins and the customers?'

'I've no idea, Dottie, darling,' said Flora.

The maid came to the door and Hardy gave her his hat and coat, and said he had an appointment with her mistress. He had rung her earlier and found that she had no guests for dinner and could see him that evening.

Mrs Gerard looked up from writing a letter. If she was surprised to see him, or even dismayed at all, she quickly concealed it, very graciously inviting him to take a seat, adding, 'Please excuse me for a moment, Inspector, I'll just quickly finish this. You know how hard it is to keep up with one's correspondence, and I'm afraid this letter to my sister is *very* overdue. Please ring the bell for tea, there's a good fellow. Though if you prefer it, you could have something stronger.'

'Tea is fine for me, thank you.' He obliged her, then resumed his seat on the sofa facing her. He wondered what she was writing. He owed his own sister a letter, he remembered. Mrs Gerard was right, it *was* hard to keep up a regular correspondence.

The room was a peaceful one, elegantly decorated in an older style but free of the clutter so fashionable during Mrs Gerard's younger days. A great book, bound in faded rubbed leather, reposed on a table by the window and as the maid came in with the tray and paused to exchange a few words with Mrs Gerard, Hardy got to his feet and went over to take a look at it.

It was of course a Bible. He carefully opened it, and noticed it was even older than he had imagined. The edges of the pages were yellowed, in some places slightly torn or creased, and the gilt was fading here and there where many hands had touched the book to turn the pages over the decades. Inside the front cover, he was glad to see the family tree he had half-expected to find. Books like this old Bible were handed down through the family and each generation added their own names. Quite literally, their names were entered into the Book. He had only just located Mrs Gerard's name when she called to him, somewhat sharply, and asked him to join her. No doubt she was afraid he would damage her family heirloom. He closed it with supreme gentleness.

The tea was poured, the maid left the room, taking Mrs Gerard's sealed letter with her, and the lady of the house turned her attention to Hardy.

'Now then, Inspector, what can I do for you? I know you wouldn't simply pay me a social call.'

Her words reminded him of the visit to the Manderson house a few short weeks earlier. 'I might,' he had said to Dottie then, hoping she would flirt with him. It seemed to him, he had spent the last few months continually hoping she would flirt with him. Coming back to his work, he smiled at Mrs Gerard.

'I'm sorry to trouble again. I just wanted to ask you for a few details, if I may. I shan't take up a lot of your time.'

'Oh, I have plenty of time for chatting with a charming young man!' His hostess gave him a broad smile in reply but her eyes remained wary.

'Well we've had a little bit of a breakthrough with these robberies,' he said. All lies, of course, there'd been no such thing. He actually had nothing but ideas, possibilities, and a great deal of guesswork. 'And that being the case, I need to verify some of the items of jewellery that have been recovered. I also need the details of your insurance claim, just for my own records, you understand. You know how tedious all this paperwork is, and how one needs to dot every I and cross every T. If I could give half the time I devote to paperwork to the investigation, I'm sure I'd be a lot further on.'

She looked uncomfortable. She congratulated him on his success, but her hands clutched at one another in her lap, trembling and restless.

'Oh dear, I'm not sure if I can remember...'

'Just the name of the company would do. I'll set my sergeant onto finding out their address, so never you mind about that.'

She still hesitated. Just for a moment he thought she was going to refuse outright, but in the end, she said, 'Well it's Rainham and Clive, in Holborn. But I haven't actually made a claim, as I was waiting until the crime was solved and my property recovered.'

Hardy poured himself a second cup of tea, and quirked an eyebrow at her, holding the pot above her cup. She shook her head.

'Oh no, Inspector, not for me.'

He set the pot down, and with a relaxed, friendly smile, he said, 'I wish all the witnesses had as much faith in the police as you have, Mrs Gerard. I don't mind telling you, some people have been very difficult, and they constantly telephone me asking for a report. It takes up so much time.'

They chatted about the weather, and by the time he took his leave, Mrs Gerard was much more relaxed. So much the better, he thought, if she was off her guard.

At the corner of the street, he hailed a cab and got it to take him back to the police station.

*

Chapter Eighteen

Maple was halfway through a sausage roll of gigantic proportions. His feet were on the desk, and on seeing Hardy suddenly appear in the doorway, Maple spluttered and almost fell on the floor.

'Bill, you blighter, you might warn a bloke!'

Hardy grinned. 'When you've finished your office picnic, I want you to contact an insurance company for me. It's Rainham and Clive of Holborn. Find out what items Mrs Gerard has insured with them, when, and for how much. Ask if she's made any claims at all.' He turned to go to his own office, then paused in the doorway. 'Oh, and find out if they insure any of the other guests at any of the robberies. Not that I'm expecting they do, it would be too much to hope for.'

'They'll be gone home hours ago. Like normal people do,' Maple protested.

'Use your initiative, then!' Hardy called over his

shoulder. Maple waited until he could be sure his boss was out of range then said several choice things about what Hardy could do with his initiative.

In his office, Hardy leaned against his desk and looked at the board again. The room was almost in darkness, the light coming through the frosted glass of the grating near the ceiling showed that outside the sky was almost black.

He stayed there, filled with a quiet sense of elation. Things were coming together.

He reached into his pocket and pulled out his wallet. Inside there was the scrap of fabric pressed flat between two pound notes. He took it out and lay it on his desk. Then crossed the room to put on the light.

Blinking in the sudden brilliance, he sat down again to stare at the tiny piece of cloth and to think about what Dottie had told him. It filled his mind with a new range of possibilities. And the things he already knew, coupled with those new possibilities began to create in his mind a complete and complex picture. He put the scrap away again, then crossed the room and put out the light. He was on the point of leaving but turned to sit back down at his desk in the darkness. There was no one waiting for him at home.

An hour later, Maple found him still sitting there at his desk, completely engulfed in darkness.

'Thought you'd gone home,' was the sergeant's comment. Silence greeted his words. 'You asleep?' he asked, louder this time.

'I know what happened,' Hardy said softly. 'I know who, almost. And I know why, more or less. I even know how. Partly. I just need to find the evidence.'

Maple leaned against the frame of the door and let out a long low whistle. 'So you've solved the case, then? Or—you know—you're getting there. Want to tell me about it?'

'It's a bit tentative, but it's the only way everything makes sense.'

'Well, life doesn't usually make sense. I mean, look what's happening in Europe. So if you've got it even half worked out, that's pretty good. Want to tell me about it?' he added, for the second time. There was a long silence.

'Bill?'

Silence again. If he didn't know otherwise, Maple could have sworn he was addressing an empty room.

'Bill!' he said again, sharply.

'Hmm?'

'Want to tell me about it?'

'Oh. No. I just want to...'

'In that case, I'll get off. I'm taking Janet to the pictures. To see that *Desert* thing you disliked so much.'

'Hmm.'

There was a long pause. Then from the doorway, Maple said, 'Good night, Frank, enjoy your evening, Frank. Give my regards to Janet, Frank.' After a moment's pause he added, 'I've left my notes on that insurance query on my desk. It's not much help, just the one pearl necklace and matching earrings and brooch on their register, as well as a few other small bits and pieces. And she hasn't even put in a claim for the pearls yet. And since the robbery it's been, what? Five weeks?'

Thirty seconds later, Hardy looked up from his desk. 'Hmm?'

The following morning, the director of the London Metropolitan Museum was not a happy man, and Hardy hadn't even asked him anything yet, apart from explaining the reason for his visit.

The director, a Mr Falke, crossed his office to open the door and speak to the efficient-looking young woman typing at the desk in the little outer room. In heavily accented but very correct English he said, 'Please bring us refreshments, Miss Walters.' She made a reply, though Hardy couldn't make out what she said.

The small errand had given Mr Falke both thinking time and the chance to compose himself. When he returned to sit behind his desk, he had quite obviously come to a decision.

'May I speak frankly, Inspector?'

Hardy nodded. 'Please do, Mr Falke.'

'Dr Melville was offered his position by my predecessor, who resigned due to ill health at the start of this year. I have serious concerns about the veracity of Dr Melville's qualifications and experience. Not that I have any fault to find with his work, you understand; that has been above reproach. And certainly, his knowledge is extensive. In addition, his exhibitions have brought in a steady stream of visitors to the museum.'

The door opened, and the secretary came in with the tray, which Mr Falke leapt up gallantly to take from her. If his manners were perfectly correct, the smile 'secretly' exchanged between the two of them was anything but, Hardy thought. Inwardly he smiled and shook his head at the romantic folly of the human race. Outwardly he preserved an impassive policeman's stare.

'And yet you're not satisfied?' Hardy prompted once the door had closed once again and the director had returned to his seat.

Mr Falke leaned his elbows on the desk and stretched his long neck forward to gaze at Hardy beseechingly. 'I just don't know what to do. Rumours have reached me of dishonest dealings and I've noticed for myself how often Melville is absent during work hours. Oh, he always has the reasons, I must have just missed him, he had to run to some department or other on an urgent matter, or he had to meet with a benefactor who wishes to make a donation to the museum. But there is something wrong here. Not financially, I don't mean that. I am talking of artefacts, potential exhibits. Treasures, if you will.'

'I understand.'

'Do you take milk or lemon in your tea, Inspector?'

'Milk, please.'

'A deplorable English habit, but one which I'm afraid I have grown to enjoy.'

'Where are you from originally, Mr Falke? If you don't mind me asking.'

'Not at all. I am from Austria. I came here originally to study history at Oxford, that was in 1913. I met my lovely wife there, and so I stayed. Sadly, she passed away two years ago. But yes, I stayed on after my degrees. All through the last war.'

'That must have been difficult for you.'

'It was difficult for everyone, Inspector. No doubt you are too young to remember. But mark my words, it will happen again.'

'So you are not an admirer of the new German Chancellor?'

'Hmm. That little man. Inspector, I tell you now, he is a warmonger and a villain. And if I were still in my native land, I would doubtless be shot just for saying so. I'm very much afraid there will soon be another 'war to end all wars'. Until we humans can change fundamentally, we will always be at war.'

It was a pessimistic view, but one that coincided very closely with Hardy's own. 'Wars and rumours of war,' he said softly. The director nodded sadly.

'Yes, exactly.'

'There are certainly a lot of changes going on over there.'

'Yes, and not for the better. This new camp now, that is most definitely not a good thing, and there will doubtless be more to follow. I believe Herr Hitler wishes to send his piggies to market.'

Hardy didn't understand. Possibly his confusion showed in his face, because Falke said in a hushed voice, 'It is just my little joke, Inspector. And not a very good one either. Because you see, we Jews do not eat the pork sausages, and this camp that Herr Hitler has created, it is really just a slaughterhouse. Just you wait and see.'

He handed Hardy his tea. Silence stole over the room. Hardy was thinking about what the man had said, and comparing it to what he had read in the newspapers. He had a sense of unease in the pit of his stomach. Could there really be another European war? Surely not. And yet...

They might have been two friends talking politics and philosophy in any gentleman's club. Hardy would have liked to stay longer, to discuss other topics. There was something about Mr Falke that reminded him of his tutors at Oxford, and he welcomed the half-forgotten stimulus to his intellect.

Mr Falke cleared his throat and brought Hardy back to the present. 'The good Dr Melville, now. I have grave doubts that he is genuinely a doctor of any kind. I have written to Edinburgh university to check, but I have not yet had their reply.'

'Surely he gave references?'

'Indeed. But I find that one reference was from Melville's own aunt.'

Hardy sat forward. 'Would that be a Mrs Gerard, by any chance?'

If Mr Falke was surprised, he didn't bother to show it, but merely nodded. 'It would. And the other referee, who spoke so highly of Dr Melville's curation of his private collection, is in fact a family friend. And so you see...'

'A Mr Smedley-Judd, perhaps?'

Mr Falke's smile was a bitter one. 'The fact that you know their names seems to confirm my worst fears.'

'I'm afraid that seems rather likely, Mr Falke.'

The secretary tapped and put her head round the door. 'Inspector? I've had a call from the police station asking for you to go back as soon as possible. A Sergeant Maple says to tell you 'we've got Daphne's bag', I do hope that makes sense?'

'That makes perfect sense, yes, thank you very much.'

Hardy left a few minutes later, and he had a lot to think about. Mr Falke, shaking Hardy's hand, promised to let him know what he heard from Edinburgh university. But no news could compare to the excitement he felt knowing that Daphne Medhurst's handbag had been found.

Back at the police station, Hardy looked at the handbag. He quickly reread the statement from the policeman who'd found it concealed by dustbins behind a shop, not fifty yards from the alleyway where Daphne Medhurst had been killed.

His initial annoyance and sense of failure that his men had not found the bag sooner was somewhat ameliorated by the fact that the shopkeeper had been having some work done the day Daphne's body had been discovered, and there had been workmen, tools and materials all over the yard behind the shop that day, making access impossible, although the night before, at the time of the crime, it had been only too accessible.

So that explained that. They hadn't been incompetent, merely unlucky. Relieved, Hardy smiled at the little diagram the policeman had provided, copied from the original one in his notebook. It showed just where all the contents of the bag had been found scattered, and their position in relation to the bag itself. A lipstick and powder compact were shown as being a foot or so to the north, a small diary-address book to the south. On the north-west side, there had been a small amount of loose change, whilst the south-west was the site of the empty purse, and a handkerchief, still bearing the outline of Daphne Medhurst's painted mouth.

The illustration included a partial footprint, which was unfortunately plain and ordinary, with no distinguishing characteristics. Still, Hardy gave the young man ten out of ten for effort, and felt certain it wouldn't be long before the bright youngster was in plain clothes.

The lining of the bag had been ripped out, shredded into tatters of frayed artificial silk of a rather bright pink. The bag was a small one, for evening use, decorated with probably hundreds of tiny black beads, and with a flimsy narrow chain for a handle. Not an expensive item, but Hardy knew how important bags were to women. This one had clearly been thoroughly searched for something. And Hardy had a good idea what that something might be.

Hardy was more than usually nervous at the prospect of interviewing the man he had been ordered to detain after delivering his latest report to his superiors. He had requested, and been denied, time to obtain further information and evidence. So here they were. Hardy pulled out the chair and sat down. Ian Smedley-Judd had, of course, refused to speak without his solicitor being present. They had therefore been obliged to wait. The solicitor, seated beside his client, was an expensive one, and not the sort to tolerate young police officers with little experience. For that reason, Superintendent Edward Williams sat beside Hardy. And even though the man had many more years' experience than either Hardy himself or Sergeant Maple, it had been a long time since he had interviewed a suspect, and Hardy would have felt ten times more confident with his sergeant by his side.

He tidied his papers and cleared his throat. 'Mr Smedley-Judd, it seems clear from my enquiries that you are deeply involved in the perpetration of these dinner-time robberies that have been taking place.' He knew he didn't sound very confident, or very sure of his facts, but he had been planning on elaborating on his opening sentence. A glance up and he saw that Smedley-Judd was staring at him, or more correctly right through him, looking rather bored. Neither Smedley-Judd nor his solicitor spoke.

But the superintendent, at this point, leaned towards Hardy and said, rather too loudly for a whisper, 'You'd better leave this to me, son. I've got a bit more experience than you. I'll soon break the blighter. He'll be singing in no time, if he knows what's good for him.'

It was an unfortunate comment, as not only did it cause the solicitor to lodge a formal complaint, but it also heralded the start of a long and frustrating three-hour stint of the police asking questions which Smedley-Judd and his solicitor steadfastly refused to answer.

At length, just as it was growing dark outside, the prisoner was returned to his cell and his solicitor went with him for a further discussion. The superintendent and Hardy retired to Hardy's office for a very welcome cup of tea and a conference.

Hardy didn't feel able to suggest that his superior should stand down and allow Sergeant Maple to take his place in the interview room, yet at the same time he couldn't see any other way to break through the prisoner's reserve. He stared glumly into his tea as Williams propounded one idea after another for getting 'the Toff to crack'. Privately Hardy thought the superintendent had seen a few too many detective thrillers at the pictures. That, or possibly not enough. Whatever the reason, the man clearly was not good at reaching people.

They had Smedley-Judd's belongings in a large envelope on the desk in front of them. Automatically Hardy began to check through the contents. There was a soft metallic sound and thinking there were coins in the bottom of the envelope, he shook out the rest of the items onto his desk blotter. When he saw what was there, he smiled and said, 'Sir, I need a warrant to search Mr Smedley-Judd's art collection room.'

'His...? I thought you had already...?'

'Er, no, sir. His wife said she had no key for the room, and I wasn't able to arrange a meeting with Mr Smedley-Judd. Every time I called I was told he was out.'

'But what about when you picked him up? Why on earth didn't you go to the house with a warrant at the time?'

Hardy hesitated. But then, reminding himself it wasn't his fault, he said, 'We searched the rest of the house, but Mr Smedley-Judd said he'd lost the key for that room. The chief superintendant refused a warrant, saying we'd get everything we needed from Mr Smedley-Judd himself, or if not, I could apply for one later.'

'Ah.'

'I'm sure it could yield something useful,' said Hardy, cautiously but persistent.

'Very well, I'll go and deal with that. Pop down and make sure the so-and-so gets his hot meal, will you. I don't want him saying he was mistreated on top of everything else. Then get over to the house. I presume you'll need some men.'

'Just Sergeant Maple, sir.'

'Really?' The superintendent gave him a long, doubtful look, then nodded. 'Very well. I just hope to God you find something.'

'Me too, sir.' Hardy said. He went to give instructions to the officer in charge of the cells. Not that it was necessary, he knew he could rely on the prisoner being properly cared for. But on the off-chance that the superintendent might ask if he had done so, he wanted to be able to say quite truthfully that he had.

Hardy rounded up Maple and they took a police car to the Smedley-Judd residence in Kensington.

Mrs Smedley-Judd was at home, Morris informed them, and about to sit down to dinner. Hardy was worried she might have her nephew with her, but when he asked, Morris said she was dining alone. The butler's manner was rather less friendly than it had been the last time Hardy spoke with him.

Mrs Smedley-Judd was none too happy at being told they planned to search her husband's art collection room, and again said she had no key to give them access, and that it was absolutely out of the question that they should break the door down.

'No need for that,' Hardy said, and held up the key that had been in her husband's personal belongings. She took one look then turned and walked away.

The walls of the collection room were bare, as were the table tops, the cabinets and the shelves. The collection—all the fine religious treasures Ian Smedley-Judd had so cherished—were gone. The room stood, neat and bare, like an empty guest room, awaiting the next arrival.

The two men stood in the doorway and stared in dismay. Maple swore loudly and furiously, whilst Hardy leaned back against the doorframe, his eyes closed.

'Well, now I know why I never managed to catch him at home,' he said.

'Getting shot of the loot.'

'Exactly.'

Maple employed a number of other colourful phrases to demonstrate his opinion of Mr Smedley-Judd. Then said, suddenly inspired, 'His wife might know.'

'I'm sure she does,' Hardy responded, 'But she'll never tell us. I think we'll be very lucky if we find anything of her husband's collection. He knew we'd be coming, and he made preparations. Just like his ancestors hundreds of years ago.'

With a heavy heart he turned to leave the room. A thought made him glance back at the little side-table just inside the door. Bending, he saw something that finally gave him cause to smile.

'Evidence envelope, please, Frank.'

Maple puzzled, handed one over, and watched in silent curiosity as Hardy picked up a tiny scrap of fluff off the carpet, and with as much care as if it had been a sacred relic, placed it inside the envelope which was then sealed, labelled and dated.

'We've got him,' he said. Maple looked sceptical.

*

Chapter Nineteen

The next morning, he had no sooner sat down at his desk than his phone rang. 'Hardy speaking.'

'Front desk sir, I just wanted to let you know that we've had a call from the butler of a Mrs Gerard. Says you know him. Chap called Aitchison? Apparently, they've just found Mrs Gerard dead.'

'What?' Hardy was on his feet. 'Phone him back, tell him I'm on my way.'

'Yes sir.'

'Sergeant!' Hardy yelled as he reached the hallway.

Maple came running, grabbing his coat.

'Mrs Gerard is dead,' Hardy said.

Maple swore. 'Is that the end of our case, then?'

'I have no idea. I hope to God not.'

When they arrived at the house, the butler was already standing in the open doorway, watching the street for them. He was pale but composed. As he showed them into the drawing room he told Hardy, 'I've called the doctor though I'm sure he can't do anything, and Mrs Gerard's priest is already here, he's in the kitchen having a cup of tea. Sir, when you've finished here, I'd like a word, if I may. It's quite important.'

'Of course.' Already Hardy was looking about him, taking in the scene. The room was largely the same as when he had last been there, although the curtains were still closed and the lights were on. The fire had been lit the night before but was now just a heap of cold ash. He was glad nothing had been touched. But his immediate instinct as he took in the scene was that this was a suicide.

Mrs Gerard was stretched out on a sofa. Her shoes sat neatly side by side on the carpet beside her. A pillow propped the lady's head, a light, crocheted coverlet draped her body from feet to chin. On the small side-table was an empty bottle. The label indicated that it had contained sleeping pills though of course he had no idea how many had actually been in it. Beside the bottle was a decanter of water and a glass tumbler. The lady's spectacles sat neatly folded on the side-table, placed on the top of an envelope. Even from his place by the door, he could read the address on the envelope in Mrs Gerard's large, clear hand. 'Inspector Hardy.'

Her eyes were closed. Her hair and face were—as always—immaculate, and her hands were folded on her breast, the string of her rosary caught between her fingers. On her lap lay the massive family Bible he had admired. It lay open at the page showing the Gerard family tree.

For form's sake, though it seemed a foregone conclusion, Hardy felt for a pulse. The wrist was chilled and heavy to his touch. There was no sign of life.

From the doorway, next to the large shape of Sergeant Maple, Aitchison gnawed his knuckle, and watched anxiously. As Hardy stepped away, Aitchison called in a hushed voice, 'I'm not wrong, am I? She *is*...?'

'Oh yes, I'm afraid she is dead.' Hardy looked around. He said to Maple, 'Call the fingerprint chappie, just get him to take a look at the bottle and the glass. I don't think for a minute there's any need, but we'd best cover ourselves. I doubt he'll need to do anything else in the room. Then get the bottle, the glass and the Bible wrapped and taken back to the station. Tell them to be careful with that Bible, it's a family heirloom. Send for Dr Garrett, too. I'm going to speak with the staff.'

'Shall I send that letter too, or do you want to keep it with you?'

'I'll keep it with me.' Hardy turned to Aitchison. 'Let's go to the kitchen. I presume everyone's there?'

'In the staff sitting room, sir, just off the kitchen.'

'Staff sitting room, eh? Very nice.'

'She was a wonderful lady sir, a pleasure to work for. An absolute pleasure, one of a kind, I can tell you.' Aitchison's composure threatened to falter. Hardy patted him on the shoulder.

'Come on. Let's go and have a cup of tea.'

On his return to his office late that afternoon, Hardy finally found time to read the letter attentively. He'd glanced through it at the house, and seen her statement at the beginning that she intended to take her own life. He saw too the big flourish of a signature at the end, and taken with everything else, was satisfied everything was as it seemed. Mrs Gerard had committed suicide. Not that she saw it in quite those terms. Certainly she didn't feel she would be committing a sin. The priest had confirmed as much, saying she was adamant her death would have a purpose.

Now, all the interviews at her house had been completed and it was clear beyond doubt that there were no suspicious circumstances. Maple had stayed behind to finish off assisted by a couple of constables.

Hardy took out the letter he had so carefully folded and placed in his wallet. As he did so, the tiny scrap of fabric fluttered in the air to fall and lay on the carpet. He stooped to pick it up, thinking he still didn't know quite why it was so significant.

Opening the envelope, he pulled out the foolscap sheet of paper, closely written on both sides in the same handwriting as the envelope, as the notes in the Bible, that Aitchison had confirmed was Mrs Gerard's own hand.

Mrs Gerard wrote:

'I am not insane. Some may think one has to be insane to take one's own life, or else very weak, but I say to them, sometimes it is saner and more courageous to see one's future, unendingly forlorn and bleak in a prison cell, and to make an alternative choice. I see myself as a martyr, like so many of my ancestors, giving up my life voluntarily in the hope that something useful may come of it.

'I would like to explain what has been going on. It's a little complicated, but it's vital that you, my charming Inspector Hardy, understand why I, and my associates, did what we did. Yes, it was in part for mere material gain—I'm by no means as financially secure as you probably imagine. And Ian and Gareth, my old friends, go through money like it was water running through their hands.

'But there was another reason, far more important, to me at least.'

Hardy paused, turned to look around the room, with a strange sense of coming out of a dream. He saw his desk and chair and went to sit down to read the rest of the letter in comfort.

'In 1305, my ancestors, and a few other wealthy landowners, commissioned the creation of a new set of vestments for the little church that opened up on our estate. We were minor royalty then, and aspired to greater status in King Edward's realm. A marriage was arranged between the eldest son of the Gerard family and a princess from Navarre. So the vestments were in part to honour the coming princess, and to impress her family with our piety and wealth.

'By the time Henry VIII betrayed our Faith, the vestments were already very old and quite fragile. In 1605, three hundred years after the original commissioning of the vestments and the marriage of that young couple, James I was relentlessly pursuing and destroying Catholic churches, families and estates. My ancestors, the Gerards, and three of their closest Catholic connections: The Garnetts, from one of whose daughters the Smedley-Judds are proudly descended; the Moyers in Hertfordshire, another proud old family, and a family by the name of Radleigh, once Catholic but they recanted to save their worthless hides five hundred years ago, though the new Bishop is a sympathiser and closet Papist. These families divided the most precious vestment, the Gerard Chasuble, as it was then known, into five pieces, in the fervent hope that one piece at least, but God willing, all five, would survive the turbulent times and see the restoration of the Faith. The plan was to protect the parts at all costs, until such a time as they could be sewn back together and take their place once more in the celebration of the true rites and ceremonies of the Church.

'No doubt at this point you are shaking your head. No doubt you think, why all this fuss for a bit of old cloth. I could ask you why young men in their thousands, even tens of thousands, died for the sake of a flag—another bit of old cloth—in the Great War. It is the same principle. The cloth is a symbol of something far, far greater than oneself. In the case of the Gerard Chasuble, my ancestor, Lord Hugh Gerard referred to it as 'The Mantle of God'. For him, it was more valuable than his own life.

'I may say, Inspector, that I have been terribly frustrated by that little scrap you have. I can only guess where you obtained it, and if you hadn't given it to lovely little Dottie, I would never have known that someone close to me socially or geographically was the bearer of the fifth piece. You have no idea how I was at once tortured by not knowing exactly where it was, yet exultant at knowing it had survived after all these years. How wonderful!'

The rest of the letter went on to explain how she, and James Melville, whose real name was Jimmy McKay, and who was the illegitimate son of her sister, had met up with Mrs Gerard's acquaintances the Smedley-Judds, and hatched a plot. With the aid of two former cell-mates of Melville's, one of whom was Cedric Meyer, along with three men recruited by Gareth Smedley-Judd, they had perpetrated the robberies to obtain all the Catholic relics they could, with special emphasis on searching for the fifth piece of the chasuble, the right sleeve, which still eluded them. Mrs Gerard was very vexed over the location of this last piece of the mantle. The second piece had been carefully preserved in Ian Smedley-Judd's collection, the Moyer family had hidden the third piece carefully away, and the fourth piece, one of the sleeves, had been discovered in a drawer in Bishop Radleigh's home, but was still in Dr Melville's possession. The members of the gang had taken it in turns to participate in the robberies, imagining it would make the cases harder to solve if they were not always carried out by the same people. They always had someone at the party who would disappear to the W.C. at the crucial moment and let the robbers into the house, tipping them off regarding the number of staff and their whereabouts. It was a system that had worked very well for them for a time.

Mrs Gerard had closed the letter with, 'That is everything I wanted to tell you. I have taken the pills, and already, I feel so drowsy. I am grateful that I will sleep my way into the next world, and I fully believe I will receive my crown for a race well run. Sincerest regards, Millicent Gerard.'

Hardy read through the letter four times, made notes regarding the criminal activities mentioned, then sat for a time deep in thought.

'It's not Duck,' announced Maple, bursting in to disturb his thoughts an hour later. 'The tattoo. Remember the witness said it looked like it said duck? But it's not. Leastways, not according to this. I think you're going to be pleased when I tell you what just came through in a telegram from Scotland.'

Hardy set down his pen and leaned back in his chair. He couldn't imagine what Maple was going to tell him, but he could tell from his expression that it was good.

'Well?'

'It's Duke.'

Hardy was still none the wiser. Maple perched on the end of the desk and handed Hardy the telegram. Hardy looked at it and let out a long, low whistle.

'I never would have guessed that in a million years.'

'I know! Don't that beat all! Duke Street prison in Glasgow. Well, someone did say they thought it could be a prison tattoo, so hey presto! I've sent them a further request for information about the conviction, the dates and so forth. I told them it's urgent so shouldn't be too long, I hope. But they says it's quite common for the convicts to do their tattoos themselves, usually on their arm or shoulder, in that blue ink like the sailors use. It starts out that quite bright blue but usually fades to a horrid kind of messy navy-blue over time. Anyway. So now we know.'

'Right,' Hardy said, unable to disguise his sense of triumph, 'We've got him! We're going to the London Metropolitan Museum.'

'Day trip or work?'

'Work, of course. I'm going to make your day.'

'Ooh, are we arresting that idiot Melville?'

'We are,' Hardy confirmed with a grin.

The London Metropolitan Museum had closed by the time they arrived. But Maple pounded on the door until the night-watchman, pulling out a cosh, came to threaten them with the police. At that point Hardy pulled out his warrant card and the night-watchman, red-faced, let them in.

The defiance went out of James Melville as soon as he looked up and saw them at his door. In Melville's office, Hardy pulled out a drawer at random, and was pleasantly surprised by what he found there. Pulling out his ever-useful handkerchief, he took careful hold of the item and held it up.

Melville glanced at the object then turned away, briefly closing his eyes and giving a small involuntary shake of the head.

'I assume this is not yours?' Hardy asked. Melville said nothing, trying to back away, but

Maple was there, solid and blocking the whole of the doorway. 'I think you probably intended to dispose of it, and then you forgot, didn't you?' Hardy continued with an exaggerated sigh. 'Out of sight, out of mind, don't they say? I'm the same. Always forget the little details.'

He opened the catch, still with the handkerchief wrapped around his hand, fumbling with it and wondering how women managed to open and shut their bags with one hand and without even looking. He got it open, and peered inside.

The first thing he saw was her purse. The second thing he saw was his own handkerchief, given to her months ago, and now laundered and pressed and lying at the bottom of the bag. A soft warmth stole over him. He looked at Maple.

'Arrest him for the mugging of Miss Dorothy Manderson. There may be further charges relating to his involvement in armed robbery and also three charges of murder.'

'Now wait a minute...!' Melville shouted, but was marched away, protesting all the while. Maple had Melville by the arm and was stating the caution. But Hardy didn't hear. He turned his attention back to the bag.

The lining had been ripped out, just as it had in Daphne Medhurst's handbag. The only difference here was that Dottie was—mercifully—still alive. The various items were also still all there inside the bag.

In the drawer there were two further items of interest. One was a tiny pot of make-up. The other was a large piece of undyed silk wrapped around something soft.

As soon as he began to unwrap the silk folds, he knew what it contained. The hair stood up on the back of his neck, and he could feel goosebumps prickling his forearms. With the utmost care he spread it out on Melville's desk. He didn't realise he was holding his breath.

It was a large square of fabric—actually not quite square—there was a slight curve to one side, and neat stitching along that length told Hardy that it was, in fact, a hem. He rotated the fabric, and now he could make sense of the picture. Two figures knelt in prayer beside a tree. At the base of the tree and running in front of the figures, was a narrow river, worked in tiny pearls which glistened in the electric light. The fruits on the tree were undoubtedly rubies. The hair was stitched with gold thread, and the stitching went first in one direction, then in another, creating the effect of waves of hair. Rubies and emeralds adorned the garments, whilst sapphires made their eyes. And beside the tree, curling suggestively around the gold-worked trunk, was the dark form of a snake, its tongue forked menacingly and even after all these hundreds of years, still glittering with silver strands.

The mantle of God.

Hardy felt a strange and almost overwhelming emotion wash over him. He felt awestruck, yes, by the resilience of the delicate and very fine workmanship, and that this section of the garment had survived. But through all of that, was his sudden desire to protect the mantle at all costs. Even if it cost him his life. It wasn't just a bit of old cloth, it was—a symbol. He just wasn't quite sure what it represented to him.

Most of the surface of what Dottie had told him was probably velvet had gone long ago. In several places the fabric was worn right through to the base warp, threadbare. Yet here and there a glorious emerald green shone out, vibrant and still alive, more than six hundred years after it was first commissioned and created.

With a sigh, Hardy wrapped it up again with the greatest care. Debating what to do with it next, and recalling the heavy rain outside, he pressed it as carefully as he could into Dottie's handbag, and with that under his arm, he took a last look around the room, and then left, snapping off the light and closing the door on James Melville's little empire.

'Where's the last piece of the mantle?' was Hardy's question, and it was clear from the look on Melville's face that it was an unexpected one.

Melville had intended to remain silent, but ignoring his solicitor, he leaned forward, his elbows on the table. The tattoo, no longer covered with make-up, was clearly visible, and it did indeed say 'Duke St.' Hardy now knew that Dr James Melville, really just plain Jimmy McKay, had spent two years incarcerated for theft, at Duke Street prison in Glasgow.

Melville said, 'What do you know about the mantle?'

'Why don't you tell me about it? I'm sure you'd welcome the chance to show us what you know, *Dr Melville*.'

'I could have been a doctor. I've done enough research, all meticulously conducted within the ethical and procedural guidelines of the universities of both Oxford and Edinburgh. But it was my background, you see. It tells against me. Oh, it's all perfectly acceptable on my mother's side—but my father, oh dear me no. A simple dockyard worker, hers for one glorious weekend, leaving her with me as a little memento, before returning to his wife. And then of course, there's my little falling out with the law in my younger days. So no, all in all, not quite the right kind of person to be awarded a professorship, in spite of my academic achievements.'

'No one could doubt either your knowledge or your commitment to your studies,' Hardy said. 'Even Mr Falke said he had nothing to fault in your professional ability.'

'That weasel!' Melville snarled. 'Always sniffing around, trying to find out what I was up to. What research has he ever carried out, that's what I'd like to know!' He realised he was getting too loud, for he halted abruptly and took a sip from his glass of water before continuing in a quieter voice. 'Aye, well, they were happy times, this last couple of years at the museum. I suppose I knew it wouldn't last forever.'

'And the mantle?' Hardy repeated gently.

'Well, my aunt Mrs Gerard has one piece, the top back section. And Ian Smedley-Judd has another, the left front. I have the third piece no doubt you've found it, and some people in Hertfordshire have another. We're not sure where the fifth piece is, we've looked everywhere we could think of.'

'And when you say you've looked everywhere, you mean you've searched the houses where the robberies that *you* were involved in, took place?'

Melville gave Hardy a knowing look. Hardy realised he should have been more subtle. Why would Melville compromise himself at this stage? Hardy realised he should have led around to the robberies more carefully, he might have got more out of Melville if he had. But there was one piece of information he had that Melville didn't know. He leaned forward to say, with genuine sympathy, 'I'm sorry to have to inform you that your aunt Mrs Gerard took her own life last night. She was found dead this morning by her butler, Mr Aitchison.'

For a moment no one spoke, nothing moved. Time seemed to stand still as Melville absorbed this information. Colour drained slowly from his face. In a voice scarcely more than a whisper he said, 'She's dead?'

Hardy nodded. 'I'm very sorry,' he said. 'I wouldn't make a thing like that up. I can allow your solicitor to take some time to confirm it for you if you wish.'

'How?'

'Sleeping pills.'

Melville heaved a long slow sigh, and stared at his hands folded on the table in front of him. After another moment he said, more to himself than anyone else, 'Auntie Millie is dead.'

'I'm afraid she left a very full account before she died,' Hardy felt almost guilty at giving him this information, yet he wasn't manipulating Melville: it was the truth, after all, and Melville had a right to know. He saw from his expression that Melville knew exactly what the implication of that information was. He sat up straight in the chair and Hardy knew he was about to hear Melville's confession.

The solicitor, clearly sensing the shift in the room, leaned forward to whisper something to Melville, who shook his head impatiently. Melville responded by answering Hardy's previous question.

'I admit I have searched all those houses where the robberies took place, and a few others besides. I admit I was involved in the robberies. And I also admit I attacked Miss Manderson, which I deeply regret. I am very glad she suffered no serious injury. Other than that, I have never hurt anyone.'

'You held people at gunpoint. Elderly people, pregnant women, young people. You held *Dottie* at gunpoint.'

'True.' Melville bit his lip. 'I would never have hurt her. Or anyone else.'

'You would never have hurt her? You mugged her in the street and left her lying on the pavement! And what about Daphne Medhurst?'

'That wasn't me. It was that ass Smedley-Judd.'

'Which one?'

'The youngster, Gareth. The stupid one.'

'And Muriel Carmichael? What about the young police constable shot at the Mandersons' house? He was only twenty-one, he had his whole life ahead of him.'

Melville was clearly shaken. But his response was short. 'The same.'

The solicitor, a look of alarm on his face, hurriedly interposed. 'I'd like some time in private with my client. I'm afraid I really must insist.'

Melville gave him a scornful glance. 'I'm going to

tell them everything. What's the point now of keeping anything back? I just need you to keep me from the gallows. I didn't kill anyone, or even hurt them.'

Maple produced his ink bottle and pen, and laid the statement form on the desk in front of him, then Dr James Melville began his confession. It was fast approaching ten o'clock in the morning. They worked all through lunch and tea. At last by six o'clock, and at length, with every I dotted and every T crossed, Hardy felt he could finally leave.

*

Chapter Twenty

There were not many mourners at the graveside as Daphne Medhurst was laid to rest. Her father was there, of course, looking shrunken and aged, his expression one not of grief but of confusion, as if he couldn't understand how his daughter came to be lying under the ground in a pine box.

His sister had travelled up from Southsea, and she was there only to support her brother, Hardy quickly determined. Her mouth was set in a line, her jaw tense, and at every stage her hand was on the Major's arm, guiding and consoling. The police were represented by Hardy and Maple, the two of them together forming a substantial percentage of the total number of mourners, as the only others in attendance besides the vicar were Mr and Mrs Manderson, with Dottie and Flora.

It was a miserable service. A fine spring morning, the sun shone, the sky was blue, daffodils bobbed vivid heads here and there. Halfway through the final prayer, a squirrel scampered over to look at what was going on and sat observing them for several minutes. If the weather was anything to go by, it should have been an occasion for happiness.

They struggled through a stretched-thin version of *Abide With Me*, and then it was all mercifully over. Miss Medhurst led her brother away to a waiting taxi. She'd already thanked everyone for coming before the service started, and had made it clear that they would not be invited to return to the Major's house for refreshments afterwards.

'He's not at all well,' she confided to Hardy. 'I'm going to take him back with me right away. We'll get someone to sort out everything at the house later. I just need to get him away.'

The Major, as biddable as a child, looked vaguely round then at a soft word from her, got into the taxi and they drove away.

Hardy felt the weight of Daphne's death hanging about his shoulders.

Maple murmured something about getting off, and Hardy nodded. In another cemetery across the city, another service was about to take place, this time for Constable Daniel Paige, only twenty-one years of age and killed in the line of duty. The commissioner and the assistant commissioner had promised to attend and offer the Met's sympathies to the young man's mother and father. There were already plans for a special honour to be posthumously awarded.

'Bill,' Flora's voice cut into his reverie, and he felt a slight surprise at her addressing him so informally. Not that he minded at all. 'Will you come back to our house for coffee and sandwiches? You can't go straight back to work without any lunch.'

He was so tempted to accept. His stomach growled, though mercifully not loudly enough for anyone else to hear. Dottie was watching him, and he oh-so-nearly accepted Flora's offer. But he had Ian Smedley-Judd in a holding cell. He needed to get back. He made his apologies and turned away before Dottie's smile and her lovely eyes persuaded him to follow her to the ends of the earth.

Dottie watched him go with something approaching rage. She couldn't make him out, as she told her sister at the first available opportunity.

'One minute he's my best friend, holding my hand and telling me things about the investigation and looking as though he wanted to kiss me, then in the very next he's ignoring me and rushing off!'

Laughing and shaking her head at Dottie's temper, Flora said, 'Dottie, darling! You know how busy he is. And it's such a responsible job. He can't just do what he wants all the time. He's got to find out who did these terrible things.'

'He already knows that!' Dottie exclaimed. 'So why can't he simply arrest them and then come and take me out dancing?'

'*Does* he dance?' Flora asked. Dottie frowned.

'If he doesn't, he'd better soon learn. I'm not marrying a man who can't—or won't—dance.'

Flora laughed again. 'Oh, so we're planning our wedding now?'

'I've got to marry him,' Dottie grumbled, 'it's the

only way I'll ever see anything of him.'

'Good afternoon, it's Inspector Davies here, of the Hertfordshire Police. We had the pleasure of you chaps paying us a visit a couple of weeks ago. I've got something I think you're going to like.'

Hardy smiled. Not that his colleague at the other end of the line could see it, of course. 'What is it, Inspector? Please tell me you've just solved my case for me.' His case was coming together well, but he was always ready for more good news. After being up half the night all he wanted was to close the case and get something to eat and then get some sleep.

'I wish I could, old chap. But we might be able to give you a hand. We went to Smedley-Judd's to follow up on some of that information you sent us, and what do you think? While we were there, the London brother's butler rang up from Kensington and thinking my sergeant was the other butler, told him that Ian Smedley-Judd, Mrs Gerard and the Scot had been arrested, that the police knew everything, and that if Mr Gareth knew what was good for him, he'd clear out to South America while the coast was clear.' Inspector Davies paused to draw breath, adding somewhat ruefully, 'We brought Mr Gareth in on the strength of that, but he's not saying anything, I'm afraid.'

'Don't worry,' Hardy told him. 'Just tell him you don't need him to talk as his brother has already told us everything, that Gareth was the mastermind behind the whole thing, the robberies and the three murders. That should get him talking. There's nothing like a bit of sibling rivalry to loosen the tongue. Oh and, let him know Mrs Gerard has killed herself, and left a signed confession.'

'Is that true?' Davies sounded excited.

'Oh yes,' Hardy said, 'the last bit's true. Not the bit about his brother. *He* hasn't said a word either, up to now at least. I think he'll tell us plenty now he knows we've got his little brother. But Mrs Gerard did kill herself in the early hours of yesterday morning, and she left a note which explicitly states that the Smedley-Judds and Melville were members of the gang. That's all perfectly true.'

'What's that?' Ian Smedley-Judd asked. Hardy had just placed a small brown envelope on the table as he sat down opposite Smedley-Judd and his solicitor. A lot of the bluster had gone out of the prisoner since their conversation the day before, Hardy noticed. The stubble and lank hair made the stockbroker look a lot less imposing than was customary, and his cheeks were pale. Perhaps that was what a night in police custody did for you? Or possibly it was just the terrible food.

'It's something from your special art collection room,' Hardy said.

'That room's empty,' Smedley-Judd replied. His voice held a triumphant note.

'It is now,' Hardy said, unruffled. 'I'm sure you thought you'd covered your tracks. But I found this,' he patted the envelope. 'It's not much, but taken with everything else we have, I'm sure it will be enough to ensure you pay the ultimate price for what you've done.'

'And what precisely *has* my client done, I'd very much like to know, Inspector.' The solicitor imbued the title with as much distaste as possible. His complacency irked Hardy, and suddenly, and for the first time, he felt glad that fate had ensured he ended up on this side of the interview table, instead of on the other, defending snakes like Smedley-Judd or Melville.

Hardy ticked it all off on his fingers. 'We have a confession from a Mr Wotherspoon about his involvement in the receipt and disposal of stolen goods. We have a confession from Mr Wotherspoon's son-in-law, Cedric Meyer, who has told us about you and your chums using his taxicab to travel to the houses where the robberies took place, here in London, in Oxfordshire and in Hertfordshire.'

'Once again, Inspector, it seems I must explain to you that my client has no involvement in these terrible crimes. Nor are *any* of these people known to him. Really, Inspector, this is a disgrace. I must insist...'

Hardy continued as if the solicitor hadn't spoken. 'We have a confession from James Melville, also known as Jimmy McKay. He has a record for theft and robbery with violence, and has told us a great deal relating to his own role in the robberies, and how you were related to those too.'

'Jimmy McKay?' Smedley-Judd was if possible even paler.

His solicitor began to shake his head. 'Once again, Inspector...'

'Yes, Jimmy McKay,' Hardy said to Smedley-Judd. 'His aunt, Mrs Millicent Gerard, committed suicide the night before last. Before she did so, she made a full and frank confession to her priest, and then she wrote it all down in a letter for me. As soon as Jimmy heard about his aunt, he told us everything.'

Smedley-Judd seemed to have nothing to say, though Hardy could see he was thinking furiously. Hardy went on, 'In addition, we have witness statements, we have just received a phone call in which the main points of your brother's confession were read to us. I'm sorry to say he did not manage to evade police in Hertfordshire. In fact, it was the local police who intercepted the phone call you instructed your butler Morris to make, telling your brother to get out while he could.'

Hardy put the envelope back into his pocket. He looked at Smedley-Judd, looking right into his eyes 'If I were you, I'd make a full confession too, in the hope of clemency. I'm afraid there's not much doubt that you will be convicted. Now, it's almost four o'clock. I'll get some tea sent in, and we can make a start. How about it?'

'Mr Smedley-Judd, I really must advise...'

'You can go, Brownlow. I've made up my mind. I can see I'm not going to get out of this. Will my brother hang, Inspector?'

Hardy barely noticed the solicitor pick up his attaché case and with an air of injured pride, leave the room. 'For the murder of two innocent women, Daphne Medhurst and Muriel Carmichael, not to mention a young policeman? Yes, I'm afraid there's very little doubt about that.'

Ian Smedley-Judd hung his head. His shoulders heaved. 'My little brother,' he said, his voice distorted by emotion. 'He has grown up to be the most cold, ruthless...You'd never believe he could become upset about the death of a pet rabbit, would you? And yet he was such a sensitive little boy. As a man...' he sighed. 'It's all over, I know that. None of this was supposed to happen. No one was supposed to get hurt. It was Melville who knocked down the first girl and ran off with her bag. Not that it contained what we were looking for. I didn't have the stomach for hurting anyone, it all got too brutal for my taste. Gareth couldn't believe Melville let her live. So he took over. It was Gareth who had the next go at getting the scrap. That was the girl at the cinema. Of course, it was only later we realised Gareth had killed the wrong girl. He thought it was Miss Manderson again. A terrible business. I know Major Medhurst. As one father to another, I know what a dreadful thing we've done. Will you let him know how sorry I am? It was never meant to be like this. Never.'

'Will you tell us how it was meant to be? Sergeant Maple will write down what you say. I'll send for that tea. We might as well be comfortable, we'll be here for a while.'

'Speaking of which, perhaps I might use the—er—the facilities before we get started?' Smedley-Judd said.

'Yes, of course. Sergeant Maple will send for someone to escort you.'

'Go and see what's keeping them, will you Frank? It's been ten minutes.' Hardy said. Maple leapt to his feet and left the room. Steam curled up into the air above the three teacups on the table in front of him. It was colder in the room than he'd realised, though outside it was a lovely, if chilly, Spring day. Summer would soon be here, he thought. He thought of Dottie, thought of her in a light pretty dress, thought of walking hand in hand with her somewhere leafy with flowers and birdsong, and then he would kneel before her and say...

'He's dead!'

Snapping out of his daydream, and surging to his feet, Hardy stared at Maple.

'What?'

'Hung himself in the lav. Nothing can be done for him, he's a goner. I can't believe it.'

Hardy raced up the stairs to the gentlemen's WC. On the tiled floor was Smedley-Judd, Dr Garrett was kneeling beside him and already shaking his head. In the corner of the room, the young police constable stood wringing his hands in despair. It was the same bright young chap who had found Daphne Medhurst's handbag. No doubt this new blot on his record would outweigh his usefulness on that occasion. There was no need to remind him that even for a call of nature, prisoners were not to be left alone.

Hardy, furious and frustrated, slammed back against the wall. Although he already knew the answer, he asked, 'What happened?'

Almost in tears, the young constable said, 'Well sir, he went into the stall, to—you know, relieve himself—and it seems he stood on the side of the toilet, wrapped the chain around his neck and then just—jumped. I heard the noise, well, it was...he almost knocked down the door as he fell against it, and he pulled the cistern down as he went, which is why...'

'Why we're up to our ankles in water.' Hardy turned to Garrett, already knowing it was hopeless. Garrett simply shook his head and put his stethoscope away.

She was waiting for him by the window and spotted him immediately as he came up the steps to the house. She ran to open the door, and he couldn't help himself, he was so glad to see her, he simply swept her up into his arms.

But before he could kiss her, her mother appeared, saying severely, 'Please close that door, Dorothy, there is such a cold breeze today. Inspector Hardy, how are you? Do go through to the drawing room. I'm afraid my husband is out, and I am just about to go out myself, but I imagine that will not inconvenience you. Dorothy, do ring for some tea for the inspector, I'm sure he could do with it. He looks as though he has had a long day.'

Meekly Hardy went into the drawing room. Dottie, equally meekly, rang for tea. They sat in opposite armchairs, and didn't know quite how to start. Mrs Manderson, popping in briefly to say goodbye, appeared to approve their arrangements.

He showed Dottie the letter Mrs Gerard had left. She was distressed to hear of the old woman's suicide, but her sorrow was soon forgotten as he began to tell her everything, explaining about Melville's involvement and that Gareth Smedley-Judd, inconsolable at the death of his brother, had also made a full confession. Then of course, Hardy had needed to write up his reports, and meet with his superiors to discuss the case and agree that it was now closed. The chief superintendent had not been happy that two of the perpetrators had been allowed to take their own lives, though as the Commissioner himself had pointed out, it saved the public the expense of two trials, and said that considering his lack of experience, that Hardy had acquitted himself admirably.

The Daughters of Esther had taken off their cloaks.

They stood about awkwardly, as if feeling naked. Their new, self-proclaimed leader, the redoubtable Mrs Manderson, surveyed them with approval. With embarrassment the women began to meet the eyes of the others they had known were in the order but had pretended not to recognise.

'Now then,' Mrs Manderson said briskly. 'Let's have our tea and I will tell you about the further changes I plan to make. We'll have no more secrecy, no more pretence. We are going to be openly doing good in the community and proud of our achievements. Just as Queen Esther helped her people in a time of crisis, so shall we. I shall canvass you all for ideas of how to raise funds and expand our spheres of influence.'

Within ten minutes, animated conversation of an unprecedented volume had broken out amongst the women. One woman was even heard to laugh. It was a liberating sensation for them all.

Exhaustion had finally claimed him, and his eyes closed, his head sank against the cushioned winged back of the chair, and he went down into a deep sleep. He had barely slept in the last twenty-four hours, or indeed for several days before that.

Dottie gently removed the cup and saucer from his hand, and set them on the tray which sat on the table. She looked at him for a moment, a little embarrassed, yet aware for the first time of a curious sense of possessiveness. After a brief hesitating doubt, and a glance at the door to make sure it was closed, she went to him, and stooping over him, loosened his tie and undid the top button of his shirt. His eyes fluttered open for a single fleeting second, and his smile was warm and unguarded, a lover's smile.

She paused once more, then she turned and ran lightly into the hall, up the stairs to her room, caught up the counterpane from her bed and hurried back down with it. She caught her breath on the threshold, half afraid her mother, or anyone else, would have unexpectedly come home to intrude, or that he would be wide awake again. She pushed the door open.

He still slept. No one else was there. Dottie covered him with the counterpane, brushed his hair back from his eyes with a flutter of her fingers. At the touch, his eyes opened again, hazy with sleep, and he murmured, 'This is how it will always be,' then he slept again. She passed two fingers over his cheekbone, tracing the contours of his face, down towards his chin, feeling the roughness of the stubble against her fingertips. He didn't stir. Bolder, she touched his lower lip with her forefinger. Then stroked her finger up again, along his eyebrow and down the straight line of his nose. She breathed out softly, and clasped her hands together. If they were married, she thought, she could snuggle into the chair with him, under the same counterpane, put her arms around him and sleep with her head on his shoulder.

Idiot, she reminded herself, if they were married he wouldn't have had to sleep in the chair. He could have gone up to bed. And she too could have...She blushed at the thought of sharing a bed with him, this stranger, this man, of feeling his arms about her, the taste of his lips on hers, then with a guilty start, she thrust the thoughts away, thinking of what her mother would say about such disgraceful imaginings.

Dottie backed away to sit in the chair opposite him, busying her hands with another shawl for her sister's coming baby, her eyes fixed on his face and her own jumbled thoughts.

When her mother came home two hours later, he had gone, and the counterpane was back on Dottie's bed.

*

Epilogue

It was almost a year later that the Mantle of God finally went on display at the London Metropolitan Museum. On the day that the display was opened to the public, James Melville, also known as James McKay began his twenty-five years for armed robbery, robbery with violence, conspiracy to commit a violent crime, and as an accessory to three murders. Three other men were convicted of similar crimes, and were to serve sentences of ten to twenty-five years. Wilfred Walter Wotherspoon and his son-in-law Cedric Meyer both received two-year suspended sentences in return for their help in the capture of the other members of the gang.

Gareth Smedley-Judd, sentenced to death for the unlawful killing of Daphne Medhurst, Muriel Carmichael and the killing of the young police constable, Daniel Paige, was hanged in a gloomy prison yard on a wet Thursday, and was mourned by no one.

At the museum, with his secretary, now also his fiancée, Miss Walters hovering in the background, Mr Falke proudly showed William and Dottie the huge glass case where the chasuble held pride of place. Her hand through William's arm, Dottie stood before the case and with the others, a silence descending on them as they looked at the garment.

The five pieces had been reunited, and the seams that joined them together were almost invisible. The mantle was draped on a dummy rather like a dressmaker's form, to give the full effect of the front and back of the garment.

Dottie had a lump in her throat as she looked at the embroidered scenes: the Garden of Eden and the Expulsion from Paradise on the left front, the baptism of Jesus and the beheading of John the Baptist in his prison cell on the right front, the first miracle at the wedding in Cana on the bottom half of the back panel, and at the top in the centre of the back, the Annunciation: the figure of Mary adorned in pearls and rubies, gold thread and silver, a gleaming halo surrounding her entire form, and the wings of the angel still gloriously bright more than six hundred years after they were created. Tucked away at the top of one sleeve was a green-worked hill and a cross, whilst on the other sleeve, the one that had so frustratingly evaded Mrs Gerard and her cronies, the one where a tiny piece had been cut off but had been so carefully reattached, there was a glorious starburst, and beneath it, a tiny manger, filled with gold straw and waiting...

Was it worth the lives that had died to protect it? She couldn't say for sure, but as she drank in the ancient workmanship—*workwomanship*—she corrected herself, thinking of those women who had laboured to create the glorious wealth of colour and design, she thought if it was hers, she might, just might, have given her life to keep it safe.

THE END

ABOUT THE AUTHOR

Caron Allan writes cosy murder mysteries, both contemporary and also set in the 1920s and 1930s. Caron lives in Derby, England with her husband and two grown-up children and an endlessly varying quantity of cats and sparrows.

Caron Allan can be found on these social media channels and would love to hear from you:

Twitter:
https://twitter.com/caron_allan

Also, if you're interested in news, snippets, Caron's ~~weird~~ quirky take on life or just want some sneak previews, please sign up to Caron's blog! The web address is shown below:

Blog: http://caronallanfiction.com/

ALSO BY CARON ALLAN:

Criss Cross: book 1: Friendship can be Murder

Cross Check: book 2: Friendship can be Murder

Check Mate: book 3: Friendship can be Murder

Night and Day: Dottie Manderson mysteries Book 1

Scotch Mist: Dottie Manderson mysteries Book 3: a novella

The Last Perfect Summer of Richard Dawlish: Dottie Manderson mysteries Book 4

The Thief of St Martins: Dottie Manderson mysteries book 5

The Spy Within: Dottie Manderson mysteries book 6

Printed in Great Britain
by Amazon